STUCK-UP
SUIT

VI KEELAND
PENELOPE WARD

Stuck-Up Suit

Cover model: Dusan Susnjar
Photographer: Tijana Vokovic
Cover designed by Letitia Hasser, RBA Designs
Interior Formatting & Proofreading by
Elaine York/Allusion Graphics, LLC/
Publishing & Book Formatting
www.allusiongraphics.com

This book is dedicated to all the little girls who want to wear neon green to dance class when all the others are wearing pastel pink.

CHAPTER 1

soraya

MY RIGHT FOOT STEPPED ONTO THE TRAIN, and I froze mid-step spotting him already in the car. *Shit!* He was sitting across from my usual seat. I backed up.

"Hey, watch where you're going!" A suit bobbled his coffee, barely keeping it upright as I reversed out of the third car without looking and smashed into him. "What the hell?"

"Sorry!" I offered a fleeting apology and kept going, ducking down below the train's window as I ran down the platform a few cars. The small lights next to each door began to flash red, and a loud buzzer sounded signaling the train was about to depart. I jumped into car seven just as the doors started to slide closed.

It took a full minute to catch my breath from running the length of four train cars. *My ass definitely needed to get back to the gym.* I found an empty forward-facing seat, settling in next to someone rather than sit in one of a half dozen vacant interior facing seats. The man lowered his paper as I settled in next to him. "Sorry," I offered. "I can't ride facing sideways." The two seats in front of him were empty. Proper train etiquette would have been to take one of those, but I figured he preferred cozy seating to vomit.

He smiled. "Neither can I."

Popping in my earbuds, I breathed a sigh of relief and shut my eyes as the train started moving. A minute later, there was a light tap on my shoulder. The passenger next to me pointed to the man standing in the aisle.

I reluctantly pulled out one earbud.

"Soraya. I thought that was you."

That voice.

"Umm...hi." What the heck was his name again? Oh, wait...how could I forget? Mitch. *High pitch Mitch.* I still wasn't speaking to my sister for that disaster. Worst. Blind. Date. Ever. "How are you, Mitch?"

"Good, actually great now that I ran into you. I tried to reach you a few times. I must have typed in the wrong number, because you never responded to my texts."

Yeah. That's it.

He scratched his crotch through his trousers. I had almost forgotten about that little gem. It was probably a nervous habit, but every time he did it, my eye followed his hand, and it was all I could do not to crack up. *High pitch Mitch with the Itch. Thanks, Sis.*

He cleared his throat. "Maybe we could get some coffee this morning?"

The suit next to me lowered his paper again and looked at Mitch and then to me. I just couldn't bring myself to be mean to the poor guy; he was nice enough.

"Umm." I put my hand on the shoulder of the suit next

to me. "I can't. This is my boyfriend, Danny. We got back together a week ago. Right, honey?"

Mitch's face fell. "Oh. I see."

Fake Danny joined in. He put his hand on my knee. "I don't share, buddy. So take a hike."

"You don't have to be so rude, Danny." I glared at the suit.

"That wasn't rude, babe. This would be rude." Before I could stop him, his lips were on mine. And it wasn't a quick peck either. His tongue wasted no time pushing its way into my mouth. I shoved hard at his chest, pushing him off of me.

I wiped my mouth with the back of my hand. "Sorry, Mitch."

"It's okay. Umm...sorry to have interrupted. Take care, Soraya."

"You too, Mitch."

The second he was out of earshot, I scowled at Fake Danny. "What the hell did you do that for, asshole?"

"Asshole? Two minutes ago I was honey. Make up your mind, sweetheart."

"You have some balls."

He ignored me, reaching into the inside pocket of his suit jacket to grab his buzzing phone. "It's my wife. Can you keep it down for a minute?"

"Your *wife*? You're *married*?" I stood. "God, you really are an asshole."

His legs were stretched out, and he didn't move them to let me out, so I stepped over. As he lifted the phone to his ear, I grabbed it out of his hands and spoke into the mic without listening. "Your husband is a giant asshole."

I tossed it back into his lap and walked away in the opposite direction that Mitch disappeared.

And it's only damn Monday.

This kind of shit was the story of my life. Running into bad dates. Men who turned out to be married.

I made my way into another car so that I didn't have to look at either "Danny" or Mitch again.

Much to my delight, this car wasn't as crowded, and there was an empty seat that was forward-facing. My blood pressure immediately went down as I sank into it. I shut my eyes for a moment and let the swaying motion of the train calm me.

A man's gruff voice disrupted my serenity. "Fucking just do your job, Alan. Do your job. Is that too much to ask? Why am I paying you if I have to micromanage every last goddamn thing? Your questions make no sense! Figure it out then come back to me when you have a solution that's worth my time. I don't have time for stupid questions. My dog could probably come up with something more intelligent than what you just brought to the table."

What a dick.

When I looked over to catch a glimpse of the face from which the voice came, I couldn't help but laugh to myself. *Of course.* Of course! No wonder why he thought he could shit all over everyone. With looks like that, people probably dropped to their knees around him all of the time, both literally and figuratively. He was gorgeous. Beyond gorgeous, reeking of power and money. I rolled my eyes...but still couldn't look away.

This guy was wearing a fitted, pinstriped shirt that made it easy to figure out the sculpted silhouette beneath. His expensive-looking navy jacket was draped over his lap. The black pointy dress shoes on his large feet looked like they'd just been shined. He was *totally* one of those guys who let people shine his shoes at the airport while he avoided making eye contact with them. His most notable accessory, however, was the angry glare on his perfect face. He was off the phone call now, looking like someone just pissed in his Cheerios. A vein was popping out of his neck. He ran his hand through his dark hair in frustration. Yup. Switching to this car was definitely a good decision for the eye candy alone. The fact that he was so oblivious to everyone else around him made it easier to ogle him. He was fucking hot when he was mad. Something told me he was *always* mad. He was like a lion—the type of species best admired from afar, whereby any actual contact could lead to irreparable harm.

His sleeves were rolled up, showcasing a massive and expensive watch on his right wrist. With that sourpuss expression, he stared off out the window as he fidgeted with the watch, twisting it back and forth. It looked like a nervous habit, which was ironic considering I was sure he made plenty of people nervous himself.

His phone rang again.

He picked it up. "What?"

His voice was the type of raspy baritone that always hit me straight between the legs. I was a sucker for a deep, sexy voice. It was rare that the voice actually matched the man, too.

Holding the phone in his right hand, he used his other hand to continue messing with the metal of his watch.

Clickety Click Click.

"He's just going to have to wait," he snarled.

"The answer is I'll be there when I get there."

"What part of that is unclear, Laura?"

"Your name is not Laura? What the hell is it then?"

"Then...*Linda*...tell him he can reschedule if he can't wait."

After he had hung up, he muttered something under his breath.

People like him fascinated me. They felt like they owned the world just because they'd been blessed by genetics or handed opportunities that put them in a higher financial bracket. He wasn't wearing a wedding ring. I bet his day consisted of nothing but self-serving activities. Expensive espresso, work, eating at high-end restaurants, loveless fucking...repeat. Shoe shining and maybe racquetball somewhere in between.

I bet he was also selfish in bed. Not that I'd throw him out of bed—but still. I couldn't say I'd ever been with anyone as powerful as this guy, so I wouldn't know from experience how that translated into the bedroom. Most of the guys I'd dated had been starving artists, hipsters, or tree huggers. My life was far from *Sex and the City*. It was more like Sex and the Pity. Or Sex and the Shitty. I guess I wouldn't mind playing Carrie to this guy's Mr. Big for just one day, though. Or Mr. Big Prick in this case. *Absofuckinglutely*.

One flaw in this little fantasy of mine: I was definitely not this dude's type. He was probably into submissive high-society waifish blondes, not curvy Italian girls from Bensonhurst with snarky attitudes and multi-colored hair. My long, black tresses hung down to my ass. I looked like a cross between Elvira and Pocahontas with a big ass. The ends of my hair were dyed a different color every couple of weeks depending on my mood. This week was royal blue, which meant things were going pretty well with me. Red was when you'd have to stay out of my way.

My random thoughts were interrupted by the screech of the train coming to a halt. Suddenly, Mr. Big Prick got up, a cloud of expensive cologne saturating the air in his wake.

Even his smell was obnoxiously sexy yet overbearing. He rushed out the doors, which closed behind him.

He was gone. That was it. Show over. Well, that was fun while it lasted.

My stop was next, so I walked over to the same door that he'd just exited. My foot hit something that felt like a hockey puck, prompting me to look down.

My heart started to beat faster. Mr. Big Prick had apparently left a piece of himself behind.

He dropped his phone.

His fucking phone!

He'd flown out of the train so fast, it must have slipped out of his hand. I'd apparently been too busy admiring his juicy, trouser-hugged ass to notice. Picking the iPhone up, it felt hot in my hands. The case smelled of him. Wanting to sniff it closer to my nose, I restrained myself.

I covered my mouth and looked around. If my life were a TV show, the laugh track would have been inserted right about now. No one was looking at me. No one seemed to care that I had Mr. Fancy Pants' phone.

What was I going to do with it?

Placing it inside my leopard-print purse, it felt like I was harboring a bomb as I made my way out of the station onto the sunny Manhattan sidewalk above. I could feel the phone vibrating with text notifications, and it rang at least once. I wasn't ready to touch it again until I'd had my coffee.

After stopping at my regular street vendor, I sipped my cup of Joe as I walked the two blocks to work. On this particular day, I was running late, so I decided to forego uncovering Mr. Big Prick's life until after lunchtime.

When I arrived at my desk, I took the phone out and realized the battery was in the red, so I connected it to my charger. My position as an assistant to a legendary advice columnist was certainly not my dream job, but it paid the bills. Ida Goldman was the owner of *Ask Ida*, a daily column that had been around for years. Ida had been trying to groom me lately, asking me to try my hand at writing some of the responses. Select write-ups were printed in the paper while answers to other submissions were posted on Ida's website. Part of my job was to screen the questions that came in and decide which ones to pass along to my boss.

While Ida's advice was always sensitive and politically correct, my take on things tended to be more to the point, basically cutting out the bullshit. As a result, she never actually published my responses. Occasionally, I couldn't resist taking it upon myself to answer some of the questions that didn't make the cut—the ones that would have ended up in the trash bin anyway. Some of these people really needed a clue, and I felt it was a disservice to ignore their pleas for help.

I just recently discovered that my husband has a porn stash. What do I do? –Trisha, Queens

Score! Invest in a good vibrator. Make sure you put everything back the way it was after you get your rocks off while he's at work.

I got drunk at a party and kissed my best friend's boyfriend. Now I can't stop thinking about him. I feel horrible but think I might be falling

for him now. Any words of wisdom? — Dana, Long Island

Yes. You're a cunt. C you next Tuesday, Dana!

My boyfriend recently asked me to marry him. I said yes. He's the sweetest, kindest man I've ever known. Problem is, the diamond he gave me was smaller than I hoped for. I don't really want to hurt his feelings. I need to know a polite way to express my disappointment. —Lori, Manhattan

God has the same dilemma when it comes to you, sweetheart. P.S. When your fiancé dumps your selfish ass, give him my number.

Answering a few emails in an honest and forthright way always seemed to give me the energy I needed to jumpstart my day. The morning went by quickly. By noontime, Mr. Big Prick's phone was now fully charged, so I took it with me into the break room. I had ordered Thai food in for both of us.

After we finished lunch, Ida left the room, giving me about ten minutes of privacy to sift through the phone. Luckily, it wasn't password protected. First stop: photos. There weren't many of them, and if I thought I was going to be able to collect clues as to who this guy was based on the pictures in his library, I had another thing coming. The first photo was of a small, fluffy, white dog. Looked like a terrier of some kind.

The next photo was of a woman's bare tits with a champagne bottle planted in the middle. They were pale, perfectly round and totally fake. *Yuck.* Then there were more photos of the little dog followed by a picture taken of a group of elderly women who looked like they were in a Jazzercise class. *What the hell?* I couldn't help but laugh out loud. The last photo was a selfie of him and an old lady. He was dressed more casual, his hair a little mussed, and was actually smiling. He looked so incredibly handsome in that shot. It was hard to believe that this was the same stuck-up guy in a suit from the train, but the gorgeous face confirmed it was him.

Five more minutes until I had to return to my desk. There was no email account linked to the phone, so I opened his contacts instead and decided to call the very first name on the list: Avery.

"WELL, WELL. GRAHAM MORGAN. It's been a long time. What happened? Have you run through the entire alphabet so soon and now you're starting back at the beginning again? You remember I wasn't one of your playthings, right?" I heard the blare of a horn and traffic in the background, followed by a car door slamming that muffled the city sounds. "To the Langston building. And don't take the park. The cherry blossoms are in bloom, and I don't need puffy skin before my meeting." She finished barking at the driver and remembered the phone. "So, what is it, Graham?"

"Umm. Hi. It's not Graham, actually. My name is Soraya."

"Sor —what?"

"Sore-ah-yuh. It's Persian for princess. Although I'm not Persian. My father just thought—"

"Whatever your name is, tell me what you want and why you are taking up my valuable time. And why are you calling me from Graham Morgan's phone?"

Graham Morgan. Even the damn name was sexy. It figured.

"Actually, I found this phone on the train. I'm pretty sure it belongs to a man I saw this morning. Late twenties, maybe? Slicked back dark hair, kind of long for a suit-type, curled up at the collar. He was wearing a navy pinstripe suit. Had on a big watch."

"Gorgeous, arrogant and pissed off?"

I chuckled a little. "Yes, that's him."

"His name is Graham Morgan, and I know just where you should bring the phone."

I fished a pen from my purse. "Okay."

"Are you anywhere near the 1 train?"

"I'm not too far."

"Okay. Well, hop on the 1 and take that all the way downtown. Pass Rector Street and get off at the South Ferry Terminal."

"Okay. I can do that."

"Once you're off. Take a right on Whitehall and then a left on South Street."

I knew the area and tried to visualize the buildings around there. It was a pretty commercial neighborhood. "Won't that take me to the East River?"

"Exactly. Toss that asshole's phone in, and forget you ever saw the man."

The phone line went dead. *Well, that was interesting.*

CHAPTER 2

soraya

I HAD PLANNED TO GIVE the phone back this morning.

No, really. I did.

Then again, I also planned to finish college. And travel the world. Unfortunately, the furthest I'd ventured out of the city over the last year was when my uneducated ass accidentally fell asleep on the Path train and ended up in Hoboken.

The phone safely concealed in the side compartment of my purse, I sat in car seven, one row back and diagonally across from Mr. Big Prick, stealing sidelong glances while he read *The Wall Street Journal*. I needed more time to study the lion. Creatures in the zoo always fascinated me, especially the way they interacted with the humans.

A woman boarded at the next stop and sat directly across from Graham. She was young, and the length of her skirt bordered on inappropriate. Her tanned legs were toned, bare and sexy, even *my* eyes lingered for a moment. Yet the lion never pounced. He never even seemed to actually notice her as he alternated between reading and mindlessly clicking that big watch of his. *I totally would have taken him for more of a whore than that.*

When his stop came, I made the decision that I'd give him back the phone. Tomorrow. One more day wouldn't matter. For the rest of my trip, I went back through his pictures. Only this time, I studied them, paying close attention to the details of the background rather than the focal subject.

The photo of him and the old lady was taken in front of a fireplace. I hadn't noticed it before. The mantel was lined with a dozen picture frames. I zoomed in on the frame that was the least pixilated. It was of a young boy and a woman. The boy looked about eight or nine and was wearing a uniform of some sort. The woman—at least I thought it was a woman—had something close to a crew cut. The boy might have been Graham, but I couldn't be sure. I almost missed my stop zooming in on what turned out to be a mailman in the back of another shot. *What the hell was I doing?*

I stopped at my usual coffee truck and ordered. "I'll take a grande, iced, sugar-free, vanilla latte with soy milk."

Anil shook his head and chuckled. Every once in a while, when he had a line of women who looked like they got lost trying to find a Starbucks, I would order something ridiculous. Loudly. I'd usually get at least one who believed Anil's Halal Meat served fru fru drinks. Basically, you had four choices: black, milk, sugar, or go somewhere the hell else—he didn't even carry Equal. Dropping my buck in the cup, he handed me my usual black coffee, and I laughed as I walked away hearing a woman ask if he made Frappuccinos.

When I arrived at the office, Ida was in a particularly rancid mood. *Fucking awesome.* The whole world thought *Ask Ida* was a beloved American institution; only a select few knew the truth. The woman who delved out heaping doses of sugary advice got her jollies from screwing people and being cheap.

"Find a number for the Celestine Hotel," was how she greeted me.

I powered on the tower to the old desktop computer she had me work on. The Internet on my phone was much faster, but I wasn't using up my data because she refused to move into the twenty-first century. Five minutes later, I brought her the number in her office.

"Here you go. Would you like me to make a reservation for you?"

"Grab the travel folder from the file cabinet."

I handed it to her and waited since she never answered my question. Ida flipped through the bulging file until she found a small, folded card—the kind the hotel leaves with the maid's name on it. She read it and then held it out to me. "Call the hotel. Tell them Margaritte doesn't know how to clean a room. That the last time I stayed at the Celestine, the carpet wasn't properly vacuumed, and there were black hairs on the wall in the shower."

"Okay..."

"Mention Margaritte by name and that I specifically want a room cleaned by someone else. Then ask for a discount."

"What if they won't give a discount?"

"Then book the room anyway. My room was perfectly clean last time."

"You mean the carpet and shower weren't dirty?"

She let out an exasperated sigh as if I was trying her patience. "Their room rates are highway robbery. I'm not paying $400 a night."

"So instead you want me to possibly get someone fired?"

She raised one thick, drawn-on eyebrow. "Would you rather it be you?"

Yeah. This bitch should be giving advice on morality.

LUCKY FOR ME, IT WAS WEDNESDAY—the day Ida met her editor each week. So, at least, I only had to put up with her for half a day before she left me with a page long to-do list:

Order new business cards. (Make them less colorful this time, I run a business not a circus.)

Update blog. (Yellow folder has daily letters and responses. Do not improvise as you type. *Ask Ida* does NOT suggest doing it doggy style to cheer up your boyfriend who just lost his beloved Jack Russell terrier).

Enter bills in blue folder into QuickBooks. (Take all discounts, even if past the discount date.)

Send contracts to Lawrence for review. No direction on this one. I'd figure out why shortly after. She had written across every single page of the document with a bright orange marker. *Ridiculous. Not acceptable.*

Pick up dry cleaning. (Ticket on my desk. Do not pay him if the mark on the left sleeve of my mohair jacket did not come out.) *What the hell was mohair anyway?*

Delivery from Speedy Printing this afternoon. (No tip. He was ten minutes late again last week.)

The list went on and on. I had to stop myself from scanning it and posting it on the blog under the last response she gave to an employee who was having trouble with her boss. Instead, I cranked up the tunes (Ida didn't allow music in the workplace), tipped the printer delivery guy twenty bucks from petty cash, and took a one-hour break with my bare feet up on the desk to play with Mr. Big Prick's phone some more. Looking down at my wiggling toes, I admired Tig's latest handiwork—two feathers tatted on the top of my right foot that dangled from a leather ankle bracelet. Very Pocahontas. I needed to stop back at the shop so he could take a picture for his wall, now that the swelling had gone down.

I was nearly at my data usage limit for the month, so I popped *Graham Morgan* into Google on his phone. I was surprised when the search returned more than a thousand results. The first one was his company's website—Morgan Financial Holdings. I clicked on the link. It was a typical corporate website, all very sterile and businesslike. The list of holdings was a page long, everything from real estate to a financial investment firm. The site reeked of old money. I would have bet Daddy still had a big corner office and visited every Friday after golf. The common theme of the site also seemed to summarize the business—wealth management. *The rich get richer*. Who was managing my assets? Oh, wait. That's right. I had none. Unless you counted my great rack. And I currently had no one managing that either.

I clicked over to the *About* tab, and my jaw dropped open. The first picture was of the Adonis himself, Graham J. Morgan. The guy was seriously gorgeous. A strong blade of a nose, chiseled jaw, and eyes the color of melting milk chocolate. Something told me he might have Greek in his ancestry. I licked my lips. *Damn*. Underneath, I read his bio. Twenty-nine, Summa Cum Laude at Wharton, single, blah blah blah. The only thing that surprised me was the last sentence: Mr. Morgan founded Morgan Financial Holdings only eight years ago, yet its diverse client portfolio rivals the oldest and most prestigious investment firms in New York City. *Guess I was wrong about Daddy.*

After wiping the drool off the keypad, I moved on to the *Team* tab. Thirty different directors and managers were outlined. There was a common theme there, too. Over educated and scowling. Except for one lone renegade who dared to smile for his corporate photo. Ben Schilling, who was apparently a marketing manager. Bored with corporate life, but still not ready to go back to my to-do list, I scrolled through Graham's contacts again. I passed over Avery's name and wondered if it was only women who Mr. Big Prick managed to piss off. A few names down from Avery, I landed on the first male name: Ben. *Hmmm.* Without overthinking it, I thumbed off a text:

Graham: What's up?

I got excited when I saw the three dots start bouncing, indicating he was typing a response.

Ben: Working on that presentation. I'll have it ready tomorrow as planned.

Graham: Great. Tell Linda to get you set up on my calendar.

At least, *I* had gotten her name right. I watched the three dots start and then stop. Then start again.

Ben: I didn't think Linda was coming back anymore. After what happened at the meeting yesterday.

Now we were getting somewhere. I sat up in my chair.

Graham: A lot happened at the meeting yesterday. What, specifically, are you referring to?

Ben: Ummm...I meant when you yelled you're fired, get the hell out of my office.

This guy really was a total prick. Someone needed to

fix his ass. I launched Safari and reopened the last page I had visited. Halfway down, I found what I was looking for: Meredith Kline, Human Resources Manager.

Graham: Maybe I was a little harsh. I'm in meetings all afternoon. Could you stop over and tell Meredith in HR to make sure Linda gets a month of severance?

Ben: Of course. I'm sure she will appreciate that.

If I was too nice, I thought he might have suspected something.

Graham: I appreciate not getting sued. What she appreciates isn't my concern.

I figured I had pushed far enough, so I tossed the phone into my purse before I could do any more damage. Tomorrow I would return it. And I was looking forward to meeting the jerk in person.

CHAPTER 3

soraya

MORGAN FINANCIAL HOLDINGS occupied the entire twentieth floor according to the sign in the lobby. My stomach growled as I waited for an elevator. Seeing as though I'd just had my breakfast, I knew it was nerves, and that pissed me off.

Why was the thought of coming face to face with this jackass making me nervous?

His looks.

Deep down, I knew it was his looks, and that was ridiculous. I wasn't a superficial person, but a part of me couldn't help swooning over this jerk. That part of me really needed to shut up right now.

The elevator made a dinging sound and opened up, allowing myself and an older businessman to enter. It was just the two of us as the doors shut. When the man scratched his balls, I looked down at the feather tattoo on my foot to distract myself from it. Why was I a magnet for men who scratched their junk? Thankfully, the car arrived at the twentieth floor soon enough. I exited the elevator, allowing the man free reign to go to town on himself in private.

A black sign with gold lettering that read *Morgan Financial Holdings* hung atop two clear glass doors. Taking a deep breath in and adjusting my little red dress, I made my way through the entrance. Yes, I'd gotten dolled up for this shit. Don't judge.

A young, redheaded receptionist smiled at me. "Can I help you?"

"Yes, I'm here to see Graham Morgan."

She looked like she was about to laugh at me. "Is he expecting you?"

"No."

"Mr. Morgan doesn't see anyone who doesn't have an appointment."

"Well, I have something very important of his, so I really need to see him."

"What is your name?"

"Soraya Venedetta."

"Can you spell your last name for me? Vendetta? Like a vendetta against someone?"

"No, it's Ven-E-detta. There's an E in the middle. V-E-N-E-D-E-T-T-A." If I had a nickel for every time someone screwed up my last name...well, I'd be richer than Graham J. Morgan.

"Okay. Miss Venedetta. Well, if you like, you can take a seat right there. When Mr. Morgan arrives, I will ask him if he's willing to see you. "

"Thank you."

Straightening my dress, I took a seat on the plush, microfiber couch diagonally across from the front desk.

It shouldn't have surprised me that Mr. Big Prick wasn't here yet, since he wasn't on the usual train this morning. I wondered exactly how long I'd have to wait; I only took a half-day and was due back at Ida's after lunchtime.

Mindlessly fishing through some financial magazines, I almost hadn't looked up when the doors opened. My heart started pounding when I noticed Graham, looking angry as ever. He was decked out in black pants and a crisp white shirt that was rolled up at the sleeves. There was that gleaming watch wrapped around his wrist. He was holding a burgundy tie in one hand and a laptop in the other. When he passed by, a waft of his intoxicating cologne immediately hit me like a punch in the nose. He was looking straight ahead, completely oblivious to me or anything else around him.

The receptionist lit up as he walked by her. "Good morning, Mr. Morgan."

Graham didn't respond. He simply let out a barely audible groan in response as he swiftly passed us and disappeared down the hall.

Really.

I looked over at her. "Why didn't you tell him I was here to see him?"

She laughed. "Mr. Morgan needs time to decompress in the morning. I can't hit him with an unannounced visitor the second he walks in the door."

"Well, exactly how long am I going to have to wait?"

"I'll check in with his secretary in about thirty minutes."

"Are you kidding?"

"Absolutely not."

"That's fucking ridiculous. It's going to take two minutes to do what I need to do. I can't wait all morning. I'm going to be late for work."

"Miss Vendetta…"

"Ven-E-detta…"

"Venedetta. Sorry. There are certain rules here. Rule number one is, unless Mr. Morgan has an important meeting scheduled in the morning, he is not to be disturbed as soon as he arrives."

"What exactly will he do if you bother him?"

"I don't want to find out."

"Well, I do." Getting up from my seat, I charged down the hall as the redhead scurried behind me.

"Miss Venedetta. You don't know what you're doing. Get back here right now! I'm serious."

I stopped when I came upon a dark, cherry wood door with the name Graham J. Morgan engraved into a placard upon it. The shades to the glass windows surrounding the door were completely closed.

"Where is his secretary?"

She pointed to an empty desk across from his office. "She normally sits right there, but she doesn't appear to be in yet. So, that's even more of a reason why I cannot disturb him right now because he's probably angry about that."

She looked over at another female employee who was working in a nearby cubicle. "Do you know why Rebecca isn't here yet?"

"Rebecca quit. The agency is looking for a replacement."

"Great," the receptionist huffed. "And she lasted all of what…two days?"

The woman laughed. "Not bad, considering…"

What the hell kind of a person was this Graham Morgan? Who did he think he was?

Adrenaline suddenly coursed through me. I walked

over to the secretary's empty desk and pressed the intercom button that was labeled GJM.

"Who the fuck do you think you are...The Wizard of Oz? I'm pretty sure I'd have easier access to Queen Elizabeth."

The fear in the receptionist's eyes was palpable, but she knew it was too late, so she just stayed on the sidelines and watched.

There was no response for about a full minute. Then came his deep penetrating voice. "Who is this?"

"My name is Soraya Venedetta."

"Venedetta." He'd repeated my name clearly. It wasn't lost on me that unlike everyone else, he had pronounced my name precisely.

When he didn't say anything else, I pressed the button again. "I've been waiting patiently to see you. But apparently, you're whacking off in there or something. Everyone here is scared out of their wits of you, so no one wants to tell you I'm here. I have something I imagine you've been looking for."

His voice came on again. "Oh really?"

"Yes. And I'm not going to give it to you unless you open that door."

"Let me ask you something, Ms. Venedetta."

"Okay..."

"This thing you claim I'm looking for. Is it the cure for cancer?"

"No."

"Is it an original Shelby Cobra?"

A what?

"Um...No."

"Then, you're wrong. There's nothing you could possibly have that I'm looking for, that would make opening that door and having to deal with you worth it. Now please leave this floor, or I'll have security escort you out."

Eff this. I wasn't going to deal with this crap anymore. I didn't want anything to do with him from this point forward, so I decided I would leave his stupid phone. Grabbing my own phone, I got an idea. A parting gift. I snapped three pictures of myself: one of my cleavage with a big middle finger in the middle, one of my legs and one of my rear end. I then programmed my number into his phone, naming myself *You're Welcome Asshole*. I specifically chose not to show my face since I didn't want him to recognize me on the train.

I sent all three pictures and followed them up with one final text.

Your mother should be ashamed of you.

I handed the receptionist the phone and said, "Make sure he gets his phone back."

I sashayed out of there despite feeling a little defeated and a whole lot irate.

My mood had only worsened by the time I got back to work. The only good thing was that Ida had an unexpected out of office meeting, so I didn't have to deal with her. I ended up taking advantage and leaving for the day an hour early.

After work, I ventured over to see Tig and his wife, Delia, before heading back to my apartment. He and I had been best friends since we were little, growing up next door together. Tig and Del owned Tig's Tattoo and Piercing on Eighth Avenue.

I could hear the sound of Tig's needle buzzing in the corner; he was busy with a customer. Tig handled all things ink and Delia was in charge of piercings. Whenever I was in this kind of unstable mood, I tended to get very impulsive. I'd already decided that tonight at home I was going to dye the ends of my hair red, but that didn't seem like enough to satisfy me.

"Del, I want you to pierce my tongue."

"Get outta here." She waved her hand dismissively. She was well aware of my mood swings.

"I'm serious."

"You said you would never get a piercing. I don't want you coming back and blaming me when your mood switches back."

"Well, I changed my mind. I want one."

Tig overheard us and turned his attention away from his customer for a second. "I know you. Some shit must have gone down today for you to want to pierce your tongue all of a sudden."

Letting out a deep breath, I said, "Some shit, alright."

I proceeded to tell them the full story, from finding Graham's phone to his rudeness toward me over the intercom today.

Tig spoke through the sound of the needle. "So, blow it off. You don't have to deal with that prick anymore. You're letting it get to you. Just erase him from your memory."

I knew Tig was right. I just couldn't figure out why Graham's rejection was having such an effect on me. I wasn't going to overanalyze it tonight or relate it to my issues of rejection by my father. Maybe I was just expecting to be pleasantly surprised today instead of utterly disappointed. Something was keeping me from just letting it go. There was more I had hoped to discover about Graham that I would now never get to uncover. I didn't understand why it mattered so much, and until I could figure it out, I would take it out on myself.

"I still want you to pierce my tongue."

She rolled her eyes. "Soraya..."

"Come on, Del. Just do it!"

My tongue was stinging on the train ride home. Reading over the list of after-care instructions, I couldn't help but chuckle to myself.

Don't kiss or engage in other oral activities until you are completely healed.

Yeah...that wasn't going to be a problem, seeing as though I had no one to partake in said activities with. All of the instructions seemed easy enough until I got to the last one.

Don't drink acidic or alcoholic beverages while the wound is still healing.

Well, crap. I'd shot myself in the foot with that one, deciding to pierce my tongue on a night where I really needed to drown my sorrows in some booze.

Arriving back at my apartment, I took off my clothes and started the process of dying the tips of my hair red, which signified my worst possible state of mind. Just when I thought I knew exactly how this night was going to go, the last thing I ever expected happened.

CHAPTER 4

graham

MY DAY HAD BEEN TAKEN OVER by a faceless pair of tits and a feather tattoo. Worse, they could talk.

Out of all the fucking things that she could have texted to me along with those body shots, she had to choose *those* words. She had to send the one message that would undo me and completely fuck up the rest of my day. Perhaps my week.

Your mother should be ashamed of you.

Fuck you, Soraya Venedetta. Fuck you, because you're right.

This strange woman had gotten under my skin.

She'd said her name once through the intercom, but it stuck with me. Normally, names went in one ear and out the other.

Soraya Venedetta.

Well, technically, her full name was *Soraya You're Welcome Asshole Venedetta.*

How did she get my phone?

The text continued to haunt me as I read it over and over.

Your mother should be ashamed of you.

Each time, it made me angrier than the last, because deep down, I knew there were no truer words. My mother *would* have been ashamed of me, the way I treated people on a daily basis. Everyone deals with tragedy differently. After my mother died, I'd chosen to shut people out of my life, focusing all my energy on schooling and my career. I didn't want to feel anything anymore, didn't want to connect with anyone. The easiest way to go about achieving that was to scare people away. If being an asshole were an art form, then I'd mastered it. The more successful I became, the easier it was.

It was amazing what a man of my position and appearance could get away with. Almost no one called me out on my crap or questioned me. They just accepted it. In all these years, not one person had spoken to me in my place of business the way Soraya Venedetta had today. Not one.

While her ballsy attitude over the intercom impressed me, I'd almost forgotten about her until Ava, the receptionist, knocked on my door and handed me my phone.

And now, hours later, I was still sitting here completely obsessed with the deep realization that came from Soraya's words. And completely obsessed with the set of tits pouring out of a dress that was the color of the devil.

Fitting.

Soraya Venedetta was a little devil.

She'd left me unable to focus on work, so I canceled the one afternoon meeting I had and left the office.

Back home, I sat on my couch and sipped cognac while continuing to ruminate. Sensing that something was off with

32

me, my West Highland terrier, Blackie, just sat at my feet, not even bothering to try to get me to play with him.

My Upper West Side condo overlooked the Manhattan skyline. It was dark out now, and the city lights illuminated the evening sky. The more I sipped, the brighter the lights seemed, and the more my inhibitions slipped away. Somewhere out in the vast city, Soraya was feeling satisfied with her little act, unaware that she'd wrecked me in the process.

Staring at the image of the feather tattoo on her foot again, it occurred to me that she didn't show her face because she was probably ugly as hell. At that thought, my own laughter echoed throughout the stone cold, empty living space. I wished I knew what she looked like. I wished I had opened that office door so that I could have shut her up to her face.

My finger lingered over her name, *You're Welcome Asshole.* I wanted to make her feel as crappy as she'd made me. I was not beyond going there. So, I did. I answered her text.

My mother is dead, actually. But yes, I suppose she would be ashamed.

Maybe five minutes went by before my phone chimed.

Soraya: I'm sorry.

Graham: You should be.

I should've let it be. She would have felt like shit, and that would've been the end of it. But I was buzzed. Not to mention fucking horny. Staring at her tits, legs and ass all day had gotten me all worked up.

Graham: What are you wearing, Soraya?

Soraya: Are you serious right now?

Graham: You ruined my day. You owe me.

Soraya: I don't owe you anything, you fucking perv.

Graham: This from the woman who sent me a shot of her cleavage. Nice tits, by the way. They're so big, at first, I thought it was a picture of an ass.

Soraya: You're the ass.

Graham: Show me your face.

Soraya: Why?

Graham: Because I want to see if it matches your personality.

Soraya: Which would mean what?

Graham: Well, that wouldn't bode well for you.

Soraya: You won't ever see my face.

Graham: Probably better off. So, give me a hint about what you're wearing.

Soraya: It's red.

Graham: So you haven't changed out of that dress?

Soraya: No, I'm naked with dye dripping down my body and my tongue is throbbing thanks to you.

That was an odd thing to say.

Graham: That's an interesting visual.

Soraya: You are seriously crazy, dude.

Graham: I AM a little crazy, actually. I probably need my head checked because I've been fantasizing about a headless person all day.

Soraya: Well, the naked pic ain't gonna happen.

Graham: How about I go first?

She must have been shell-shocked because she never responded again after that. Deciding to stop messing with her, I threw my phone across the couch and lifted Blackie onto my bare chest where he stayed until I fell asleep.

I'D MANAGED TO GET SORAYA out of my head somewhat the following day, but two mornings later, the obsession came back in full force.

The morning train was particularly crowded, and I didn't get a seat. Hanging onto a metal pole for balance, I looked around me. I almost never actually paid attention to the people on the train, and now, I was reminded of why.

Fucking freaks.

At one point, my eyes wandered to the ground, to a woman's foot diagonally across the aisle. My heart pounded furiously as my eyes landed on the same feather tattoo as Soraya's. The toes of this foot were also painted the same shade of red.

Holy fuck.

It was her.

She took the same train! That must have been how she found my phone.

I couldn't look up. I didn't want to be disappointed. It would be much better to just keep the fantasy going without actually having to face reality.

But God, I had to. I had to know what she really looked like.

Counting to ten slowly, I let my eyes slowly travel up the length of her legs that were crossed. Black leather skirt, leopard-print purse at her side, bright purple low-cut shirt showcasing in the flesh the rack I'd been fantasizing about. Then, my eyes landed above the neck.

Fuck.

Fuck.

Fuck.

She was looking straight ahead. Silky, straight black hair, dyed blood red at the bottom, tied back into a ponytail, displaying a long, delicate neck. Bright red lips in the shape of a perfect bow. Pinned-up nose. Big brown eyes like saucers. What do you know, the devil had the face of an angel. In fact, Soraya Venedetta was a bombshell. My dick twitched in excitement. If I was trying to forget her before, it was going to be impossible now.

When she turned and noticed me looking at her, our eyes locked. Unsure of whether she knew who I was, my heartbeat accelerated. Then, she simply looked away unaffected toward the train window.

Did she not know what I looked like?

I wracked my brain. There were only a couple of pictures of me in the phone, ones where I was dressed casually while visiting my grandmother. Maybe she hadn't gone through the photos. No, Soraya Venedetta would have definitely opened her big mouth if she recognized me.

She didn't know.

Letting out a sigh of relief, I continued to stare at her beautiful face in awe that this was the same person who had turned my life upside down the other day. A vacant seat caught my eye, so I sat down, took out my phone, and scrolled down to her name.

This was going to be fun.

Graham: Is your hair long or short?

It was the most innocuous thing I could think of to say. I figured if I'd started off telling her what I fantasized about in the shower this morning—oiling up those big, incredible tits and slipping my cock in and out—she might not respond again.

36

Soraya: Do you have a preference?

Graham: Long. I love a woman with long hair.

I couldn't look in her direction, but I realized if I looked out the window I could watch her reflection. Her head lifted, and she glanced my way before looking back down at her phone.

Soraya: Short. I have very short hair.

Liar.

After she sent the text, a sly smirk tempted at her lips. *I'd fix her.*

Graham: That's too bad. I had a recurring fantasy all day yesterday about you having hair long enough to tie around my waist.

I got a thrill watching that sly smirk disappear. Her lips parted, and I was certain if I were closer I would have heard a sharp intake of breath. She fidgeted in her seat for a minute before responding.

Soraya: Sorry. No can do. I'm under strict instructions not to engage in any oral activity for a while.

What the fuck?

Graham: From who?

Soraya: Whom. From whom would be the proper phrasing.

Graham: Proper text etiquette from a woman who sends porn to strangers.

Soraya: I don't send porn to strangers. You just pissed me off. I wanted to show you what you were missing refusing to step down off your throne and see me.

Graham: If that's the result, I plan to piss you off again. Often.

She stared out the window for a while. It was getting close to my stop. This woman had a way of getting under my skin, and I knew I wouldn't be able to focus on my eight o'clock meeting with her oral activity restriction comment hanging in the air. So I caved.

Graham: From whom?

Soraya: Delia

Fuck. Was she a lesbian? That thought had never even crossed my mind. What kind of a lesbian sends skin shots to a man?

Graham: You're gay?

The train slowed as we pulled into my stop. If I didn't have an important meeting, I would have stayed on just to see where she got off. Against my better judgment, I let my eyes wander to her before I stood to leave. Her head was down as she texted, but there was a smile on her face. A gorgeous, real smile. Not one of those plastered, practiced-in-the-mirror smiles that most of my dates seemed to perfect. No. Soraya Venedetta really smiled. It was a little crooked and a lot fucking beautiful.

My phone flashed indicating a new text had arrived. Thankfully, it pulled my attention from staring at her before I got caught.

Soraya: LOL. No, I'm not gay. Delia pierced my tongue two days ago. Hence the strict ban on oral activities until it's had time to heal.

Fuck.

I shut my eyes in an attempt to calm myself, but it only made things worse. A visual of her sweet little face with that wicked pierced tongue going down on my cock had my eyes springing back open.

Completely distracted, I barely made it out of the train before the door closed. How the hell was I going to accomplish anything today with that new piece of information?

CHAPTER 5

soraya

IT WAS A BEAUTIFUL, NOT A CLOUD in the blue sky, kind of day. I stared out the window trying to figure out what the hell had gotten into me. I'd been around good-looking men before, dated some even. So why did being anywhere near Graham J. Morgan knock me back to being thirteen years old and nervous when the cute boy sat down across from me in the school cafeteria?

I hated the reaction my body had to him. There was a chemistry that came naturally and was nearly impossible to clamp down. I couldn't fight what came over me the same way that I couldn't force the chemistry that was missing with Jason—the last nice guy I dated.

Being on an earlier train this morning, I totally wasn't prepared to come face to face with Graham. When our eyes locked, his pupils dilated and for a split second, I thought maybe he was having the same physical reaction to me that I had being near him. But then he looked away completely unaffected. His barely acknowledging my existence was a virtual rejection, yet my hands were still shaking when his first text came in. The only good thing was, at least the shock of seeing him didn't appear to have registered on my face. He had no idea who I was, and I planned to keep it that way.

Ida interrupted my thoughts. She plopped a thick stack of unfolded letters on my desk. Who really writes a letter and mails it to an advice column in this day and age? *Hello, email? Are you there? It's me, the twenty-first century.*

"Think you can work on some responses for the Internet column?"

"Sure. I can do that."

"Maybe this time, you can make the advice appropriate."

I was feeling pretty fucking *in*appropriate this morning. "I'll try."

"Try isn't good enough. Get it right this time." She slammed the door to her office, and I stuck up my middle finger. *I told her.*

I spent about an hour sifting through the pile until I found a few letters I thought I was capable of responding to Ida-style. My first few drafts resulted in wadded up balls of paper that missed the garbage can. Then I realized there was a trick to shoveling out shitty advice. First, I would draft the response how I thought it should read. Then, I would change each sentence to the exact opposite of what my advice would be. Amazingly enough, the two-step process seemed to really generate that Ida-esque vibe.

Dear Ida,

Last year I caught my boyfriend cheating on me. He said it was a terrible mistake and promised it was a one-time thing. After a lot of heartache, I agreed to stay committed to our relationship. But I just can't get over it. There is a man at work who I'm very attracted to. I think that if I slept with him, it might help me. Can two wrongs save a relationship?

Paula, Morningside Heights

Step 1.

Dear Paula,

Yes! Two wrongs don't make a right, but they make a hell of a good excuse! Go for it! Sure, a relationship requires commitment, but then again so does insanity. Cheating isn't a mistake; it's a choice. Be real. Once a cheater, always a cheater. Get even, ride that hottie, then leave before your boyfriend does it again.

Step 2.

Dear Paula,

No. Two wrongs never make a right. If you are truly committed to saving your relationship, you should avoid temptation at all costs. People make mistakes, but they can also learn from

them and change. To err is human, to forgive divine. Be divine. Trust that he won't do it again. Ride it out if you truly love him.

After I had gotten the hang of it, I knocked out two days' worth of responses before giving them to Ida to review. When my phone buzzed mid-day, I was excited, expecting it to be Graham. As ridiculous as it was, I really looked forward to his angry, horny texts. Disappointment settled in finding a text from Aspen. I had forgotten all about our date for tonight. My immediate reaction was to cancel. But instead, I lied and wrote back I was looking forward to tonight. He was a friend of a friend who I met at a party and seemed like a really nice guy. Plus, sitting home and waiting for a text from a man who would never have an interest in a woman like me, was just plain sad.

After work, I made an extra effort to look nice hoping it would change my mood. I slipped into some tight jeans and a bright purple shirt that showed off my abundance of cleavage. Adding a sexy pair of strappy, black-studded sandals, I looked in the mirror. I looked damn good. *Screw you*, Graham Morgan who didn't think I was worth a second glance.

Living in Brooklyn, I usually met my dates wherever we were going. Public transportation wasn't exactly conducive to picking people up, which worked for me since I wasn't particularly fond of giving virtual strangers my address. But Aspen planned to take me somewhere out on Long Island, so he had picked me up.

"I hope you don't mind. I just need to make a quick stop."

"Sure, no problem."

Unlike when we had met at the party, the car ride was filled with awkward conversation. I had to ask questions to keep the conversation going.

"So where are we headed? You mentioned a club."

"It's a comedy club. I don't go on until nine."

"You're performing?"

"Yeah." He shrugged. "Figured two birds, one stone."

Something about his response bothered me. It implied our date was a task. But I tried to make the best of it. It had been a long time since I went to a comedy club, and maybe he was trying to show off to me. When my phone buzzed in my bag, I peeked to see who it was. I hated to admit it, but part of me wanted it to be Graham.

Aspen pulled into the lot and parked. "I'll just be a few minutes."

He was leaving me in the car? "Where are we?" I looked around in the darkness. There was a 7-Eleven to the left and White's Funeral Home to the right.

"I have to stop in at White's. My aunt died."

"Your aunt died?"

"Yeah. I'll just be ten minutes." He started to get out. "Unless you want to come in with me?"

"Umm...I'll just wait here."

What the hell?

I sat there dumbfounded in the parking lot. He was essentially taking me to his aunt's funeral then to work. When my phone buzzed again, I figured I could use the distraction.

Graham: How's your tongue?

Soraya: Better. The swelling has gone down.

Graham: I've been worried about it all day.

Soraya: Is that so?

I smiled. My conversation with the gorgeous perv might be the highlight of my date with Aspen.

Graham: What are you doing right now, Soraya?

I heard his sexy voice rasp the question in my ear as I read his text. The hair on my arms stood up. My body had it bad for this man, regardless of what my brain said.

Soraya: I'm on a date, actually.

My phone went quiet for a long time. I started to think that was that. But then it vibrated again.

Graham: Is it safe to assume it isn't going well since you're texting during it?

Soraya: That would be a safe assumption.

Graham: What's his name?

Soraya: Why do you want to know?

Graham: So I have a name to put with the man I suddenly dislike.

Again I was smiling at the damn phone.

Soraya: Aspen.

Graham: He's an idiot.

Soraya: And you know that because of his name?

Graham: No. I know that because you're texting another man during his date.

Soraya: I suppose if I were with you, I wouldn't be texting.

Graham: If you were with me, you wouldn't care where your cell phone was.

Soraya: Is that so?

Graham: It most certainly is.

Oddly, I tended to agree with him. I sighed and decided to share the details of my pitiful date.

Soraya: He took me to a funeral.

Graham: For your date?

Soraya: Yep.

Graham: I hope you're texting me as you walk to the closest train.

Soraya: The funeral is out on Long Island. I'm kind of stuck with him for the rest of the date.

Graham: There's more than just a funeral?

Soraya: Yes. He's taking me to work next.

Graham: Come again?

Soraya: LOL

Graham: Where are you? I'll come get you.

Was that...nice from Mr. Big Prick?

Soraya: Thanks. But I'm good.

He stopped texting after that. Worse, Aspen returned to the car. Things got progressively worse from there. Upon arriving at the comedy club, my date proceeded to down two vodka tonics. When I mentioned he was driving us home, he told me he knew his limit. Apparently, he didn't know mine. Three minutes after he got on stage and told his first few bad jokes, I took a trip to the ladies room, then slipped out the back door. Eleven dollars in cab fare later, I was waiting for the first of what would be three trains to get back home. Maybe I needed to take a hiatus from dating for a while.

CHAPTER 6

graham

I WAS IN A PISS POOR MOOD all morning. Come to think of it, my anger started to surface sometime last night. Right about the time the woman with the body of the devil and face of an angel told me she would rather be on a date with some asshole who took her to a funeral for a date, than have me pick her up.

If I didn't have an early meeting again this morning, I would have gotten on that train and told her exactly who I was. Staring at the image of her luscious tits on my phone again, I realized *exactly who I was*...pretty much a stalker lately. And that pissed me off even more. *Screw her and her date.*

"Rebecca!" I pressed the intercom and waited for my secretary to respond.

Nothing.

"Rebecca!" The second time, I roared so loud, the

intercom wasn't necessary. The whole fucking office had to have heard me.

Still nothing.

Throwing a file on my desk, I stomped out to my secretary. A redhead was sitting at her desk.

"Who are you?"

"I'm Lynn. Your secretary for the last two days." She furrowed her brow as if I should know what the hell she was talking about.

"What happened to Rebecca?"

"I don't know, Mr. Morgan. Would you like me to find out?"

"No. I'd like you to get me some lunch. Turkey on lightly toasted whole wheat with one slice of Alpine Lace Swiss. Not two. One. Coffee. black."

"Okay."

"The receptionist at the front desk controls petty cash. Talk to her."

She smiled at me but didn't budge.

"Well, what are you waiting for? Go."

"Oh. You wanted me to go now?"

I grumbled and headed back into my office.

It was early afternoon when my phone vibrated and flashed a new picture of Soraya's legs. She had never initiated our texts before.

Fuck me.

This woman was going to be the death of me. I needed to get her to agree to see me.

Graham: *Show me more.*

Soraya: *That's all you're getting.*

Graham: *You're such a tease. Open them for me.*

Soraya: *No way.*

Graham: Suddenly you have morals?

Soraya: I have my limits, and showing you between my legs is definitely a hard limit.

Graham: And there is definitely no limit as to how HARD that would make me. In fact, just imagining it is giving me a hard on right now.

Soraya: Perv. Aren't you at work?

Graham: You know I'm at work. Why did you text me your legs then? You're trying to rile me up.

Soraya: It doesn't take much.

Graham: You won't show me your pussy. At least let me hear your voice.

Soraya: You've already heard my voice before.

Graham: Yeah, but you were being belligerent. I want to hear how you sound when you're wet and horny.

Soraya: And how do you know I'm wet and horny?

Graham: I can just sense it.

Soraya: Really...

Graham: Yeah.

My phone started to vibrate. *Soraya.*

My voice was intentionally low and seductive. "Hello, baby."

"Don't baby me."

Just the sound of her voice made my body buzz with excitement.

My voice sounded strained. "I want to see you. I need to know what you look like."

God, I need to touch you.

"I don't think that's a good idea."

"Why not?"

49

"I don't think we're right for each other. I'm not your type."

Raising my brow, I asked, "And what exactly is my type?"

"I don't know...a snobby, rich bitch? Someone who compliments a stuck-up suit such as yourself."

A deep laughter rolled through me. "A stuck-up suit, huh?

"Yes. You're pompous, and you think you can walk all over people."

"Well, there's only one person I want to be all over right now, Soraya. All. Over. You."

"How did you get to be such a prick anyway?"

"Why is anyone the way they are? We're not born that way. It's learned."

"So, being a jerk is an art you've mastered?"

"I'm a jerk because..." I hesitated. "Because I don't want to deal with the bullshit that inevitably comes when I let my guard down."

"What happened to make you want to put your guard up?"

"What's with the deep questions, Soraya? I don't open up to women I haven't even fucked."

"If I let you screw me, you'll tell me all your secrets?"

My dick twitched just thinking about being with her.

"I'll tell you whatever the fuck you want to hear if sex with you is on the table right now."

"Exactly. My point exactly!"

Even though we were arguing slightly, I could sense the humor in her tone. I somehow knew she was smiling along with me and enjoying our little exchange.

Clearing my throat, I said, "Alright...let's turn the tables on you. How did you become such a snarky little pistol?"

"I've always been this way."

I chuckled to myself. Somehow, I believed that. She seemed to be naturally spunky, not putting on a show. This was who she really was.

"What do you for a living anyway, Soraya?"

"What do you think I do?"

"That's a loaded question." I scratched my chin and put my legs up on my desk. "Based on the little I know about you...an amazing set of tits and legs...I'd say maybe you're a go-go dancer in some dark, smoky club."

"Well, you got the dark and smoky part right. My office is dreary, and my boss likes to sneak butts."

"It better not be your butt he's sneaking."

Jesus. Pipe down before she thinks you're a jealous lunatic.

"He is a she...and they're *cigarette* butts she sneaks behind closed doors in her office. I work for an advice column. It's a lame job, just pays the bills."

"I actually think that sounds very intriguing. What column is it?"

"I'm not sure I should tell you. You might try to stalk me at work."

"Wouldn't that be ironic? Are you not remembering how I was first introduced to *you*?"

"It's Ask Ida."

"I feel like I know that name."

"She's been around for years."

That's right. Mom used to read it.

"My mother used to read that column. What do you do there?"

"I weed through and answer some of the submissions that come in through the website, and I assist Ida."

I laughed. "So, you give advice to people?"

"What's so hard to believe about that?"

"I need some advice."

"Okay…"

"How do I get you to agree to see me?"

"Trust me. Sometimes, it's better to keep things a mystery. I don't think anything good can come of us getting together."

"Why is that?"

"You'd just be using me for sex."

I had to ponder whether she was right. The sexual attraction was off the charts. But deep down, I knew this connection with her was far deeper than that. I just couldn't figure out where it was coming from or what it meant. Soraya had lit some kind of fire in me that I couldn't extinguish. Getting her naked beneath me was definitely a goal, but it wasn't just that. I needed to figure it out.

"Not to be a dick, but I can get ass anytime I want from almost anyone. That's not what this is about."

"Then, what is it?"

"I don't exactly know," I said, truthfully. "But I want to find out."

She was silent for a few seconds then seemed to withdraw. "I think I should go."

"Is it something I said?"

"I just need to go."

"Alright then. When will we talk again?"

"I don't know."

Then, she just hung up.

Soraya Venedetta fucking hung up on me. An urge to chase her down overtook me.

Calm your dick, Graham.

My stomach growled, making me realize that incompetent Lynn never returned with my sandwich and coffee.

Approaching the front desk, I asked, "Where the hell is my secretary? She was supposed to be back with my lunch."

"I'm afraid she notified the agency that she's not coming back."

Fucking great.

My head ached from caffeine withdrawal. I returned to my office and grabbed my jacket before heading out to the deli down the street.

Opening my laptop at the table, a brilliant idea came to me. I looked up *Ask Ida's* website and decided to submit a question in the hopes that it would reach Soraya. I began to type.

> **Dear Ida,**
> **There's this woman I can't seem to get out of my mind. She texted me pictures of her tits, legs, and ass, but won't let me see her in person. The only reason I can think of is that she's really ugly and afraid to show me her face. How can I get her to agree to see me and to understand that not all men are as shallow as she seems to think?**
> **—Stuck-Up Suit, Manhattan**

Laughing to myself, I closed the laptop and finished my Pastrami on Rye. This woman was even making me eat like shit. I made a few business calls and checked in on Meme at the nursing home before opening my laptop once again. A response from *Ask Ida* was sitting in my inbox.

Dear Stuck-Up Suit,
It's quite possible you are drawing the wrong conclusion. There is no evidence to suggest that this woman is ugly. Perhaps, she is just not that into you. You may also want to look in the mirror and consider the fact that an ugly personality is a far greater deterrent than an ugly face ever could be.

Bending my head back in laughter, I marveled at this woman's wit. That mouth on her...I couldn't wait to fuck it. Aside from the fact that she was funny, honest, beautiful, sexy, and unlike anyone I'd ever been with, there was a part of her that seemed vulnerable and guarded. I wanted to know more about why she was so afraid of me. This kind of curiosity was not characteristic of me at all. While that was unsettling, my need to get to know her superseded everything else.

SITTING ACROSS FROM HER on the train without blatantly ogling her was truly an art form. Much like a ventriloquist who operates a dummy without moving his lips, I had to somehow stare at her without her knowing.

This particular morning, it was really a challenge to keep it subtle, not only because she looked so goddamn hot, but because she wasn't alone. A heavily tattooed man who looked way more her type than I was, sat next to her. They were talking and laughing, and I wanted to basically snap his pencil neck.

My blood really started pumping when he leaned over and kissed her. I couldn't tell if it was on her face or her lips because of my only being able to sneak glances. He then got up and exited the train, leaving her behind.

The jealousy within me that previously had been lingering under the surface had now become blinding. It was so blinding, in fact, that I wasn't even thinking when I suddenly typed out a text.

Who the fuck is he?

She seemed to freeze before slowly looking over at me. Her already pale skin turned nearly white. Her head had lifted and met my gaze instantaneously. She knew it was me.

Had she always known we took the same train?

I thought about it some more. Without any hesitation, her eyes had landed straight on mine, as if she knew exactly where to look.

She'd been pretending not to know who I was all this time.

She must have looked up my picture online. I couldn't figure out how else she knew it was me, but that really didn't matter anymore. All that mattered was that I was now face to face with the woman who had infiltrated my mind, body, and soul from the moment she opened her big mouth on that intercom.

My stop was next, but I wasn't going to get off. Well, truthfully, I was getting off on something else: this highly tense staring contest. It dawned on me that she was also absorbing the fact that I, too, knew her identity.

She suddenly got up. Her stop must have been coming up next. I followed suit, walking over to the exit and standing right behind her. She was staring at my reflection in the glass of the doors. My mouth curved into a smug smile. I was like a Cheshire cat who'd finally caught his little mouse. A hint of amusement shone through her expression.

When the doors opened, I followed her out, walking quietly by her side. We were both moving very slowly, unsure of where to go or what to do. When the rush of people seemed to all disappear up the escalator to the second level, we were nearly alone on the subway platform. I suddenly gripped her waist, forcing her to turn around and look at me.

Soraya's chest was heaving, and I could feel her body trembling. My own heart was racing. To know that I was having that kind of an effect on her was surprising—arousing. So fucking arousing.

The smell of her powdery skin was practically making me high. That, in combination with the warmth of her body so close to mine, had given me a raging hard on. I was like a teenager about to cream my pants in a three-thousand-dollar suit.

When I slowly moved toward her, she walked backward toward a large, concrete pillar. I backed her up against it and wrapped my hands around her cheeks, planting my lips over her mouth. She opened for me as my eager tongue went in search of hers. All life around me disappeared. The sound of surrender she made into my mouth egged me on to kiss her deeper. Her warm, ample tits felt like an electric blanket on my chest. The cold metal of her tongue ring against the heat of my own tongue sent what felt like spasms through me. If we weren't in public, I couldn't imagine being able to stop at just kissing her. I wanted nothing more than to take her on this platform.

She pushed me off of her and cleared her throat. "How did you know it was me?"

I caressed her bottom lip with my thumb. "I'm not

answering that until you tell me who that guy was kissing you."

"That wasn't a kiss. It was a peck on the cheek. It was my friend, Tig. He met me for an early breakfast this morning."

"Friend, huh?"

"He's very married. His wife is also a good friend."

"So, there's nothing going on there?"

"No, but if there were, I wouldn't owe you an explanation." She wiped her mouth, which was likely still sore from my attack. "So, tell me how you knew it was me."

"The feather on your foot, genius. Your feet were in the picture of your legs. I used that tattoo to identify you. I've been watching you for days. You were apparently doing the same to me."

She didn't deny that she knew who I was the entire time.

I moved my mouth closer to hers. "Did you like what you saw? Is that why you kept texting me? When I first realized it was you, I couldn't believe how fucking beautiful you were."

"So, all that talk about you thinking I might have been ugly was—"

"A crock of shit. I'm so unbelievably attracted to you, Soraya. And your body right now is telling me you feel the same way about me."

"It doesn't matter how good-looking you are. You're a dangerous human being."

"You have no idea how dangerous I am when I want something. I will stop at nothing to get it. And there's nothing more that I want right now than you. But if you can honestly tell me that you have no interest in me, I will walk away, and you'll never hear from me again. If the fact that you're shaking in your boots right now is any indication, you're feeling exactly what I am."

"I don't *want* to feel this way about a guy like you."

Hearing her say that was a real buzz kill. What the fuck kind of a human being did she take me for? I might have treated people like crap from time to time, but I wasn't a goddamn criminal for Christ's sake.

"Let me tell you something, Soraya. I may not be the nicest guy on the planet or even the best fit for you. In fact, I know I'm not. But you can't deny what's going on between us. There's only one end to this."

"And what's that?"

"Me buried deep inside of you."

"That can't happen."

"Every damn night, I dream about that fucking tongue ring swirling around my cock. You're all I can think about. In fact, you were all I could think about before I even saw your gorgeous face. But after that happened, I was a goner." I caressed her cheek again. "Just spend time with me."

"If I told you I don't want to sleep with you, would you still want to see me?"

Closing my eyes briefly, I opened them and said, "I would respect that."

"I've been hurt too many times in my life. I've vowed not to give myself to anyone that way again unless I was sure of their intentions. So, if you want to be with me, then there's no sex. You want to talk to me? Fine. You want to get to know me? Fine. But it stops there. Is that what you really want?"

"I want it all, but I'll take what I can get...for now."

"So, when is this gonna happen?"

"Tonight. I'll pick you up, and I'll take you on a real date that doesn't involve someone's decomposing body in the next room."

"You're such a romantic."

"I'll go along with the no-sex thing, but mark my words. When the time comes, I'm not gonna be the one begging for it."

For the rest of that day, the prospect of seeing her later consumed me. To pass the excruciating wait, I decided to write to *Ask Ida*.

> **Dear Ida:**
> **I'm seeing a woman who has made it clear that she doesn't want to have sex with me. The thing is, she doesn't know what she's going to be missing. I'm thinking there must be something I could do to change her mind? – Stuck-Up Suit, Manhattan**

About an hour later, a response showed up in my inbox.

> *Dear Stuck-Up Suit:*
> *I get the sense that perhaps you just assume that all women should want to open their legs to you. I am guessing there is a reason that this woman feels that having sex with you would be detrimental to her well-being. Maybe try getting to know her for a while, give her a reason to trust you. Prove that you are invested. In*

the meantime, YOU should invest in a nice cold shower. Sounds like you're going to need it.

CHAPTER 7

soraya

SORAYA: WHERE ARE WE GOING?

I'd left work an hour early to get ready. More than half the clothes I owned were in a heaping pile on my bed. Normally, whatever mood struck dictated my outfit. I wasn't finicky. To me, style was an expression of your own individual personality, not following the latest trends from the runway or from one of the Kardashians. So it was freaking-me-the-fuck-out that I was on my tenth outfit.

Graham: To a restaurant, unfortunately. Unless you've changed your mind. I'm more than accommodating if you'd prefer I feast on you at my place.

If it were anyone else, all of the little pervy comments would piss me off. But for some reason, Graham's made me smile. My answer to his invitation to screw was always to screw with him.

Soraya: Actually, maybe I have changed my mind.

Graham: Give me your address. I'm still at the office, but can be there in ten minutes, wherever the hell you live.

I chuckled at his desperation. As much as I thought he was full of himself, there was something very endearing about the honesty he displayed wanting to be with me. Normally, to a guy like him, showing desperation was a sign of weakness. It almost made me feel bad about toying with him. *Almost.*

Soraya: I meant about us having dinner tonight. I'm not sure it's such a good idea.

Graham: Bullshit. If you don't show up, expect a knock on your door.

Soraya: You don't even know where I live.

Graham: I'm a very resourceful man. Try me.

Soraya: Fine. I'll be there. But you only gave me an address. Where are we going? I need to know what to wear.

Graham: Wear whatever you're wearing right now.

I looked down.

Soraya: A hot pink lace bra and G-string? Where are you taking me, a strip club?

It was a solid five minutes before he responded.

Graham: Don't tell me shit like that.

Soraya: Not a fan of hot pink?

Graham: Oh, but I am. The shade will look lovely as a handprint on your ass if you don't stop messing with me.

Spanking wasn't something I was ever into. *Wasn't* being the key word. Yet the thought of him stinging my ass had my body humming. I was growing aroused from a text. *Jesus. This man was dangerous.* Needing a break, I tossed the phone on my bed and dug back into my closet. A little black dress shoved in the back caught my eye. I'd bought it for a funeral. I cracked myself up thinking I should have worn it the other night for my date with Aspen. When I slipped it from the hanger, my phone was flashing a new incoming text message had arrived.

Graham: You've stopped responding. I'm going to take that to mean you're busy fantasizing about my hand swatting that fine ass.

He had an uncanny ability to turn a simple question into something dirty.

Soraya: I'm busy trying to figure out what to wear. Which brings me back to the original question I texted, where are we going?

Graham: I made a reservation at Zenkichi.

Soraya: In Brooklyn?

Graham: Yes, in Brooklyn. There's only one. You said you lived there, and since you refuse to let me pick you up, I chose a place close to you.

Soraya: Wow. OK, great. I've wanted to try that place. It's sort of a pain in the ass for you to get to from your office, though.

Graham: Fitting. Since you're such a pain in my ass. See you at 7.

The subway station was about a block and a half from the restaurant. When I turned the corner, there was a black town car pulling up outside. I have no idea why, but I ducked into a doorway to watch the person get out. My gut told me it was Graham.

My gut wasn't wrong. A uniformed driver got out and

opened the back door, and Graham stepped out onto the sidewalk. *God, the man oozed power.* He was dressed in a different expensive suit than he was wearing this morning. The way his suits fit him, there was no doubt that he had them custom made. Although it wasn't the fancy suit that he was wearing that gave him the air of supremacy; it was the way *he* wore the suit. Standing in front of the restaurant, he stood tall and confident. His chest was open and broad, shoulders were back, legs apart and firmly planted. He looked straight ahead, not fiddling with his phone or staring at his feet to avoid eye contact. One hand was in the pocket of his trouser pants, his thumb outside of the pocket. *I liked the thumb hooked on the outside.*

I waited a few minutes, and when he eventually looked in the other direction, I slipped out from the doorway. When he turned back and caught sight of me, I became self-conscious of my walk. The way he watched every step I made, a part of me wanted to run the other way, but the other part of me *liked* the intensity of his stare. *A lot.* So I tapped down my nerves, added some sway to my hips and decided I would not be a mouse to his cat. I would be the dog.

"Graham." I nodded as I stopped in front of him.

"Soraya." He mimicked my business-like tone and nod.

We stood looking at each other on the sidewalk, a safe distance between us for the longest minute in the history of minutes. Then he growled, "Fuck this." Stepping forward into my space, he wound a fistful of my hair around his hand, used it to tilt my head where he wanted it, then his mouth devoured mine.

For a split second, I tried to resist. But I was an ice cube trying to fight the heat from the sun. It was impossible. Instead, I melted right into the blinding light. If he hadn't wrapped his other hand snuggly around my waist, there was a good chance I'd have been on the concrete. My mind wanted to fight him at every turn, but my body couldn't resist giving in. *Traitor.*

He spoke over my lips when he finally released my mouth. "Fight it all you want, you'll be begging one day. Mark my words."

His arrogance brought me to my senses. "You're so full of yourself."

"I'd much rather be filling you."

"Pig."

"What's that say about you? You're wet for a pig."

I tried to push back from the grip he had wrapped around my waist. But it only made him clutch me tighter. "I'm not wet."

He arched an eyebrow. "Only one way to verify that."

"Back off, Morgan."

Graham took a step back and raised both his hands in surrender. There was a glint of amusement in his eyes.

Inside, Zenkichi was dark and not what I had expected. The traditionally dressed Japanese woman led us down a long hall that was made to feel like outside. The walkway was lined with rocks and slate stones, as if we were walking a path through an outdoor Asian garden. Both sides were lined with tall bamboo and lit with lanterns. We passed an opening to a large seating area, but the hostess kept going. At the end of the hallway, she seated us in a private booth, enclosed with luxurious, thick drapes. After she had taken our drink order, she pointed out the buzzer built into the table and told us we would not be intruded on unless we wanted to be. Then she disappeared, pulling the curtains closed. It felt like we were the only two people in the world, instead of inside a busy, posh restaurant.

"This is beautiful. But odd," I said.

Graham took off his jacket and settled into his side of the table with one arm casually slung over the top of the booth. "Fitting."

"Are you saying I'm odd?"

"Are we going to fight about it if I say yes?"

"Probably."

"Then, yes."

My brow furrowed. "You *want* to fight with me?"

Graham tugged at his tie, loosening it. "I find it turns me on."

I laughed. "I think you need counseling."

"After the last few days, I believe you may be right."

The waitress returned with our drinks. She set a highball glass down in front of him and a wine glass in front of me.

Graham had ordered Hendrick's and tonic. "That's an old man's drink, gin and tonic," I said as I sipped my wine.

He swirled the ice around in his glass, then brought it to his lips and looked at me over the rim before drinking. "Remember what arguing with me does. You might want to look under the table."

My eyes widened. "You aren't."

He smirked and cocked an eyebrow. "Go ahead. Put your head under. I know you're dying to take a peek anyway."

After we both finished our drinks, and some of my nerves had started to calm, we finally had our first real conversation. One that wasn't about sex or tongue rings.

"So how many hours do you work a day in that big fancy office of yours?"

"I usually go in by eight and try to leave by eight."

"Twelve hours a day? That's sixty hours a week."

"Not counting weekends."

"You work weekends, too?"

"Saturdays."

"So your only day off is Sunday?"

"I actually sometimes work in the evening on Sunday, too."

"That's nuts. When do you find time to enjoy yourself?"

"I enjoy my work."

I scoffed. "Didn't sound that way when I stopped in the other day. Everyone there seems afraid of you, and you refused to open the door."

"I was busy." He folded his arms over his chest.

I did the same. "So was I. I took two trains to personally deliver that phone, you know. And you didn't have the decency to even come out and say thank you."

"I didn't know what was behind the door waiting for me, or I would have come out."

"A person. A *person* was behind the door. One who went out of her way for you. If I were a sixty-year-old married woman with blue hair, you should have come out to thank me."

He sighed. "I'm a busy man, Soraya."

"Yet here you are on a weeknight at only 7PM. Shouldn't you be working until eight if you're so busy?"

"I make exceptions when warranted."

"How big of you."

He arched an eyebrow. "You want to look under the table, don't you?"

I couldn't help but laugh. "Tell me something else about you. Aside from you're a workaholic with a superiority complex who drinks fancy drinks. All of that, I could have guessed from my observations on the train."

"What would you like to know?"

"Do you have any brothers or sisters?"

"No. I'm an only child."

I mumbled under my breath. *Gee, I never would have guessed that one.*

"What did you say?"

"Nothing."

"How about you?"

"One sister. But I'm not speaking to her at the moment."

"And why is that?"

"Bad blind date."

"She fixed you up?"

"Yep."

"With the guy who took you to the funeral? What was his name, Dallas?"

"Aspen. No, she didn't fix me up with Aspen. I picked that disaster all on my own. She fixed me up with a guy she used to work with. Mitch."

"And it didn't go well, I take it?"

I fixed him with a stare. "I nicknamed him High Pitch Mitch with the Itch."

He got a chuckle out of that. "Doesn't sound so good."

"It wasn't."

He squinted at me. "And will I have a nickname tomorrow?"

"Would you like one?"

"Not if it's anything like High Pitch Mitch with the Itch."

"Well, what did you have in mind?"

The wheels spun in his head for about thirty seconds. "Morgan with the Big Organ?"

I rolled my eyes.

"You can fact check under the table at any time." He winked.

I continued to try to get to know him, even though all roads led to between his legs. "Any pets?"

"I have a dog."

Remembering the little dog from my snooping in his cell phone, I said, "What kind of a dog? You seem like the type to have a big scary one. Like a Great Dane or a Neapolitan mastiff. Something representative of what you keep goading me into looking at under the table. You know, big dog, big d—"

"The size of a dog is not a phallic symbol," he interrupted.

So, it was his cute little dog in the pictures.

"Really? I think I read a study once that said men unknowingly purchase dogs that represent the true size of their penis."

"My dog was my mother's. She passed away when he was a puppy, twelve years ago. "

"I'm sorry."

He nodded. "Thank you. Blackie is a West Highland terrier."

"Blackie? Is he black?" The little dog in the photo had been white.

"He's white, actually."

"So why Blackie? To be facetious? Or is there another reason for the name?"

His response was clipped. "There's no other reason."

Just then, the waitress served our dinner. I ordered the Bonito Shut fish entree, basically because the menu said it was for adventurous eaters only. And Graham ordered Sashimi. Both our dishes looked more like art when they arrived.

"I hate to eat it; it's so beautiful."

"I have the opposite problem. It's so beautiful; I can't wait to eat it." His smirk told me his comment had nothing to do with his fancy looking dinner.

I shifted in my seat.

We both dug into our meals. Mine was incredible. The fish literally melted in your mouth. "Mmm...this is so good."

Graham surprised me by reaching over and forking a piece from my plate. He didn't seem like a plate sharer. I watched him swallow, and he gave a small nod of approval. Then I reached over and forked a piece of his meal. He smiled.

"So. You've told me about Mitch the Itch and Funeral boy. Do you date a lot?"

"I wouldn't say a lot. But I've met my fair share of assholes."

"They were all assholes?"

"Not all of them. Some were nice guys but just didn't work for me."

"Didn't work for you? How so?"

I shrugged. "I just didn't feel *that way* about them. You know. Like nothing more than a friend."

"And do you have any more dates in your forthcoming calendar?"

"My forthcoming calendar?" I let out a ladylike snort. "You go from dirty talk to sounding like a snobby college professor pretty easily."

"Does that annoy you?"

I thought about my answer for a moment. "I wouldn't say annoy. More like amuse."

"I'm amusing?"

"Yes. Yes, you are."

"Pretty sure I've never been called amusing before."

"I'd bet that's because most people only see the asshole you show on the outside."

"That implies that I'm more than just an asshole on the inside."

Our eyes locked when I responded. "For some reason, I believe that you are. That there is more to you than just an asshole with a sexy exterior."

"You think I'm sexy." He grinned, full of himself.

"Of course I do. I mean look at you. You have a mirror. I'm guessing you figured that out all by yourself by now. It must not be difficult to fill up the evenings on your *forthcoming calendar.*"

"Are you always such a wiseass?"

"Pretty much."

He shook his head and grumbled something. "Speaking of forthcoming calendars. I would like yours cleared of any more dates. Other than me, of course."

"We're halfway through our first date, and you're telling me, not asking me, to not date other people?"

He straightened in his seat. "You told me you weren't going to sleep with me. That we were going to date and get to know each other. Does that still stand?"

"It does."

"Well, if I'm not fucking you, no one else should be either."

"How romantic."

"It's a deal breaker for me."

"And that would go both ways? You wouldn't be seeing anyone else either?"

"Of course."

"Let me think about it."

His eyebrows jumped in surprise. "You need to think about it?"

"I do. I'll get back to you on it." It was, without a shadow of a doubt, the first time that Graham J. Morgan was not getting his way with a woman.

Hours later, my phone buzzed in my bag. It was Delia checking on me since she knew I was out on a first date. I shot off a quick text to let her know I was safe and glanced at the time on my phone. We had been sitting in the restaurant for more than three hours. It wasn't lost on me that it was the first time I had even thought about my phone.

"Well, you were right about one thing."

"You'll have to be more specific. I'm right about most things."

I shook my head. "And here I was about to give you a compliment, and you go and ruin it with your arrogant self."

"I believe arrogance is when you have an exaggerated sense of your own abilities. I don't exaggerate. I would be a realist."

"Stuck-Up Suit is truly a fitting name for you, isn't it?"

Ignoring me, he asked, "What was the compliment?"

"When we were texting during my funeral date the other night, you said if I were with you, I wouldn't care where my cell phone was. Until it buzzed just now, I hadn't even noticed I never took it out."

That pleased him. A little while later, Graham paid the bill, and I made a quick stop in the ladies' room. Freshening up, it struck me that I really didn't want our date to end. The thought brought on almost a melancholy feeling that surprised me.

Outside of the restaurant, Graham's black car was already

curbside. He must have had it waiting and called the driver when I went to the restroom.

"If you're not going to come home with me, I insist on at least giving you a ride home to your place."

"The subway is right around the corner. I'm good."

He shot me an annoyed glance. "Give a little, Soraya. It's a ride home, not a ride on my cock. And I think you know by now that I'm not a serial killer."

"You're so crass."

He put his hand on the small of my back and steered me to the waiting open car door. I didn't put up a fight. Graham was right, I was being stubborn while he had pretty much agreed to anything I demanded. Something told me it was a rare occasion when the man was this flexible.

When we arrived at my apartment, Graham walked me to the door.

"When will I see you again?"

"Well, tomorrow is Saturday, so I suppose maybe Monday on the train."

"Have dinner with me again tomorrow?"

"I have plans."

His jaw flexed. "With whom?"

We embarked into a lengthy stare off. His gaze was hard. When neither of us gave for a few minutes, he grumbled *Christ* under his breath, and before I realized what was happening, my back was against the door, and his mouth was on mine.

He kissed me as if he wanted to eat me alive. Before releasing my mouth, he took my lower lip between his teeth and tugged. Hard. With his lips vibrating up against mine, he spoke. "Don't push me to my limit, Soraya."

"Why? What will happen?"

"I'll push back. And I'm trying not to do that with you."

He was being honest, and I realized I should appreciate that. "To my sister's house. It's my niece's birthday party. That's where I'm going tomorrow night.

He nodded. "Thank you."

It took every bit of my willpower to go inside and shut the door behind me. I leaned my back against the door, unable to remember the last time I was so hot and bothered. Maybe not ever. His mouth was sinful; the thought of what he could do with that wicked tongue *other* places on my body kept me in a state of arousal that bordered on frenzied. But it was more than that. The way he was so dominating and controlling, yet exercised restraint to respect my wishes, was the sexiest thing I'd ever seen. The man stimulated something that had been sleeping inside of me. I needed a glass of wine and an orgasm. Not necessarily in that order. If I was going to be firm on my stance that we get to know each other and not have sex, then taking things into my own hands was absolutely essential.

In my bedroom, I stripped out of my clothes. I didn't sleep naked every night, but tonight was definitely a bare evening. As I slipped into bed, my cell rang.

"Is phone sex on the table?" Graham's voice was a needy rasp. Whatever cooling off my body had done since I left him on the other side of the door was instantly reheated. His voice could definitely speed things up for me. But...

"Sex is off the table. That should probably include all types of sex. Intercourse, oral, phone."

He groaned. "*Oral.* God, I want to taste you. And feel that metal tongue ring on my cock. You have no idea how difficult it was to control myself tonight every time I caught a glimpse of that metal when you spoke. It's like you're taunting me with every word. What are you wearing, Soraya?"

That voice. I needed to record him saying *What are you*

wearing, Soraya? So I could play it over and over again in a loop when I needed to satisfy my own needs. "I'm actually not wearing anything. I just got undressed and slipped into bed."

"You sleep naked?"

"Sometimes."

He actually growled. "Touch yourself."

"I plan to. But I think I'm going to need both hands tonight. So I'm going to hang up first."

"How long do you plan on driving me crazy, Soraya?"

"Good night, Graham." I hung up without waiting for him to respond. Even though my body physically ached for the man, I wasn't ready to open that door with him just yet. Although as I glided my hand down my body alone in my bed, the only thing I could think of was *God, I wish it was his hand.*

CHAPTER 8

graham

I DIDN'T HEAR FROM HER ALL DAY Saturday, not that I'd expected to. Soraya Venedetta was intent on driving me fucking nuts. I'd never been in this position before. I'd relentlessly pursued business ventures that I wanted until they inevitably gave in when I sweetened the pot and gave an offer they couldn't refuse. But pursuing a woman was new to me. Sure, there were a few who made me chase for a first date. But by the end of the night, I was always certain what it was that made them tick. They wanted to be wined and dined, flattery, a business connection, a certain lifestyle. It wasn't ever difficult to figure out. *Until now.*

What makes you tick, Soraya Venedetta?

The more the woman pissed me off, the more I wanted her. By ten in the evening, I couldn't resist any longer. I was turning into an aggrieved pussy.

Graham: How was your party?

She responded a few minutes later. It gave me some sense of peace that she wasn't so enraptured with someone she met that she stopped checking her phone.

Soraya: On the train home now. Have I mentioned I don't like clowns?

Graham: You haven't. But I think that is a pretty common phobia.

Soraya: My little monster of a niece wasn't scared in the slightest. Figures. What did you do tonight?

I was sitting alone in my living room with piles of documents strewn all over my glass coffee table and a cognac in my hand. Today had been a fourteen-hour day. Every time I thought of contacting her, I forced my nose back into my work. My eyes gave out before my desire.

Graham: I worked late.

Soraya: You know the old saying...all work and no play...

Graham: Makes Graham a wealthy boy.

Soraya: Maybe. But what good is wealth if you have no time to enjoy it.

I tossed back the remnant of my glass. I'd heard those exact words too many times to count. *From my grandmother.*

Graham: Have you thought about what I asked?

Soraya: Are you referring to my forthcoming calendar?

Wiseass. It was driving me nuts to know she was out tonight and had refused to commit to not seeing other people. Yesterday, I had told her that it was a deal breaker. At the time, I was trying to push her into an all or nothing decision in my favor. But after the last twenty-four hours, I was certain there was no way in hell I could do an open relationship with this woman. Usually, it's me who avoids committing. I was getting a taste of my own medicine, I suppose.

Graham: I am.

Soraya: How about this? You'll come with me to a social event of my choosing, and I'll attend one of your choosing. If you still want to see me exclusively after, I'm game.

What did she think? That my spending time with her friends was going to make me realize we were so vastly different that it could never work? Or was it the other way around? She wouldn't fit into my lifestyle. Clearly, she overestimated the extent in which I give a fuck about what people think in either camp.

Graham: It's entirely unnecessary, but if that makes you happy, I'll do it. When can I attend a social event of your choosing?

Soraya: Thursday night. Tig and Delia are having a party at their tattoo shop. It's the one-year anniversary of the grand opening.

Graham: Friday night. The Pink Ribbon Gala at the Met. It's an annual fundraiser I support.

Soraya: A gala, huh? I'll have to dye my tips to match my fancy dress.

Graham: Is it a date?

Soraya: Two dates. And yes.

That night, I slept better than I had the last week. As usual, Sunday afternoon I visited my grandmother. She had me take her shopping and then made me one of my favorite meals. It was generally my only homemade meal each week.

Monday morning, I was up early and ran seven miles instead of my usual morning four. As I headed for the train station, I realized how much I was looking forward to seeing

Soraya. When her stop came and went, and she didn't get on, I pouted, then called my secretary to give her a list of things to do before I arrived. I knew it wasn't possible to accomplish all of them, but at least it gave me an excuse to unload my frustration on someone.

That day, I was especially cranky. By five o'clock, I found myself again writing to *Ask Ida*.

> **Dear Ida:**
> **There's a woman who I look forward to seeing on the train every day. This morning she wasn't there. I think she might be intentionally avoiding me because she's unable to fight her sexual attraction any longer and is worried she'll give in and let me have my way with her. How can I be sure?**
> **—Celibate in Manhattan**

Twenty minutes later, a response popped up in my inbox.

> **Dear Celibate:**
> **Get a hold of yourself. Contrary to what it appears you may believe, the world does not revolve around you. Perhaps this woman had an early morning doctor's appointment to refill her birth control pills. Something a celibate man like yourself might appreciate—that is, if you are ever afforded the opportunity to break that vow of celibacy. Perhaps you should**

take a different train for a while. Better yet, take a trip to your own physician for some testing. On the off chance that you have an opportunity with this mysterious train woman, you'll want to be prepared.

My day had already been monopolized thinking about why she wasn't on the train this morning. *Fucking great.* Now it would be impossible to think about anything else but coming inside of her, for the entire night.

SORAYA NEVER SHOWED UP on the train the following two days either. I got the feeling she had chosen to intentionally avoid me until our date. Thank God tonight was the night of the party at the tattoo shop. Otherwise, I might have lost my damn mind.

I was about to explode in more ways than one. My emotions were out of control, and it no longer felt healthy to hold everything in. There was only one person I could trust with details of my personal life. I normally never called my grandmother during the week, but for some reason, I felt like I needed her to set me straight today before I made a total ass of myself tonight. Pushing the pile of papers on my desk aside, I picked up the phone. It rang three times before she answered.

"Graham? Are you alright?"

"Everything is fine, Meme."

"You don't normally call me on a Thursday."

"I know."

"What's going on? You seemed preoccupied last Sunday. Is something wrong?"

"Nothing is wrong."

"Well, what is it?"

Letting out a deep breath, I cut to the chase. "Am I a bad person?"

"What kind of a question is that?"

"There's this...woman I've been seeing. She seems to distrust me. And I have to wonder if there's a legitimate reason for that. Maybe I'm not good for her. Maybe I'm not good for anyone."

Never one to mince words, Meme laughed and said, "You do have a tendency to be a dick, sweetheart. But from what you tell me, that's par for the course when it comes to your business dealings. Dealing with a *woman*, on the other hand, is a whole different ball game. And you've certainly played the field..."

"That's the thing. I have...but this one is different. It *feels* different. I don't even know how to explain it. It makes no sense, really. We're nothing alike at all. She's from Brooklyn... an Italian, hot-tempered, loose cannon with multi-colored hair. She calls me out on stuff. She can even be downright mean sometimes. Yet...I can't get enough of her. But I can tell she doesn't trust me. I don't know how to get through to her."

Meme snorted. "I'm assuming by *get through*...you also mean she hasn't allowed you to have your way with her?"

"She hasn't allowed anything to happen in that area, no."

"You're just not used to women keeping their legs closed. There is such a thing as a lady with self-respect, you know. I think I like this girl."

I sighed into the phone as she continued.

"It takes time to see people for who they really are. You need to be yourself and have patience, and eventually, she will see the real you."

"But what if the real me isn't good for her? What if I'm toxic?"

"Who said that?"

"I don't know if I am capable of love anymore..."

"Just the fact that you even care, Graham, is a good sign. If it's the right person, we're all capable of it. You fell in love with that Genevieve, didn't you?"

Just the mention of her name made my stomach sour.

"Look where that got me."

"You know what I think?"

"What?"

"I think you've been trying so hard to control everything, intentionally picking the wrong people, just so you won't get hurt. And now you're starting to believe that you're incapable of anything more. You're beginning to believe your own lies."

"Maybe."

"I think this girl...what's her name?"

"Soraya..."

"Soraya...huh...pretty."

I closed my eyes and twirled my watch around my wrist. "She is."

"Anyway, I think this girl is a wake-up call for you, that we don't always have control over things. Just go with the flow. Let things happen on their own. Give up control. But more importantly, for God's sake, don't be an asshole."

I couldn't help but laugh out loud. "I'll keep that in mind, Meme."

The realization hit that Soraya was definitely not the first woman in my life to tell it like it is.

CHAPTER 9

Soraya

AVOIDING GRAHAM OVER THE PAST COUPLE OF DAYS had been really difficult, but I felt like I needed to step back for my own good. The truth was, I couldn't trust myself. Any little bit of contact might have pushed me over the edge. It was bad enough I thought about him all day and pleasured myself to images of him at night. For all I knew, the second I gave in, he would be gone. And I didn't want this to end. I loved the excitement of wondering what he'd say or do, wondering what would happen next. I couldn't risk giving in too soon and losing this feeling...or losing him. I hated that a part of me still felt like he might disappear once we slept together.

Nevertheless, I was prepared for it whenever it might happen because I didn't really trust myself around him. Even though I vowed not to have sex with him yet, I made sure my legs were shaved and that I was wearing the laciest lingerie I had. I also made sure my birth control was up to date.

I poured orange juice and rum into the punch bowl that sat atop the buffet table we'd set up in the tattoo shop. Delia had hung up festive red Christmas lights as decorations even though it wasn't the holidays. Bob Marley was playing while she set out some appetizers. Tig was still working on the last customer in the back before closing for the party. A makeshift bar was stationed in the corner with our friend, Leroy, serving as both the bartender and DJ.

Butterflies swarmed in my stomach at the thought of Graham meeting my friends. I couldn't imagine him walking in here with his million-dollar suit, though. That was going to be a funny sight. I hoped that Tig and Delia didn't think I was crazy for bringing him here. They were already wary of him because of my initial descriptions of his glowing personality. It had been hard to backtrack and explain to them why I was suddenly enamored with Mr. Big Prick. They still called him by that name.

Checking my phone incessantly, I noticed that Graham was about five minutes late. People were starting to arrive, but he was all I could think about. I decided to distract myself by putting out some candy. That was when I heard Delia's voice. "Please tell me that Clark Kent hottie who just walked in isn't Mr. Big Prick, because I might have to fight you for him."

My heart started beating out of control at the sight of Graham in the doorway.

Oh. My. God.

He was dressed nothing like I'd ever seen before. There was no suit. Instead, he was wearing a black polo shirt that fit his chest like a glove made for pectoral muscles along with a pair of dark jeans. His hair was slicked back off to the side in a way that made him look younger. And he was wearing glasses. God, the bespectacled look really worked for him. It worked for *me*. A little too much.

My body reacted more with every step he took toward me, the punch of his signature scent nearly knocking the wind out of me. While I had been trying to restrain myself, Graham pulled me into an easy hug and buried his mouth in my neck.

"I missed you so fucking much, Soraya."

The strained sound of his words against my skin were enough to do me in. The night hadn't even started, and my panties were already wet. I was ready to pull him into a supply closet.

Jesus. Grab a hold of yourself.

Graham's brown eyes were searing into mine from beneath the lenses. They trailed down to my cleavage and back up again. I had dyed the ends of my hair purple and wore a similar color dress to match. He took a fistful of strands and gently tugged, whispering seductively in my ear, "Purple, huh?"

I cleared my throat. "Yes."

"You told me the red signified anger. What does the purple mean?"

"What's with the glasses?"

"Answer me first."

"Purple represents confusion or a dilemma."

He smirked. "I see."

"So, why the glasses?"

"Honestly, I haven't slept well. I've been worried about you but trying to give you space. When I don't get my sleep, my eyes dry up. The glasses are more comfortable than contacts."

We stood there gazing into each other's eyes for nearly a full minute before Delia interrupted our moment.

"Well, if it isn't Mr. Big Prick..."

Crap.

Graham's eyes widened as he offered her his hand before looking at me with an amused expression. "I guess my reputation has preceded me. I'll choose to believe that Soraya came up with that nickname based on the literal and not figurative translation of prick."

"It was what I called you before we met...back in the days when I was holding your phone."

"And what made you come up with that name specifically?"

"You reminded me of a jerkier Mr. Big from that show *Sex and the City*. Thus, Mr. Big Prick."

Graham slid his hand along my waist. "And who would you be...slutty Samantha?"

I squinted in surprise. "You've watched that show?"

"My mother used to watch it."

"That's funny." I smiled.

"Now that you know me a little better, do I still remind you of that guy?"

"Well, you do have a driver. So, I guess there are some similarities."

He wriggled his forehead. "Although, there's no *sex* in our city, is there?"

When I glared at him, he playfully kissed me on the cheek then ran his hand down my back, causing a shiver to run through me. This was going to be a long night.

After introducing Graham to Leroy and a few of the other guests, I brought him over to meet Tig. My friend had a cigarette hanging out of his mouth when he offered Graham a handshake. "Mr. Big Prick...how the fuck are ya?"

Graham rolled his eyes. "I'm well. You must be Tig."

"Anyway, I don't know if Soraya told you, but she's like my sister. And seeing as though she doesn't have a blood brother or even a father who's worth a piece of shit in her life, that means that if you hurt her, I'm gonna have to be the one to kick your ass. Just wanted to get that out of the way."

Graham nodded his head slowly in understanding. "I appreciate you looking out for her."

"Glad we cleared that up." Tig snickered. "I would ask you if you want a tat on the house while you're here...but something tells me you're not into ink."

"I'm into *her* ink." Graham winked at me then scratched his chin, looking like he was pondering something. "Actually, I might be interested. Do you fix tattoos as well?"

"Yeah. What do you mean specifically?"

"I have one that I don't want anymore. It was a mistake, and I'd like to ink over and around it, change it into something else."

He had a tat? No fucking way.

"Let's take a look." Tig waved his hand, prompting us to follow him.

My eyes were glued to Graham's ass, which looked amazing in those jeans. My hands longed to squeeze it. I wondered how he'd react if I did.

The muffled sounds of the guests faded into the background when we entered the quiet of the back room. My breathing quickened as Graham slowly lifted his shirt over his head, tousling his hair. It was the first time I had ever seen his rippled chest in the flesh. His physique was beautiful beyond my imagination. It was clear he worked out hard.

I couldn't take my eyes off of his six-pack. His skin was so smooth and tanned. It was everything I had fantasized about and more. My hands tingled with a desperate need to feel his skin. My eyes traveled down the thin, happy trail of hair that led into his jeans before my gaze scrolled up again and landed on it: the tattoo on the left side of his torso. I squinted my eyes. It was a name written in script: *Genevieve*. My heart dropped. Swallowing my jealousy, I specifically chose not to ask the question I was dying to.

Who the hell is Genevieve?

It felt like my ears were burning. The only thing worse than worrying about Graham being a manwhore was the possibility that there was someone out there who had actually meant something to him—meant enough to permanently mark his body with her name.

Tig looked at me, sensing my discomfort then turned to Graham. "Who's Genevieve?"

Graham looked at me when he answered, "She's an ex-girlfriend. Like I said, the tattoo was a mistake." His expression lacked humor, and it made me even more curious about what might have happened between him and this woman.

Tig took out a book that featured all sorts of designs with details that could mask the letters of the name. Graham chose an intricate tribal design.

I stood there mesmerized, listening to the sound of the needle. The tension in the air was thick as Graham would look over at me from time to time. Tig was able to color in and shade over the name so that by the end, it looked like it was never there. The new tat looked super sexy against Graham's olive skin. To be honest, I wanted to run my tongue over it.

Tig placed a clear bandage over the design and gave him after-care instructions before Graham put his shirt back on.

"Thanks, man. How much do I owe you?"

Tig held out his hands. "Please. It's on the house."

"I insist."

"Just take care of my girl. That's all I need from you. Nothing else."

Graham looked at me. "I can do that."

Placing his hand on the small of my back, Graham led me through the door and back into the main room.

"Can I get you a drink?" he asked.

"Yeah. I'll take some of that punch over there."

Graham returned with two glasses of the spiked juice, and we both gulped them down swiftly. A stream of red liquid dripped down my cleavage. Before I could wipe it off, I felt Graham's long finger running a line up the middle of my chest.

"Messy girl," he said as he licked the punch off of his index finger.

That one single swipe practically did me in. I was so incredibly attracted to him, but never had I wanted him as badly as tonight. The casual clothes, the glasses, the way he was looking at me, seeing him shirtless like that...it was all too much. But more than anything, the lingering jealousy over "Genevieve" was driving me nuts the most. A foreign and uncontrollable sense of possessiveness came over me. My reaction was a wake-up call. I was already in too deep, destined to get hurt. Take that realization, add a little rum punch, and you got one hot mess.

"You're deep in thought tonight, Soraya. Tell me what's on your mind."

What felt like a hot flash started to permeate my body. Never in my life had I ever reacted to a man this way. Never had I felt so much fear and desire at the very same time. Certainly, never had the jealousy monster reared its ugly head. I didn't want him to sense it. I needed to cool off.

"I'll be right back," I said before making my way to the back of the shop. Before I could get very far, I felt a firm hand on my waist. Then, he pulled me into Tig's office and shut the door, backing me against it with his arms locking me in on each side.

"You think you're the only one who is fucked up by what's happening here?" he groaned.

I stayed silent, trying to catch my breath.

There was no light, and he didn't attempt to find one. In the darkness of the office, I could barely see anything. I could only feel his chest against mine and his breath against my lips as he said, "You're driving me crazy. I need to touch you. Please just let me taste you... just once."

Bending my head back, I pressed his head into my chest as he ran his tongue slowly down my cleavage, moaning over my skin. He pulled the top of my dress down, exposing my breast and took my nipple into his mouth, sucking so hard that it caused me to squeal. The muscles between my legs were pulsating with need. Even though I wanted him inside of me, I was terrified. I suddenly moved my face away from him and began to cover myself.

Panting, he buried his nose in my neck and placed his hand over my heart. He pulled me closer to him. "God, listen to that heartbeat. You want me. I can feel it. But you're so goddamn scared of me. Why?"

"I don't know," I whispered.

He pulled back and cupped his hands around my cheeks.

"Talk to me. Please. Whatever happened to make you so distrusting?"

"I'm just afraid to get hurt."

"Who hurt you?"

It was hard for even me to understand where this was coming from. I hadn't even had a boyfriend who'd shattered my trust or broken my heart. It made no sense. I'd never really been in love before. The feelings that I had for Graham were new to me, but I didn't want to admit that to him. The one thing I knew for sure was that my father was somehow at the root of my paranoia. So, I decided to tell Graham a story that might explain my fear of rejection, although I couldn't say I truly understood it clearly myself. Anything was better than admitting to him that I'd never felt this way about anyone before, though.

"When I was about ten years old, my parents divorced. My father ended up marrying a woman from the neighborhood. Theresa was a widow. She had three daughters, one of whom was my age and went to my school...Brianna. Anyway, my dad pretty much became their father and spent less and less time with my sister and me as a result. There was this father-daughter rose ceremony and dance that the school was putting on for girls in my age group. The dads were each supposed to buy a dozen roses for their daughter and then take pictures together at the dance. Anyway, my mother had asked my father if he was available to take me. He never got back to her. So, I ended up showing up at the school, all dressed up and hoping he would turn up. And he did...with Brianna. There she was, holding the big bunch of pink roses in one hand and my father's hand in the other. I ran home crying, and when my mother confronted him, he said that he didn't realize I was interested in going. He said that since

Brianna's dad was dead, it was important that he be there for her. He said he thought I would understand. Anyway, this has nothing to do with you, Graham. You asked why I have trust issues, and my father is really the only reason I can think of."

He took my face in his hands again and planted a firm and passionate kiss on my lips. My body relaxed into him, and when he pulled away, I longed for him to just keep kissing me.

"I'm sorry that happened. That is so incredibly shitty. And it does explain a lot."

"Yeah...thank you."

"I was pretty much an only child," he said. "My father was never in the picture, which might have been better than a rejection later on. I don't know."

"So, it was just you and your mother?"

"Yes."

"How did she die?"

"Lung cancer when I was a teenager."

"I'm so sorry."

"Thank you." He paused then said, "It was hard. I vowed never to allow myself to become attached to anyone after that. I didn't ever want to suffer that kind of loss again. My mother's death is a big reason I am the way I am...closed off and cold. At the same time, it motivated me to be the best that I could be in other ways, to make her proud. So, some good and bad came of it."

My stomach churned as I prepared to ask the question I needed an answer to. "Did you become attached to Genevieve?"

"Yes," he simply said.

My heart was palpitating. "How long were you with her?"

"Two and a half years."

"I see."

When I looked down, he placed his hand on my chin and moved my face to meet his eyes in the darkness. "What do you want to know, Soraya? Ask me."

"What happened with you and her?"

"Genevieve took a job with me as a broker right out of school. We were serious...or so I thought. Anyway, to make a very long story short, I actually started my company with a friend of mine named Liam Gainesworth. Liam, Genevieve, and I worked very closely together. I eventually found out they were having an affair behind my back. Liam went on to start his own company, which is now one of my competitors and took Genevieve with him."

Wow.

"That's awful. I don't even know what to say. I'm sorry."

"Don't be. It wasn't meant to be."

"I know, but I can tell that it hurt you."

"I'm here with you, aren't I?"

"What does that have to do with it?"

"Because I don't want be anywhere but here. If anything were different in my life, I might not be. I don't understand it, either, Soraya. This. What's happening between us. I can't make any promises. I just know I don't want it to stop."

Neither do I.

"We'd better go back out before they think we're—"

"Fucking?"

"Yeah."

He buried his face in my neck and chuckled against my neck. "God forbid."

"Thank you for being patient with me."

He growled, "Patient isn't the right word..."

"Maybe not."

As I took his hand to lead him out of the room, he nudged me back for a moment. "Hey..." When I turned to face him, he leaned his forehead against mine. "I'll wait as long as you want me to. I'm not going anywhere."

"Thank you."

We were both much more relaxed after our talk. We spent the rest of the night quietly listening to the conversations around us at the party. I leaned my back into Graham, who wrapped his arms around my waist, the warmth of his body balancing out the goosebumps from the contact. I didn't know where this was going, and for the first time, I resolved not to analyze it.

CHAPTER 10

Soraya

THE NEXT DAY AT THE OFFICE, they kept coming in droves. Dozens of roses. Pink ones, red ones, yellow ones. A new dozen was delivered every hour. It took me a bit to figure out why he was doing it. It was the story I told him about my father and the rose ceremony. I later found a card that had fallen off of the first dozen that read, *These are long overdue.* My heart felt heavy and filled with something unidentifiable all at once.

Tonight was the gala I was supposed to be attending with him. It was going to be way out of my comfort zone, and nervous jitters followed me around all day. I'd picked out two different formal dresses at Bergdorf's on my lunch break.

When I got back to the office, there was a plate of Indian food at my desk. The smell of curry was nauseating.

"Ida? How did this food get here?"

"A delivery guy left it, said it was for you. I thought you ordered it."

"I get Indian for you, but you know I hate it."

Then, a thought crossed my mind. I took out my phone.

Soraya: You didn't order me Indian food, did you?

Graham: I did.

Soraya: Why?

Graham: I thought you liked it? I saw you going to pick it up.

Soraya: Um...how is that? You were following me?

Graham: It was only one afternoon. I missed your face. I was gonna pull up next to you like Mr. Big, surprise you and take you out to lunch. Then I saw you rushing out of Masala Madness and figured you already had plans.

Soraya: LOL. I was getting lunch for Ida. Indian gives me heartburn.

Graham: I need to work on my stalking skills.

Soraya: That was really sweet of you, though.

Later that afternoon, Graham sent me another text.

Graham: Hey, I heard they changed the name of the gala in honor of me.

Soraya: Really?

Graham: It's now called the Big Blue Ball.

Soraya: LOL.

Graham: They're giving out swag bags with ice packs and ibuprofen.

Soraya: You're crazy.

Graham: For you, I am.

Soraya: What time are you picking me up?

Graham: Holy shit. Am I actually allowed at your door?

Soraya: Yes.

Graham: 7:30 then.

Soraya: I'll need your approval on my attire. I have two dresses on hold at Bergdorf's and still can't decide.

Graham: You know I'm gonna veto whatever it is, just so I can watch you undress.

Soraya: How's your tattoo?

Graham: Fine. We can play I'll show you mine/ you show me yours if you want later.

Soraya: I have a few you haven't seen.

Graham: I'm painfully aware of this.

Soraya: Maybe if you're good tonight, I'll let you see one.

Graham: And if you're good, I'll let you look under the table.

Soraya: LOL

Graham: You're evil, Soraya Venedetta. Taunting me with your tattoos. How the fuck am I supposed to work now?

Soraya: ;-)

After work, I went by Bergdorf's to purchase my dress. I had two on hold and hadn't decided which I liked best. At the fitting room, I gave my name and waited for the salesperson to return with my selections.

"Here you go, my dear."

"Thank you. But that one isn't mine." I pointed to a gorgeous green dress. It was actually the first dress that had caught my attention earlier in the day, but it was a designer I could never afford. The price tag was almost ten times the other two put together.

"That's the one your husband added this afternoon."

"My husband?"

"I assumed he was your husband. I'm sorry, I didn't ask his name. Boyfriend, perhaps? Not very many men who look like that walk into the women's dress parlor. Or pay the bill for that matter."

"Pay the bill?"

"The gentleman who added this dress to your selections. He also paid the bill for the green one. And instructed the manager to put any other dresses you like on his account as well. He also had us pick out shoes to go with the green and paid for those as well." She hung the dresses in a fitting room and disappeared for a moment. When she came back, she opened the box to show me an amazing pair of Louboutins that I could never afford.

I shot off a text before stripping out of my clothes.

Soraya: Do you shop in the ladies department often?

Graham: That was a first. You should see the items I took with me.

Soraya: You purchased other items?"

Graham: Yes. The woman in lingerie looked at me like I was Caitlin Jenner.

Soraya: LOL. You went to lingerie, too? What did you buy?

Graham: Those purchases you won't get to see so soon. Since I won't be seeing them modeled quite yet. Unless you've changed your mind...

The idea of Graham shopping in the lingerie department both amused and aroused me. I pictured him running his hand through his hair in frustration, completely hating that he was doing it, but not being able to stop himself.

Soraya: The green dress is beautiful, but I can't accept it. It's too much.

Graham: It's final sale. Donate it if you don't like it.

Seriously? The dress was nearly three thousand dollars.

Soraya: You're crazy, you know that.

Graham: Does it fit?

Soraya: I haven't tried it on yet.

The rapid fire of texts we were exchanging came to a halt for a few minutes.

Soraya: You still there?

Graham: Are you in the fitting room?

Soraya: Yes.

Graham: I just had a small fantasy of you standing in the fitting room, looking at your gorgeous naked body in the mirror.

Soraya: And...

Graham: You want to hear more of my fantasy?

Soraya: I might...

Graham: I'd like to join you in that fitting room. Bend you over with your hands pressed against the mirror, fingers splayed wide, and take you from behind while you watch us. You'd still be wearing the shoes I picked out.

This time, I was the one who went quiet. I looked in the mirror and actually saw Graham standing behind me. If the illusion was that hot, there was a good chance I'd melt when the real thing happened. *When.* I was no longer even attempting to fool myself by saying *if.* Eventually, my phone buzzed.

Graham: I know what you're doing.

Soraya: See you tonight, Mr. Big Prick.

When I arrived at my apartment carrying a garment bag, I noticed a black town car parked outside. As I neared, the uniformed driver got out. *Graham's driver.*

"Ms. Venedetta, Mr. Morgan requested that this be delivered to you." He handed me two sealed manila envelopes.

"What is it?"

"I don't know, ma'am. I was instructed to deliver it, so here I am." He gave a polite nod and opened the car door. "You have a good afternoon."

My hands were full, so I waited until I was upstairs before attempting to open the envelopes. After hanging my dress, I sat down on my bed and ripped open the first of the packages. Inside was a box of *La Riche Alpine Green* hair dye. The color was an exact match for the dress.

Graham J. Morgan had a serious sweet side.

Curious, I tore open the next envelope. It was a box of green *Betty Down There Hair Color* with a sticky note that read, *I wasn't sure if the carpet matched the curtains.*

Smiling from ear to ear, I thought to myself, *you're going to find out for yourself very soon if you keep this up.*

THE BUZZER RANG AT PROMPTLY 7:30. I spoke into the intercom before pressing the button to unbolt the main door downstairs. "Is this Celibate in Manhattan?"

"Unfortunately, yes."

I buzzed him up and unlocked my door to wait.

Walking down the hallway from the elevator to my apartment, he took quick, confident strides. Each one made my pulse race a little faster. He was wearing a dark tuxedo and was quite possibly the most gorgeous man I'd ever set my eyes on. There was no doubt in my mind that he could cause traffic jams walking down Manhattan streets dressed like that. I literally licked my lips.

While I stood there salivating, Graham took my face into one hand and squeezed. "You are going to be the death of me, looking at me like that." Then he kissed me until there was no doubt what I was feeling was mutual.

I blinked myself back to reality when he released me. "I need to get dressed. Come inside."

"I haven't been able to think about anything but coming inside since you told me about your doctor's appointment to renew your birth control."

I rolled my eyes at him for being a perv, even though I secretly loved every dirty word. "I just need a minute to slip my dress on."

"Would you like help with that?"

I pointed to a chair in the kitchen. "Sit. Stay."

"Am I a dog? I'm not above begging."

I disappeared into my bedroom and slipped on the green dress. It was the most expensive thing I've ever owned. Graham wasn't lying when he said the dress was final sale. Otherwise, I wouldn't be wearing it. But I had to admit, the other dresses I picked out couldn't compare to the beauty of the one he had bought.

Unlike Graham, who strode toward me with the self-assurance of knowing his place at the top of the food chain, I was a nervous wreck to walk out of my bedroom. The dress was gorgeous; it hugged my every curve and showed off the perfect amount of skin to be sexy without tilting to slutty, yet I wasn't in my comfort zone. Looking in the mirror, my reflection was beautiful, but what it didn't reflect was...me.

Whatever doubt I had was almost fully erased when I

saw Graham's face. He was sitting at my kitchen table playing with his phone and stood when he saw me.

"You look fucking incredible."

"The dress is incredible. I still can't believe how much you paid for it."

"It's not the dress, Soraya. It's the woman wearing it."

"That's sweet. Thank you."

"Green is most definitely your color." He reached up and fingered my hair. "I can't see if your tips match with this hairdo." I'd pinned my hair up into a French twist, and tucked the colorful ends underneath.

I smiled. "They do. But I didn't want to stick out like a sore thumb. I've never been to a gala before, but something tells me I would be the only one with green in her hair."

"You don't like your hair up?"

"I like it better down, actually."

"Turn around. Let me see." When I complied, Graham slipped the pins that were fastening my thick tresses out. My long hair fell down in waves. He guided me to turn back around. "You'll stick out with it up or down, and it has nothing to do with your hair color."

"You don't mind?"

"Mind? I'm an arrogant asshole. I quite like it when others envy what I have."

"Just give me a second to fix it." I went to the bathroom and smoothed out my hair. I really did like my hair down better. When I returned, Graham took both of my hands.

"So, does it match?"

"Yes. The color is pretty close, don't you think?" I lifted my tips up against the top of my dress. The greens were almost the exact same hue.

"I wasn't talking about the dress."

"Oh. No. Thank you for the *Betty Down There*, but the curtains don't match."

"That's a shame."

I smirked. "Really? I thought you might like my set up down there."

"Your set up?"

I kissed his lips gently, then spoke against them. "There's nothing to dye. I'm completely bare down there."

GRAHAM WAS RIGHT ABOUT ONE THING; we were certainly attracting attention. Although I doubted any of the women eye fucking the man I was standing next to even noticed my hair. Graham seemed oblivious as he steered me toward the bar.

"You seem to have a fan club."

"It's more like a hate club. My business is very competitive."

I eyed one woman who was blatantly staring at us as we walked. She was wearing a red dress, and her head was following our every step. "Looks more like lust than hate."

Graham followed my line of sight. He pulled me closer to his side. "Keep away from that one."

That comment only made me stare longer. "Why?"

"I don't want her tainting your view on me any more than I accomplish on my own."

At the bar, Graham ordered his fancy drink and the wine I had at dinner last week. He got a point for remembering what I liked. While we waited, I looked around the room. The Met was an incredible place. I'd been inside before for exhibitions but never in this particular hall. The domed ceilings were a work of art in itself. It was overwhelming to take it all in. The people. The venue. The man standing next to me, most of all.

Graham handed me my drink. "How much money will something like this raise?"

"I think last year it drummed up five million."

I almost choked sipping my wine. The woman in the red dress who had been staring at us sauntered to the bar.

"Hello, Graham."

He nodded. His response was curt, and I felt his body stiffen. "Avery."

Oh, fuck. The woman I called.

"Aren't you going to introduce me to your friend?"

He drew me even closer to his side. "Actually, no. We were just about to dance. Excuse us."

Graham abruptly steered me away from the bar and the woman. I was relieved to get away from her myself, but curious at the relationship. There was a large, mostly empty dance floor on one side of the room. On our way, we made a stop at table number four and Graham set down our drinks.

Out on the dance floor, Graham pulled me close. I wasn't surprised to find he knew how to dance. The way he led with a strong hand, definitely suited his domineering personality.

"So...red dress. I take it you two have history?"

"We do. But it's not what you think."

"Meaning what? That you haven't fucked her?"

He pulled his head back and his brow arched. "Jealous?"

I looked away. The thought of him being with anyone else stirred something irrational inside of me. Graham leaned in and ran his nose along my throat. "I like that you're jealous. It means that you're possessive of me. I feel the exact same way about you."

My eyes met with his. Our gazes held for a long time

before he spoke again. "No. I haven't slept with Avery. Never laid a finger on her. She's not happy with the way I'm currently handling a business acquisition."

"Oh."

He leaned in closer, gravelly speaking in my ear. "But speaking of fucking. I've had a hard on since you told me you were bare." With his hand on my lower back, he pressed me firmly against him. I could feel his erection poking into my hip. The man was attacking all of my senses at once—the sound of his needy voice, the smell that was so male and distinctly him, the touch of his hands on my bare skin—*God, I wanted to taste him.* It didn't help that the way his body controlled mine as we fluidly swept across the dance floor reminded me how dominating he would probably be in bed. There was an unlocked closet around somewhere nearby, I was sure of it. It would be so easy to give in to him right now. But instead, I forced my usual bitchy self through the haze of lust that threatened to swallow me.

"Maybe you should see a doctor about that. Seems like you constantly have an erection. Too much Viagra, perhaps?"

"I can assure you, there is no artificial assistance needed to make my cock swell when I'm around you, Soraya. And I have visited my doctor recently. In fact, just a few days ago. I took some advice from a columnist I follow and prepared myself on the off chance that I'm permitted to break my celibacy vow. I'm clean and have the papers to prove it."

"You sound eager. Are you carrying them on your person right now?" I was joking, but Graham pulled back and patted his jacket pocket over where the inside pocket would be. I chuckled. "Are you serious? You don't actually have them on you, do you?"

"Of course, I'm serious. There is nothing more that

I want to do than come inside of you. Not a chance I was going to miss an opportunity because I wasn't prepared if the occasion presented itself. I've been carrying them with me for three days."

His admission was bizarrely endearing. Another song came on, and we danced in quiet for a while, our bodies swaying in unison.

I leaned my head on his chest and sighed. "I like this. I didn't expect to, to be honest."

He nuzzled against me. "Me, too. I normally hate these things."

My guard was slipping for this man. It didn't take long for me to be reminded to lift it back up and protect myself.

We were seated at a large round table set up to accommodate at least a dozen other guests. Graham introduced me to the couples surrounding us on either side, but a few of the chairs were still empty.

"So what do you do? Soraya, is it?" Braxton Harlow sat to my left. He was an older, yet handsome looking gentleman with silvery hair that stood in stark contrast to his tanned face. Graham was talking business to the man on his other side.

"I work for an advice columnist. *Ask Ida*."

"You're a writer. How wonderful."

"Not exactly. It's more like I run crappy errands for the writer and sometimes she lets me take a shot at answering some of the letters we get."

"I see."

"What do you do?"

"I own a pharmaceutical company."

"You're a legal drug dealer?"

He chuckled. "I suppose I am."

"Does that mean you're a doctor?"

"It does."

"Well maybe you can talk to Graham here, he seems to have a medical issue."

Just then, Graham joined our conversation. "I heard my name. Are you two talking about me?"

Braxton responded, "Soraya was just about to tell me about a medical issue you're having. Is there something I can help you with, Graham?"

Graham squinted at me and then downed the last of his drink. "I don't know, do you treat blue balls?"

At first, the man looked confused, but that quickly changed into a hearty laugh. After that, the three of us fell into easy conversation together. Graham's hand was always on the back of my chair, his fingers lightly tracing a figure eight along one bare shoulder. I was actually beginning to relax and enjoy myself, right up until I saw a flash of red across the table. Avery was seated directly across from us. Graham and the man she was with did that silent nod thing that men do.

"Looks like we're sharing a meal with your friend." I leaned into Graham.

"Ignore her."

That was easier said than done. I felt her glare, even when I wasn't sneaking peeks. For some reason, the woman was enjoying making me feel uncomfortable. She made no effort to speak to anyone else at the table.

After dinner, I excused myself to go the ladies' room. I closed myself in a stall and attempted to figure out the best way to go to the bathroom without dipping my expensive dress in toilet water, or touching the seat, or dropping my purse, or falling forward as I hovered in five-inch stilettos. I would have thought it was a much easier task.

The restroom had been empty when I walked in. I heard the entrance door open, then close, and then the clickity clack of heels stopped somewhere in the vicinity of my stall. My intuition told me who was on the other side. Taking a deep breath, I stepped out, and a flash of red immediately assaulted me. Avery was lining her lips in the mirror, but her gaze was set on me as I walked out.

"If it isn't Graham Morgan's latest plaything."

"Is this how you get your kicks? Following women into the restroom to speak ill about their dates."

She rubbed her lips together to even out the fiery red color, blotted on a tissue, and then capped her lipstick. "I'm providing a service to womankind by warning women about that man."

"What's the matter? You don't like the way he conducts his business, so you need to warn me off?"

Her mouth spread into a malicious smile. "Is that what he told you? That I simply don't like the way he conducts his business?"

Hating feeling like she knew something I didn't, I said nothing. Instead, I washed my hands and took my own lipstick out. When I was all done, she was still standing there. I folded my arms over my chest. "Well get on with it. Tell me what you are dying to enlighten me with."

She took a few steps, stopping behind me to study my reflection in the mirror. Then she spoke directly into my eyes. "On second thought, you're not worth my time. Eventually, you'll figure it out on your own. Or maybe you can ask Graham why he is set on destroying my best friend's husband's company."

I took a minute to compose myself after Avery walked out. She was every bit as big of a bitch as when I called her that first day I found Graham's phone on the train. I wanted to chalk her warning up to fierce competition between rival companies, but that didn't sit right with me. It was personal for that woman in some way.

Graham was waiting for me outside the bathroom. "Everything okay? I saw Avery follow you in."

"Fine." I forced a smile. After a few steps, I decided I needed to know more. "Can I ask you something?"

"Of course."

"Who is Avery's best friend?"

Graham raked a hand through his slicked back hair. "Her best friend is my ex, Genevieve."

CHAPTER 11

graham

SOMETHING HAD CHANGED AFTER SORAYA'S VISIT to the ladies' room last night. Before that, she was being her usual sarcastic self—charming the pants off a sixty-year-old pharmaceutical researcher by being nothing other than who she is. After, though, she was quiet and withdrawn. When we arrived back at her apartment, she didn't invite me in, and her kiss was missing the usual fire that burned between us. Afraid to push, I waited to see what would happen the next day. *Nothing had happened.* And here I was sitting in my office on Saturday afternoon staring at a pile of prospectuses. My concentration had gone to shit since that woman stormed into my life.

I picked up my phone, then tossed it back on my desk. By three o'clock, I had repeated the motion twenty fucking times. Eventually, I grumbled to myself what a pussy I was and thumbed off a quick text.

Graham: We survived the two events. Do we still have a deal?

I stared at the damn phone until the dots started to jump around. My anxiety level grew as they started, then stopped, then started again. No thought was necessary to text back that our deal of exclusivity was sealed. *What are you thinking, Soraya Venedetta?*

Soraya: Are you sure that's what you want?

There was no stopping as I texted my response.

Graham: It's what I've wanted since day one. These little tests were your idea.

Soraya: I'm nervous.

I hit call, rather than play a game of *guess what you're really thinking* texting. She picked up on the first ring.

"What did she say to you?"

"Avery?"

"Who else?"

"I told you already."

"Tell me again. I'm missing something."

"I don't remember her exact words."

"Tell me what you remember."

"Well. She basically stalked me while I peed. Then told me she was doing a service to womankind by warning me about you."

"Go on."

"There wasn't much else. She said I wasn't worth her time and that I would figure it out on my own eventually. Then she told me to ask you why you were set on destroying her best friend's husband's company."

"I had already told you about Liam and Genevieve. He's a competitor."

She was quiet for a minute. "I googled you and Liam this morning."

Blowing out a deep breath, I leaned back into my chair. "And..."

"There was a bunch of articles about how you are trying to do a hostile takeover of his company."

"That's right."

"The articles all said you were overpaying market value by almost double. I don't know much about business, but why would you do that? If it wasn't to destroy a man because you still had feelings for the woman he stole from you? The woman whose name was tattooed on your body?"

"That's what this is about?"

"I'm nervous, Graham. I feel like you could swallow me whole."

"I've been trying to."

"Yes, that, too. But you know what I mean."

"You're afraid I'm going to hurt you?"

She sighed. "Yes."

"Liam's company owns a twenty-three percent stake in Pembrooke Industries. Last year, I purchased twenty-eight percent in Pembrooke under a straw corporation to which I'm the sole shareholder. If I acquire Liam's company, it comes with his shares in Pembrooke. That would give me fifty-one percent ownership and controlling interest. That interest is worth more than double Liam's company alone. I'm after Pembrooke, not Liam. The analysts assume it's because of a grudge since he was my former employee."

"So you aren't still in love with Genevieve?"

"No. And if you're concerned, you could have come to me, Soraya."

"I'm sorry. I guess I'm just totally freaked out by what's happening between us."

"As am I. But you know what I realized?"

"What's that?"

"Freaked out or not, whatever it is that's going on, it's *going* to happen. Neither one of us has the ability to stop it. So why don't you get your ass down here to my office and tell me you're sorry for jumping to conclusions in person."

"Is that code for hop up on your desk, and we play boss secretary?"

I groaned. "Get your ass down here."

She chuckled. I'm glad my constant suffering could, at least, be of amusement to her. "No can do, Morgan."

"Stop screwing with me, Soraya."

"I'm not. I actually can't come there. I'm not home."

"Where are you?"

"Helping Delia at a trade show. We're a few hours upstate."

I muttered something inarticulate under my breath. "When will you be back?"

"In the morning. The show doesn't end until after dark, and Delia is dangerous enough driving in the light. Plus, she'll pierce a hundred walk-ins today at the show, and be cross-eyed by the time it's over. So we're going to crash at the hotel across the street from the show."

"What will you be doing all day?"

"Assisting. I swab the area before she pierces and hold hands with the chickens."

I wasn't sure I wanted to know the answer, but I asked anyway. "What will you be swabbing?"

"The usual. Ears, noses, belly buttons, tongues, nipples, a penis or two."

"Come again?"

"It's clinical."

"Yes, that makes me feel better about you swabbing a man's cock. I'm sure Delia has her M.D."

"Relax. It's no big deal."

"Yes. You're right."

"I am?"

"Sure." I partially covered the phone and yelled to my secretary, who wasn't in today. "Elizabeth? Can you come in here a minute?"

"Elizabeth? Is that your new secretary?"

"Yes. I'm going to wash her tits."

Soraya chuckled. The woman damn laughed at me. Again.

"What's so funny?"

"I've seen firsthand the way you treat secretaries. Pretty sure she wouldn't let you wash her feet, much less her tits."

Sadly, she was probably right.

"When will I see you?"

"Tomorrow night."

"Okay."

"I'll pick you up at six."

"Works for me. I have to go now. A big tatted guy just walked into Delia's booth. They usually need hand holding the most."

"Wonderful. Now I'll be picturing you swabbing some muscle head's cock while he ogles your massive rack and gets hard."

"You have a pretty vivid imagination."

"Tomorrow. Soraya."

"Later, Suit."

A few minutes after we hung up, my phone buzzed with a text from her.

Soraya: *Yes, we have a deal.*

I needed to get her mind off that shit with Avery, show her that there was nothing to be scared about when it came to me. Unable to concentrate on anything but seeing Soraya tonight, I left the office early which seemed to be the norm lately. If I didn't own the company, I would have totally fired my ass.

Back at my condo, I got to work chopping vegetables for the pasta primavera I was planning to make. I wasn't a gourmet cook by any means, but I could make a damn good al dente pasta. I'd texted Soraya earlier to let her know there was a change of plans; I was cooking her dinner for us at my place. It felt like the right change of pace after the gala fiasco. I needed to let her into my space and show her more of my casual side.

I'd just turned on the television that was built into the wall of my kitchen, selecting a show from the DVR list when the phone rang. *Soraya calling.* I grabbed a towel to wipe my hands before answering it.

"Hey, gorgeous."

"Hi..." She paused. "What is that music in the background?"

"The television."

Shit.

Frantically trying to lower the volume, I soon realized that the volume control wasn't working. My coolness factor was about to plummet.

"Was that the opening sequence to *General Hospital?*"

"No," I lied.

"Yes, it was."

Fuck. Caught in the act.

I laughed guiltily. "Ok, it was. You got me."

"You watch soap operas?"

"Only this one."

"And here I was thinking we didn't have anything in common..."

I cleared my throat and surrendered to the embarrassment. "You watch it, too?"

"Actually, I used to...not as much anymore."

"I never really got into it until my mother became sick when I was in high school. She was obsessed with GH. When she was bed-ridden, I'd curl up next to her at three in the afternoon and keep her company while it was on. I ended up getting into some of the storylines and kept watching it after she passed. It reminds me of her."

She went quiet then said, "Graham...that is...wow...I... that is really precious."

Feeling suddenly emotional, I quickly changed the subject. "To what do I owe this phone call?"

"I wanted to know if I could bring anything."

"Nothing but your beautiful ass, baby."

"Seriously. I want to bring something."

"I have it covered."

"Okay. Wine then."

Stubborn girl.

"My driver will pick you up in an hour."

"Alright."

I paused for a moment then whispered her name, "Soraya..."

"Yeah?"

"I can't fucking wait to see you."

SO IMMERSED IN SETTING UP OUR TABLE, I'd forgotten to let the doorman know to just send Soraya straight upstairs. When he rang to notify me of my visitor, I decided to mess with her a bit.

"Please put Miss Venedetta on the phone," I told him.

She came on the line. "Yes?" My dick twitched at the sound of her voice. Soraya wasn't even in front of me, but just knowing she was downstairs was making me hard.

"How can I help you, Miss?"

She giggled. "Is this *General Hospital?*"

Little wiseass.

"If you'll play naughty nurse, it *can* be. Give him back the phone and get your ass up here."

When the doorman returned to the line, I instructed him to show Soraya to the elevators. Her knock was rhythmic and loud, and Blackie immediately started barking.

I spoke to my dog as I walked to the door. "Yeah. Yeah. Just wait till you see her."

My heart started to pump faster the minute I opened it and caught sight of how breathtakingly beautiful she looked. Her hair was down but had a wild and wavy windblown look to it. The ends were still green, and she wore a matching emerald-colored blouse that was sleeveless but covered her entire neckline. There was a bow tied up at the top. Sleek black pants looked like they'd been painted on her legs. Overall, it was a teasingly conservative ensemble compared to her usual attire. Her normally bright red lips were also bare as if she knew I'd be eating them whole later.

Fighting hard to restrain myself from mauling her, I begrudgingly placed my hands at my side. I vowed not to touch or kiss her yet, fearing that I wouldn't be able to stop. So, I was going to hold back as long as I could. This night was about showing her she could trust me. Pouncing on her right out of the gate would negate that.

"Come in." I took in a long whiff of her floral scent as she entered the room.

The dog immediately started to jump all over her.

"Get off her, Blackie."

Looking amused, she handed me the bottle of wine she was carrying, bent down and lifted him up. Blackie was licking all over her face.

Damn, I wanted in on that.

Taking the dog from her, I cracked, "And you thought it would be *me* you'd need to pry off of you."

"You are being very good, Mr. Morgan."

"I'm trying," I said sincerely.

She covered her mouth. "Oh, my God! Blackie. It just hit me. From *General Hospital!* He's named after *that* Blackie."

"That's right."

She pointed at my face. "You're not embarrassed, are you?"

"No."

"Because your ears are turning red!"

Fuck.

"I think it's sweet, Graham, especially that the show reminds you of your mother. Thank you for sharing that with me."

"I don't think I've ever told anyone about that. You have a way of turning me into mush, Venedetta."

"Good." She grinned.

Circling my palms together slowly, I said, "Since we're on the subject. Let's see how good your *General Hospital* knowledge is."

She flashed the cutest smile again as she accepted my challenge. "Lay it on me."

"There's one more thing about me—a major identifier—that has a *General Hospital* connection."

"What do I get if I guess it correctly?"

"A special kiss from me later."

"Oh, yeah? A *special* one, huh?"

"I'll give you a hint."

"Alright."

"It rhymes with organ."

"Oh, *that* line again. Ok...Morgan....your last name." A realization seemed to hit her. "That's right! Oh my God. That name is from *General Hospital,* too!"

"The last name connection is purely coincidental, of course, but the J of my middle name stands for Jason."

She nodded in understanding. "Jason Morgan...like the character!"

"My mother thought it was brilliant."

"Your mother sounds like she was very clever."

"She was...clever, funny, bright, full of life...a lot like you, actually." I walked over to the granite counter and opened the Sauvignon blanc she'd brought. Handing her a crystal glass, I said, "Can I show you around?"

Sipping our wine, we toured the condo. Soraya particularly loved the electric fireplace in my bedroom. I couldn't wait to fuck her right in front of it someday.

We finally circled back around to the living room and stopped in front of the floor-to-ceiling length window overlooking the Manhattan skyline.

She gazed out at the spectacular city lights. "I always dreamt of having a view like this."

Meanwhile, I was gazing at nothing but her. "This view is yours. You can come here anytime you want."

"I can *come* here, huh?"

"I didn't mean it like that."

"Oh, I know. You're uncharacteristically polite and politically correct tonight. What's gotten into you, Graham Jason Morgan?"

"Do you not like me polite? I'm trying not to fuck anything up tonight. After what happened at the gala—"

"You're fine. You're good just the way you are. I love how honest you always are with me about your thoughts and feelings." She leaned in and gripped my wool sweater, causing my cock to swell. I felt myself unraveling very quickly as she continued, "In fact, I prefer blunt honesty to anything else. I always want you to tell me the truth, even if you're afraid it might offend me. I don't think you understand how much I just need the truth."

"I don't think you understand how much I need *you*." Now that her hands were on me, I was a goner. "And I'll give you anything you need. You want the absolute truth?"

"Yes. Tell me what you want."

"In what way? Out of life? Right now? Be specific."

"What do you really want right now at this very moment?"

"You won't fault me for my answer?"

"As long as it's truly what you're thinking...no."

My voice was thick. "I want your tongue on my cock."

Yup. I'd lost it.

Her eyelashes flickered seductively. "What else?"

"After you take me into your mouth, I want to strip you naked and eat your pussy right before I fuck you from behind with your hands plastered against this window."

"Then what?"

"I want to come inside of you."

"Then?"

"Then...we eat pasta in bed naked."

We both let out slight laughs before the tone turned serious again.

She looked around my living room. "When did it get so dark all of a sudden?"

"I don't know. I haven't noticed much else besides you since you walked in that door. That's the truth."

"Thank you for being honest with me, Graham."

It was the last thing she said before she placed her fingers on the bow at her neckline, slowly untying it. Well, fuck. This was apparently the reward for my honesty. She undid the buttons, and her satin blouse fell to the ground. When she unsnapped her black lace bra from the front, her tits sprung out. Even though it was dark, the lights of the city let in enough illumination for me to see her nipples pucker from the cold air.

Letting out a shaky breath, I said, "Let me warm you up." I bent down and sucked her breast mercilessly into my mouth. She let out a moan the second my lips touched her skin.

Soraya dug her fingers into my sweater, tugging on it and pulled it over my head. Pressing my bare chest into hers, I took her tongue into my mouth and sucked on it slowly. My cock, now fully hard, was bursting through my jeans against her stomach. Then, the feel of her little hand sliding over my crotch obliterated the last bit of the control within me.

She suddenly dropped to her knees.

I was done.

My heart seemed to be beating faster than it could handle as she unzipped me and took my cock out. It felt like time stood still as she looked up at me and slid her tongue ring in a slow circle across my crown that was already wet and ready for her mouth. My head seemed to fall back involuntarily from the sensation that could only be described as absolute bliss.

This.

This was heaven.

When she suddenly lowered her jaw, taking me fully, my balls tightened in a desperate attempt to keep from coming instantly down her beautiful throat. I realized that I was in bigger trouble than I ever imagined because there was no way I could ever let go of her now that I knew what this felt like.

All I could think about was how I couldn't wait to be inside of her, how I wanted to claim every inch of her, every orifice. I wanted to own her, but the truth was...she already owned me. I was so fucked.

"Slow down, baby."

My cell phone started to ring. *Shit*. There was no way in hell I was answering that. When the home phone started ringing immediately after, my stomach dropped because I knew it was my grandmother. Meme was the only person who had my landline home number. The answering machine picked up.

"Mr. Morgan? This is Cambria Lynch, your grandmother's social worker. She had a pretty bad fall today and is at

Westchester Hospital. I'm calling to let you know." The rest of the message was muffled.

Soraya released my cock from her mouth and jumped back when she processed the words on the answering machine. I ran to the phone and picked it up, but Cambria had already hung up.

Tucking myself back into my pants, I was in a complete fog when I looked back over at her. "I need to head to the hospital."

Soraya started frantically putting her clothes back on. "I'm going with you."

I practically tripped over Blackie, who was apparently riled up, because he was humping his toy on the ground. I prayed that one of the best nights of my life didn't turn into one of the worst.

CHAPTER 12

Soraya

MY STOMACH WAS NAUSEOUS the entire ride to the hospital.

Poor Graham.

The worry in his eyes was evident as he kept staring blankly ahead. His driver had taken the rest of the night off, so Graham drove us in his BMW to Westchester.

I placed my hand on his leg. "She'll be okay."

"Yeah," he said without taking his eyes off the road.

An hour later, we pulled up to Westchester Hospital. Graham took my hand as we scurried toward the entrance.

"My grandmother is here. Lil Morgan. Where can I find her?" Graham asked the woman at the front desk.

"Room 257," she said.

The elevator ride was extremely nerve-wracking. The antiseptic smell of the hospital made me sick to my stomach. When we got to the room, a doctor and a nurse were standing next to Lil's bed.

I immediately recognized her as the old woman with blue hair from the pictures in Graham's phone. My heart warmed at the way her eyes brightened when she saw him.

"Graham. Who told you I was here?"

"Cambria called. Are you okay?"

"I didn't want her to worry you."

"She did the right thing. What happened?"

"I don't remember. I slipped and fell, but I don't know how it happened. They're saying I broke my hip."

The male doctor held out his hand. "Mr. Morgan, I'm Dr. Spork."

"Doctor, can we speak outside for a moment?"

"Certainly."

Graham walked out of the room with the doctor, and the nurse followed them out. They'd left me all alone with Lil.

I'd still been looking out toward the door when her voice startled me.

"You must be Soraya."

It floored me that she knew my name, that he'd mentioned me to her.

"That's right. It's nice to meet you, Lil." I smiled and sat down on the chair adjacent to her bed.

"I can see now why he's so taken with you. You have a dark, natural beauty that's rare to come by."

"Thank you so much."

Her voice sounded tired and weak. "Graham is very private. He may never give me the chance to get you alone again, so forgive me if I'm laying a lot on you at once..."

I swallowed, not expecting an interrogation. "Okay."

"I know, at times, my grandson can be an absolute prick."

I let out the breath I'd been holding and laughed. "Yeah. I found that out pretty quickly when we first met."

"And I heard that you called him out on his crap."

"I did."

"Good. But you know, that's not really who he is deep down."

"I'm starting to see that."

"When his mother died, he internalized everything. It took a long time for him to put himself out there, and the one time he took a chance, he got burned."

"Genevieve?"

Lil looked shocked. "So, he told you about her..."

"Well, I know a little. I know that she's with his former friend, Liam, now."

"Yes. That situation was bad. In many ways, it undid any progress he'd made after my daughter Celia died. I honestly wasn't sure if Graham would ever open his heart to anyone again. But I sense it might be happening with you."

Hearing her say that made my heart feel like it was going to burst. "I don't know what to say."

"You don't have to say anything. I just wanted to make sure that you knew that there's a lot more to him than he shows. It seems you know more than I thought you did, which is good. Just don't let him convince you that he's unbreakable."

"I'm more afraid of him breaking *me*, to be honest."

"Don't be afraid to get hurt. It's far better than never experiencing anything earth-shattering. Even temporary joy is better than nothing at all. You're afraid of getting hurt like I'm afraid to die. That doesn't mean I'm not going to live every day to its fullest."

I placed my hand over hers. "Thank you for that advice."

Graham walked in at that exact moment. "Uh oh. I smell trouble stirring up."

Lil's face once again lit up when he entered the room. "While I wish you hadn't come all the way down here, I'm really happy to have met Soraya. I hope I didn't ruin your evening."

"Nah. We were just...eating pasta." He glanced over at me briefly, and we gave each other a knowing look.

"What did the doctor say about me?" Lil asked.

"He thinks you need hip surgery. They're gonna keep you here for a couple of days then move you to a rehab center. I'm gonna work with Cambria to make sure they put you in a top-of-the-line facility."

"I don't want you getting stressed out over me."

"You could have hit your head. You don't even remember how it happened. Of course, I'm gonna worry. I'm just glad it wasn't worse, Meme."

"Me, too," I said.

We sat with Lil for another hour before driving back to the city. Graham put on classical music and stayed completely quiet during the ride. When we finally entered Manhattan, I was the first to speak.

"Are you okay?"

"Yeah...I'm fine. It's just..."

"What?"

"It just hit me more than ever tonight that she's the only family I have. My mother was an only child. My grandmother is literally...*it*. When she passes, I won't have anyone left. It's just kind of a sobering thought."

"You'll have a family of your own someday."

He caught me off guard with a question I didn't see coming. "Do you want kids, Soraya?"

I could only give him the honest answer. "I'm not sure."

"You're not sure?"

"I can't say that I'm one-hundred percent sure. I'm hoping I *will be* sure by the time I have to make a decision."

"Are the doubts you're having because of the situation with your father?"

"Partly. I haven't really analyzed it too much, though. I just don't feel absolutely certain that motherhood is in the cards for me."

He looked pensive upon my reply. Maybe that wasn't what he wanted to hear, but I didn't want to lie to him. It was how I'd always felt.

Looking over at him, I asked, "Are you taking me home?"

"I wasn't planning to." A look of disappointment washed over his face. "Why...do you want to go home?"

"I just thought maybe with everything that happened with Lil—"

"You thought I'd want to be alone? No. I don't want to be alone, Soraya. I'm tired of being alone. I want you in my fucking bed tonight. We don't have to do anything. I...just want to hold you while I fall asleep. *That's* what I want if that's okay with you."

Even though it scared me, I wanted nothing more.

"Okay. Yeah."

Graham never had a chance to cook his pasta dish. Since it was late, we stopped for takeout Szechuan and brought it upstairs to his condo. We passed the paper containers back and forth to each other as we sat with our legs crossed on his living room floor watching *General Hospital*.

"I could get used to this," he said, slurping a noodle into his mouth. An uncharacteristically boyish charm shone through his face in that moment.

My heart clenched. Tonight was the first time that it really hit me that things were getting serious between us. As much as his question about whether I wanted children had rattled me earlier, I realized there was no going back. I needed to see where the tide took us. As Lil said, it would be better to get hurt than to never know.

After we cleaned up, Graham quietly led me into his bedroom. I watched as he pulled his sweater over his head. Admiring the tattoo that Tig had inked onto Graham's side, I licked my lips, wanting desperately to taste his skin.

He walked to the bathroom and returned with black pajama pants on then tossed a blue t-shirt at me.

"I want you to sleep in my shirt."

He watched intently as I unbuttoned my blouse. His mouth looked like it was watering, and his eyes were glued to my chest as I threw the t-shirt over my head.

I got into his massive bed, my body immediately sinking into the plush, memory foam mattress. This bed was fit for a king—or a Morgan.

He got behind me and enveloped my body in his arms. His breathing slowed, and I realized he was falling asleep, calm as a baby. I soon followed suit.

IT WAS 4AM WHEN SOMETHING woke me up. Graham was turned to me with his eyes open.

"I love watching you sleep."

My voice was groggy. "If I knew you were watching me, I wouldn't have been able to."

He chuckled. "What woke you up?"

"I don't know. Maybe it was just my intuition."

"You know what I think?"

"What?"

"I think you wanted to peek under the blanket."

"And here I thought the dirty bastard in you had taken the night off."

"Never. He's always here, even when he's quiet." He laughed, and his smile nearly melted me. He locked his fingers with mine. "Seriously, though, I think something's weighing on you."

"How do you know?"

"Your eyes."

"Your grandmother told me I shouldn't be afraid of getting hurt."

"She's a wise woman. You should listen to her. But can I tell you a secret?"

"Yes."

"You terrify me, Soraya."

"Likewise."

"But that's the very reason that I just know."

"Know what?"

"That this could be the real thing."

The real thing.

"I need to learn to stop worrying about tomorrow, just enjoy today," I whispered.

Graham brought my hand to his mouth and kissed it. "No one knows what's going to happen from one day to the next, but if the world were to end tomorrow, there's no place I'd rather be than right here with you. That tells me everything I need to know."

When he pressed his lips into mine, it felt different from any of the other times he'd kissed me, more passionate, almost desperate. It felt like he was releasing all of the pent up tension in his body into me. What started off slow and sensual soon turned wild and frenzied. No longer able to control the need for him, I made a conscious decision to let go of all of my insecurities, even if just for this moment in time. Here in this bed, I felt safe. That was all that mattered.

As if he could read my mind, Graham climbed over me, pinning me down with his arms on each side of me. He hovered over me for the longest time, just staring into my eyes. He seemed to be holding back, seeking permission. So, I silently nodded, letting him know that I was game for whatever he had in store. He closed his eyes for a moment then opened them again.

He never took his eyes off me as his large hand worked to slowly slide my underwear off. He cupped me right between the legs as I throbbed, so wet and ready for him.

He clenched his jaw. "Fuck, Soraya. I need to be inside. Now." With his boxer briefs still on, he ground his cock against me. I squeezed his ass, pushing him against my clit, so incredibly aroused.

He pulled off his underwear, and now his bare cock felt hot against my stomach. Spreading my legs as wide as they could go, I couldn't wait a second longer. Gripping his shaft, I led him into my opening. Unprepared for his girth, I gasped before slowly easing him in.

"Oh...fuck...you feel...fuck..." he muttered against my mouth as he moved slowly in and out of me. He pulled his face back to look at me. His pupils were dilated as he continued to stare into my eyes almost hypnotically with every thrust. No man had ever looked at me like that during sex. He was fucking me, body and soul, and I just knew that this was going to ruin me forever.

The room was completely still. I could hear nothing but the sound of our wet slapping arousal as he fucked me as deeply as he could. His hands were pulling at my hair harder, and when his breathing became uneven, I knew he was losing control.

"I'm gonna come so hard, Soraya." He gritted his teeth. "So...fucking...hard."

Those words were all it took as I felt my muscles pulsating around his cock. He could feel my orgasm and finally let himself go. His hips bucked as he fucked me harder, letting out a loud groan before coming inside of me.

Collapsing, he gently kissed my neck over and over, staying inside of me for the longest time. When he eventually pulled out, I could feel his hot cum streaming slowly down my inner thighs. I'd never known what that felt like because I'd never let a man come inside of me before. I was no virgin, but somehow it felt like my first real time, far more intimate and intense than anything I had ever done with anyone. It felt like I should have wanted to run to the shower, but it was just the opposite. I wanted the remnants of him to stay inside of me.

He kissed me softly until I slowly fell back asleep, wondering if anything I could ever conjure up in my dreams would top the reality of what I'd just experienced.

THE NEXT DAY IN WORK, a complete and utter fog followed me around all day. Nothing Ida was saying was registering. My mind kept replaying the events of the night before. The few hours before I was set to see him again seemed like an eternity. It felt like a drug addiction for Christ's sake.

I assumed he'd been quiet all day until I checked the *Ask Ida* email account.

Dear Ida,

This is the former Celibate in Manhattan. You might also remember me as Stuck-Up Suit. I thought it would be polite to provide you with an update to my situation, seeing as though you've been so helpful thus far. The good news: I'm happy to say that I'm no longer celibate. The bad news: Now that I've had her, I want to be inside of her every second of the day. I can't stop thinking of fucking her in every which way. I'm worried that she may eventually tire of my insatiable appetite. So, my question to you is: Is there such a thing as too much sex?

—Fucked in Manhattan

Dear Fucked in Manhattan:

Congratulations on ending your celibacy. I guess the answer to your question would depend on how good you are in bed. Assuming that your performance is favorable (which I highly suspect it is), I don't think you will have a problem. You may also be veering on the side of presumptuous in assuming that your lady friend would find an overabundance of sex unfavorable. Don't underestimate a woman's own voracious libido.

That evening, Graham was supposed to call to let me know what time his driver would be picking me up to take me to the condo. It was unlike him to be running so late without calling me. My paranoid side got the best of me as I picked up the phone and dialed him.

He answered. "Soraya..." The tone of his voice sounded sullen.

What the fuck?

"I've been waiting for your call. Is everything alright?"

He let out a deep breath into the phone. "No. I'm afraid it's not."

My heart started to palpitate. "What's going on?"

"I just got some news a little while ago."

"News?"

"It's Liam."

"Your ex-friend? Genevieve's husband. What about him?"

There was a long moment of silence. "He's dead."

CHAPTER 13

Soraya

THE ANXIOUS FEELING I HAD after speaking to Graham last night had carried over into my sleep. I tossed and turned all night, unable to settle. By morning, I was downright antsy. Graham had said he was going into the office to work on some business last night—he had planned to take over Liam's company through smart business maneuvers but had no intention of taking advantage of the man's death to get what he wanted. Although that wouldn't stop others. The vultures, he said, would be scavenging first thing this morning when news broke. Graham was going to somehow freeze out others from taking advantage and postpone his own planned takeover.

I was disappointed he wasn't on our usual train, although I hadn't really expected him to be.

Soraya: How are you this morning?
Graham: Tired. I'm still at the office.
Soraya: You mean you stayed there all night?

Graham: I did.

Soraya: I'm sorry. This must be difficult for you. Is there something I can do?

Graham: Just hang in there for me, please. I'm going to be swamped for a few days.

If I was unclear on just how affected Graham was by the news, his response solidified he was not himself. He hadn't suggested I should crawl under his desk or spread my legs when I asked him if there was anything I could do.

Soraya: Of course.

Arriving at my stop, I exited the train and began my usual morning routine of stopping at Anil's coffee truck. After I placed my order, a thought hit me.

"Can you make that two coffees and also two buttered bagels and two orange juices?" It wasn't exactly gourmet, but it would make me feel better to do *something* for him. The man had followed me and sent Indian food because he thought I liked it; a bagel and coffee was the least I could do.

Heading back to the station, I called Ida and left a message I would be late and then hopped on the A train. Twenty minutes later, I arrived at Morgan Financial Holdings. Stepping out of the elevator on the twentieth floor, the gold lettering above the glass doors suddenly made me nervous. I had started to become accustomed to the butterflies that I got around Graham, but being on his turf—in the arena where I knew he ruled with an iron fist—had me feeling intimidated. And I hated that.

I squared my shoulders and walked to the receptionist. It was the same young redhead from the day I brought back his phone.

"Can I help you?"

"Yes, I'd like to see Graham."

She looked me up and down. "Graham? You mean Mr. Morgan?"

"Yes. Graham J. Morgan."

"Do you have an appointment?"

Not this shit again.

"No. But he'll want to see me. If you can just let him know Soraya is here."

"Mr. Morgan doesn't want to be interrupted."

"Look. I know you have a job. And judging from our interactions, you're probably even good at it. You seem to do a great job of blowing people off. But, trust me on this one, you won't get in trouble for interrupting him to tell him I'm here."

"I'm sorry...he was very specific..."

Oh for God's sake. "I'm fucking him, okay? Just tell Graham I'm here, or I'm going to walk past you anyway."

The woman blinked twice. "Excuse me?"

I leaned in. "Fucking him. You know, you insert..."

"Soraya?" Graham's voice stopped me from continuing my anatomy lesson. He was coming down the hall toward me, taking long strides. I turned and waited, rather than walking to meet him. *Damn.* He was wearing those glasses again.

"What a nice surprise."

"Your receptionist didn't seem to think so."

Graham quirked an eyebrow, his lip hinting at amusement, then turned to his employee with his business mask on. "Ms. Venedetta doesn't need an appointment." He looked to me and back to his receptionist. "Ever."

He took my elbow and steered me down the hall he had just come from. The woman sitting at the desk outside of his office stood as we approached. "Cancel my 9AM call, Rebecca."

"It's Eliza."

"Whatever."

He shut the door behind us and no sooner than it closed, I was up against it, and Graham sealed his mouth over mine. The brown paper bag carrying the bagels dropped to the floor, my fingers needing to thread into his hair. He kissed me long and hard, his tongue doing that aggressive dance with mine while his hard body crushed me against the door. The desperation of his need turned me on instantly. Reaching down, he lifted one of my legs, allowing him to press deeper into me in just the right place. *Oh, God.*

"Graham."

He groaned.

"Graham."

My hand holding the coffee was starting to shake.

"I'm going to drop the coffees."

"So drop them." He mumbled against my lips and then his tongue was back searching.

"Graham," I chuckled into our joined mouths.

He hissed out a frustrated breath. "I need you."

"Can you let me put down the coffees and maybe take a look around your office before you maul me?"

He leaned his forehead against mine. "Are you asking me or telling me?"

"Considering that sounds like the answer will be no if it's a question, I'm telling you."

He groaned but stepped back.

"I love the glasses, by the way. Not sure if I told you that the other night when you wore them to Tig's."

"I'll throw away my contacts."

I walked to his desk, getting my first look around his office as I set down the coffees. Floor-to-ceiling windows overlooked the Manhattan skyline on two sides of his corner office. There was a large mahogany desk positioned at an angle that faced one glass wall. Not one, but two sleek computers were positioned next to each other on his desk. The top of the desk had various case files strewn about, and piles of documents were flipped open in mid-review.

"Your office is beautiful. But it looks like you're busy. I won't stay long. I just came to drop off a bagel and coffee."

"Thank you. You didn't have to do that."

"I wanted to." I got my first full look at him. He was still gorgeous, but he looked tired and stressed. "You look exhausted."

"I'll survive." He motioned to a seating area. "Come. Sit. Have breakfast with me. I actually haven't eaten anything since last night." The other side of the office had a long leather couch with two wingback chairs across from it and a glass coffee table separating the seating. Graham sat, and I pulled out the bagels and unwrapped them.

"I got you what I like since I wasn't sure what you liked."

"I'll eat whatever you feed me."

"In that case..."

A dirty grin crossed his face. "Don't think I won't hold you down on this couch and feast on you until my entire staff knows you're a religious girl."

I shoved my bagel into my mouth to stop myself from daring him. The minute it took to chew and swallow also let me get my libido somewhat under control. "So...were you able to ward off the bad guys?"

"I am one of the bad guys, Soraya."

"You know what I mean. To stop people from taking advantage."

"Yes. And no. It's complicated. In our business, there

are many layers of ownership. I'm working through those layers now. But it seems Liam had established a poison pill to deter a takeover from an unwanted party. That poison allows existing shareholders to purchase additional shares at a discounted price, which would dilute the value of shares and make the acquisition less attractive to prospective takeovers."

"So, he had an escape plan."

"Exactly. And it would have worked well had he granted those rights to a corporation that was trustworthy."

"I take it he didn't."

Graham shook his head. "No."

"Sounds complicated and messy."

"It is."

"How are you handling the non-business stuff?"

"The non-business stuff?"

"You lost a friend."

"An ex-friend."

I nodded. "An ex-friend. But he must have been someone you cared about for a period of your life since you started your business together."

"At one point. Yes. But as you know, things changed."

"I saw on the news this morning that it was a heart attack."

"Happened in the car. He swerved off the road and hit a tree. Was dead by the time the police arrived. Luckily, no one else was in the car. Genevieve said he was supposed to have had their daughter in the car, but she wasn't feeling well, so she stayed home. Otherwise..."

He saw the look on my face.

"I spoke to her this morning. She called for help with the business issues, but I was already working on it."

"I didn't realize you were friendly."

"We aren't. It was a business call. She knew I would help, and there would be a benefit for both of us to stop others from devaluing the company."

I nodded. It made sense. And it was ridiculous that I was jealous of a woman who lost her husband yesterday. "How is your grandmother?"

"She told Cambria to let me know she was cutting me out of her will if I didn't break her out of the hospital."

"Oh, no."

"Actually, that's good. It means she's feeling like herself again. When she's agreeable and compliant, it scares me."

The relationship he had with his grandmother was fast becoming my favorite thing about him. You can tell a lot about a man by watching how he treats the matriarch of the family. "Is she still at Westchester Hospital?"

"I had her moved to the Hospital for Special Surgery."

"That's on 70th, right?"

"It is."

"It's only a few blocks from my office. Why don't I stop in at lunch and visit her? You're swamped here, obviously."

Graham searched my face. "That would be great. Thank you."

"No problem."

"Will you stay with me tonight?"

"At your place?"

"Yes. My driver can pick you up after work and take you out to Brooklyn to collect your things and then take you to my place. I'll meet you there after I'm done here. The doorman will let you in if I'm not back yet."

"Okay."

We chatted for a while longer while we ate. After we finished our bagels, I gathered our garbage. "I need to get to the office, or Ida will come up with a list of things she needs to be done, that she really doesn't, but will keep me in the office until nine o'clock."

Graham kissed me goodbye, and I stopped it before it got too out of control this time. "Does this mean you're going to take a train since I'll have your driver?"

"It does."

"Commoner."

"Let's not forget how we met. I take the train every morning now."

"Now? You mean you didn't before?"

A smile spread across his face. "First time I'd taken the train to work in years was the day I lost my phone. My driver was on vacation that week."

"But you've been taking it ever since, too?"

"I have a reason to now."

The anticipation I'd felt since our phone call last night finally quelled a bit after leaving Graham's office. I wanted nothing more than to have trust in what was growing between us, yet a part of me was still afraid. He was so confident and fearless, and I tried to use that to reassure myself. I hated that weak and scared part of me. It was time I figured out how to get rid of it.

"MRS. MORGAN?" I CRACKED OPEN the door and peeked my head into her room. She was sitting up in bed watching TV.

"Come in, come in, dear. And call me Lil."

I'd texted Graham to find out what she liked to eat and brought her a fish filet from McDonald's, which Graham had told me was crap, but also her favorite junk food.

"I thought maybe you could use some company today. Graham's been stuck at the office since yesterday. I work nearby."

"Is that a fish sandwich I smell?"

I smiled. "Sure is."

"Graham thinks because it's not from some swanky restaurant that charges sixty dollars for a meal as big as a quarter, that it's not good food. Love the boy, but he can be a downright snob with his head stuck up his own ass sometimes."

I laughed thinking *Stuck-Up Suit*. "He does have an elitist side to him at times."

There was a snack tray on wheels in the corner, so I pulled it closer and set up her lunch, then set up mine.

"Is that a soap opera you're watching?"

"Days of Our Lives. My daughter got me hooked on them."

"She got her son hooked, too." I chuckled.

"You know about that?"

"I do. It's sort of out of character for him."

"It wasn't at one time. Believe it or not, that man used to be a mush. He was with my Celia, anyway. Boy idolized his mother. Took it hard when she passed. Probably why he's the way he is. Doesn't get attached to many women, if you know what I mean. The ones he did get attached to, didn't stick around. Wasn't my Celia's fault, of course."

I knew she was also referring to Genevieve. The first woman he opened up to after his mother died had let him down. I'd never even met the woman, yet despised her already. "How are you feeling? Graham said your surgery is Friday."

"I feel good. They keep trying to get me to take pain

medicine, but I don't need it, and it makes me sleepy. I think they just like to make old people sleep all the time, so we don't ask for anything."

I looked around the room. It was the nicest hospital room I'd ever been in. There was room for a half-dozen patients, yet there was only one bed in the room. In the corner, there was a beautiful arrangement of flowers. Lil saw me looking.

"They're from Graham. Sends me a fresh arrangement every week on Tuesday, like clockwork. I used to have a giant garden, but it got to be too much for me to manage."

"He's very thoughtful when he wants to be."

"There are two sides to that man. Thoughtless and thoughtful. Not sure he got the in-between gene."

"You sure have him nailed down."

"Somebody's gotta see him for what he is and call him on his shit."

I chuckled. "I suppose so."

"Although something tells me you'll do the same. I can tell...you're good for him."

"You think? We're sort of opposites in a lot of ways."

"Doesn't matter. It's what's inside of you both that counts."

"Thanks, Mrs. M...Lil."

I stayed for longer than my lunch hour, enjoying Lil telling me about the characters on her soap opera. The storylines were so far-fetched, I couldn't stop thinking about Graham watching them—he was so stern and pragmatic. When I went to leave, Lil took my hand.

"He's a good man. Fiercely loyal and loves his family. Very protective of his heart. But once he gives it, he doesn't take it back."

"Thank you."

"You can fix the rest. Pry the stick out of his ass and hit him over the head with it a few times. He's smart. He'll figure it out real quick."

"Now *that,* I can do."

GRAHAM WASN'T HOME WHEN I ARRIVED at his condo. Blackie met me at the door, springing up and down like a little crazy dog.

"Hey, Buddy." I lifted him, and he proceeded to lick my face. I still couldn't get over the fact that Mr. Big Prick had a small fluffy white dog. "Looks like it's just you and me for a little while."

I looked around the large open space. Aside from Blackie's panting, it was eerily quiet. The last two times I had been here, the tour had pretty much been limited to the inside of Graham's pants, so I used the time to snoop a bit.

The condo was stunning. No doubt it was professionally decorated—cool grays and sleek silver gave the place a bachelor feel. It could have been featured in *GQ,* with the owner standing in the middle of the open space, his arms folded across his chest. But as beautiful as it was, it was missing something. Personality. There was no hint to who lived here.

Curious, I wandered into the living room. There was an oversized sectional facing a large, flat screen TV hanging on the wall. Beneath it was a sleek black cabinet. It took me a minute to figure out how to open it without any handles. Inside was a DVD collection. *Caddyshack, Happy Gilmore, Anchorman.*

Huh.

I kept browsing, moving up to the next shelf. *Glory, Gettysburg, Gangs of New York.*

Hmmm.

Make up your mind, Morgan.

I ventured into the kitchen. The refrigerator was a vast smorgasbord of takeout containers. And...three containers of Nesquik strawberry milk.

Huh.

In the bedroom, I eyed the nightstand. Checking out his DVD collection and the contents of his fridge was one thing, but invading his bedside table would really be crossing a line. I looked around the room for something else to check out. It was pretty barren—no pictures, no folded pieces of paper on top of the dresser from emptying his pockets the day before. My eyes narrowed in on that nightstand again.

"No," I said out loud to myself.

I lifted Blackie up over my head, and we had a talk. "It would be wrong of me to go through Graham's drawer, wouldn't it, little buddy?"

He stuck his tongue out and licked my nose.

"I'll take that as a yes."

Inside the walk-in closet seemed more like Graham J. Morgan. Suits lined one side, mostly dark. An obscene amount of dress shirts lined the other. Everything was neat and organized.

Boring.

I walked back into the bedroom, my eyes falling immediately back on the nightstand. The damn thing was haunting me. "Maybe just one peek." I stroked Blackie, who was still in my arms. He purred at me. *Dogs purr?* A purr would be the human equivalent to a yes, wouldn't it?

Just one little peek...I won't even move anything.

Walking to the drawer, I slid it open with my pointer finger. Inside was a black velvet satchel, a clear bottle of something that could be lubricant—although the label was facing down, and an unopened box of condoms.

Okay...so maybe I needed to move one or two things.

"You think there's something good in that bag, buddy?" I was speaking to Blackie again.

But it wasn't Blackie that answered.

"I *know* there's something good in that bag." Graham's deep voice scared the shit out of me. I jumped, my arms jerking upward sent Blackie sailing into the air. Luckily, he landed on the bed right side up.

"You scared the hell out of me." My hand clutched at my chest.

Graham stood in the doorway leaning casually against one side. "You were so engrossed in your snooping, that you didn't hear me come in."

"I wasn't snooping."

Graham arched an eyebrow.

"I wasn't."

"So I must have left the drawer wide open this morning?"

I folded my arms over my chest. "Guess so."

He chuckled and walked to the table, sliding the drawer closed. "Well, if I left it open this morning and you weren't snooping, then you probably don't want to know what's in the bag."

"Not in the least."

"Shame."

"Why? What's in the bag?"

"Kiss me."

"Will you tell me what's in the bag?"

He wrapped his arms around my waist. "I'll show you what's in the bag. Now greet me properly."

I rolled my eyes as if it wasn't something I wanted to do every time I looked at his ridiculously handsome face. Then I planted a chaste kiss on his lips. But before I could pull away, he had a handful of my hair in his hand and didn't let go until he kissed me properly.

"Wouldn't have taken you for a snooper," he mumbled against my lips.

I pulled my head back and looked at him. "I'm not usually. But I can't figure you out."

"What's there to figure out?"

"Slapstick comedy or Civil War flicks? The same type of person doesn't usually have both."

Graham looked amused. "I like both."

"What's with the three quarts of Nesquik? Strawberry, too."

"I like it."

"Obviously."

"And so does Blackie."

"You feed your dog Quik?"

"I do."

"See...that's the thing. Mr. Big Prick doesn't have a cute little dog, and he definitely doesn't share strawberry milk with it."

"Maybe I'm not Mr. Big Prick like you think." He slid my hand down to his crotch. "Maybe I just *have* a big prick, but I'm not really the prick you imagine."

"What's your secretary's name?"

"Elaine."

"Eliza. She just told it to you this morning. I was there."

"I'm busy. It's hard to find a good secretary to stay very long."

"Only when you're a big prick."

"So maybe I am a big prick. But I'm not to you, am I?"

I sighed. "So what's in the bag already?"

"What if I told you it was rope because I wanted to tie you up?"

I thought about it for a second, then shrugged. "I think I could get into that."

He blew out a frustrated whoosh of air. "Damn. I should have bought rope."

"That would entail a trip to the hardware store. I'm guessing you're not a big DIY yourself kind of guy and don't even know where one is."

"How about one of those sex toy balls that strap around your face, so you can't talk. What if I told you that was in the bag, big mouth?"

"A ball gag?"

"You knew what I was talking about fast enough."

I leaned in and whispered, "I have *Caddyshack, Happy Gilmore,* and *Anchorman,* too. But instead of boring Civil War movies, I might have a few movies in a *different* genre."

He groaned. "Are you telling me you have a porn stash?"

"Maybe."

"You couldn't be more perfect if I'd made you myself."

"Thought you didn't like my wiseass mouth?"

"Your wiseass mouth makes me hard, and later I'm going to fuck that mouth. You're right, I don't know where the damn hardware store is, but I'm resourceful, and I'm sure I can find something to secure your arms and legs while I have at it."

He was only teasing, but listening to him talk about tying me up had me aroused, and Graham saw it on my face. "Fuck, Soraya."

"Yes. Please."

That was all he needed. It wasn't until hours later that I finally learned what was inside the bag—the lingerie he had bought at Bergdorf's the afternoon he went to pay for my dress for the gala. I didn't get to wear it that night, but I did get a promise from Graham that the drawer would be filled with more interesting things for my next snooping session.

The next morning, I woke to a fully dressed Graham stroking my cheek. My eyes fluttered open. "Hey. Did I oversleep?"

"No. I'm early. I have a busy day and wanted to get an early start."

I stretched my arms up over my head, causing the sheet to slip down and expose my bare breasts. The morning chill made my nipples instantly hard.

"Don't do that. I'll never leave." Graham rubbed two fingers over one of the stiff peaks.

"Mmm..."

"Soraya..." he warned.

"What? That feels good. Don't touch it if you don't want my reaction."

He shook his head. "Will you stay with me tonight again? I'm going to be late, but I'd love to come home to this beautiful sight in my bed."

"You have to work late?" I looked out the bedroom window. "It's not even light yet, and you're already planning on working until after it's dark."

"No. I need to go by the wake tonight. There's a session from seven to nine this evening, so I'll probably stay at the office until then."

"Oh."

"Will you be here when I come home?"

"Why don't I go with you tonight? To the funeral parlor. You shouldn't have to do it alone. I can't imagine it will be pleasant, your ex-best friend whose company you were trying to buy and his grieving wife who also happens to be your ex-girlfriend. You could use some company."

"You'd do that for me?"

"Of course. Although it seems to be a thing for me lately. Funerals and dates."

Graham chuckled and kissed me gently. "I'll pick you up at 6:30. And thank you."

After he left, I lay in bed for a little while before getting up. I couldn't stop thinking...*tonight was going to be interesting.*

CHAPTER 14

graham

I SHOULD HAVE BEEN WORKING instead of fucking around. My desk was piled with stacks of documents, there were, at least, a hundred emails in my inbox that I needed to respond to, and here I was writing to a sixty-year-old advice columnist again.

> **Dear Ida,**
> **The woman I've been seeing has recently expressed an interest in being tied up. I was wondering if you could provide some guidance for a first-time bondage novice. Would rope be a good investment? Or do you suggest something along the lines of fur-lined handcuffs? Perhaps some silk ties that are less likely to leave marks on her wrists? I should note that I plan to**

> **bury my face in her tight little cunt, so there will be a good deal of tugging on the restraints while she is writhing on the bed from multiple orgasms.**
> **-Fifty Shades of Morgan, Manhattan**

It only took twenty minutes for a response to appear in my inbox. I had expected a lengthy response full of her usual sarcasm. I should have known better than to think I could anticipate anything to do with Soraya Venedetta.

> **Dear Fifty,**
> **Might I suggest checking your partner's bedside nightstand? Perhaps since this woman you're seeing expressed an interest, she went shopping after lunch for some supplies.**

This woman was going to be the death of me; I just knew it.

An hour later, my secretary buzzed in through the intercom. "Mr. Morgan? You have a phone call on line three."

"Didn't I ask not to be interrupted?"

"Yes. But they said it was urgent."

"Who is it, and what do they want?"

"Umm. I didn't ask."

"Listen..." What the hell was her name? Ellen? *God damn it.* "The bulk of your job is to screen phone calls, am I correct?"

"Yes."

"And would you consider interrupting me when I've asked not to be interrupted, without having the name of the caller, doing your job correctly?"

"I..."

My patience was running thin. "Find out the name of the caller and the nature of the so-called urgent matter."

A minute later the intercom buzzed again. "What?"

"It's a Ms. Moreau. She said to tell you the nature of her emergency is that her husband is dead."

I picked up the phone. "Genevieve."

"Graham. I need your help."

"I'm working on it. I told you that yesterday."

"I need more than that."

I took off my glasses and tossed them on my desk. Scrubbing my hands over my face, I inhaled a deep breath. It had been years since I had a civil conversation with her, but contrary to popular belief, I wasn't a total prick. She had just lost her husband to a heart attack at the age of thirty-one.

Leaning back in my chair, I exhaled a breath of venom and sucked in fresh compassion. "What can I do for you, Genevieve?"

"I don't want to run a company by myself. I can't do it."

"Of course you can. You'll hire someone you can trust if it's overwhelming."

"I trust *you*, Graham."

I used to fucking trust you, too. It was physically painful to bite my tongue. "You're not in a state to discuss business right now."

"I'm always in a state to discuss business. So are you. It's the one thing we have in common. Our emotions take a backseat to a deal."

"I think you're wrong, and you're just unable to see that clearly right now. But what is it you think you'd like me to help with?"

"I want to merge with Morgan Financial Holdings."

"You want me to buy Gainesworth Investments? As in take it over completely?"

"No. Gainesworth Investments and Morgan Financial Holdings combined would be a powerhouse. I want to run it with you."

"Excuse me?"

"You heard me right. I want to merge. Be a team again."

"Genevieve, I don't want to be tactless, but...you just lost your husband. Don't you think you should take some time before seeking a new teammate? Grieve a little perhaps? You're not thinking clearly."

She sighed. "Liam and I were separated."

"I wasn't aware."

"I caught him fucking my twenty-three-year-old assistant."

"I'm sorry to hear that."

"No, you're not. You're thinking what comes around goes around. I would be, too."

Surprisingly, I actually wasn't. "You still suffered a loss. Your daughter must need you right now. Let me finish freezing out shareholders from acquiring too much stock, and keep your leverage safe. We can discuss business after you've had time to think clearly."

"That's Graham-speak for we'll have a conversation after I've already decided what I want."

"Genevieve, go be with your family. Business can wait."

"Fine. But check your calendar. You have an appointment this Friday with a Ms. More at ten—it'll say it's a referral from Bob Baxter. It's not. That's me. More—Moreau. I made the appointment two weeks ago. I was planning on coming to you about this anyway."

"I'll see you at the service tonight, Genevieve."

After I hung up, I clicked on my calendar. Sure enough, there was an appointment for a new client consultation with a Ms. More on Friday. And it was noted as a referral from Bob Baxter. I had to hand it to her. Normally I would call someone who refers a new client, flush out some information on the referral. But Genevieve was smart. She knew there was no way I was calling Bob Baxter. There was no such thing as a ten-minute call with that man. He would have had me on the phone for three hours and made it impossible to decline a dinner invitation before I hung up, too.

Unable to concentrate, I decided to go to the gym for a while. Running and lifting always helped me clear my mind. Around mile three on the treadmill, my head was still spinning. Flashes of my life were flickering through my mind randomly.

Soraya's eyes fluttering open this morning snuggled in my bed. Smiling as she found me looking at her.

Genevieve and I popping open a bottle of champagne in the office the night our asset management portfolio reached a billion dollars for the first time.

Soraya, kneeling, looking up at me as she slid that ball of silver around the head of my cock.

Walking into Genevieve's office after arriving back early from a business trip, ready to celebrate another closed deal. Finding her kneeling, taking Liam's cock down her throat.

I ran faster and faster. But the faster I went, the faster the flash just played in my head.

Watching Tig's needle pierce my skin and the ink bleed over Genevieve's name.

Liam and I, arm in arm, watching as they hung the first sign at our office three weeks after graduation.

My mother. *My mother.* Frail, lying in the hospital bed, trying to pretend she was fine.

What the fuck?

I ran faster.

Soraya's feather tattoo.

Genevieve sitting on the corner of my desk.

Liam running next to me on the treadmill.

I looked to my left. Fucking Liam was running next to me. The vision was so clear, for a heartbeat I really thought it was him.

When I finally stopped, I had been running so fast, it took me a full five minutes to catch my breath. Leaning down with my hands on my knees as I panted, sweat dripping from everywhere, I squeezed my eyes shut. *Fuck. Fuck. Fuck.* Just when everything finally started to seem so simple, why did it suddenly feel complicated?

I had no idea at the time, but the feeling was a premonition of things to come.

I wasn't a huge drinker, never took drugs. *Sex* was my only vice. And when I was stressed out, I needed it even more. Like a fiend.

I knew I shouldn't have been thinking about fucking Soraya on the way to a wake, but I couldn't help myself. She looked absolutely stunning in that little black dress. She'd done her hair up, even though I knew she didn't like it that way. She probably felt that she needed to hide the colored tips again. She looked nervous, too. Fuck me, if that rare vulnerability she was exhibiting didn't make me want to screw her senseless even more. The divider separating us from the driver was completely closed, and that wasn't helping. The temptation to lift her onto my lap was getting stronger by the minute.

She must have been reading my mind when she said, "You look like you want to attack me, Morgan."

"Would you lose respect for me if I told you that despite where we're headed tonight, all I can think about is slipping your panties off and letting you come on my face?"

"I already know you're a dirty bastard. So, that's not surprising. But this just might be a new low for you," she joked.

"Something you'll figure out about me...when I'm under stress, I get particularly horny. Sex diverts my mind from whatever is bothering me. It's really the only thing that helps."

"I see. Are you looking for *my* help, Mr. Morgan?"

"Don't call me Mr. Morgan unless you're going for a submissive vibe, in which case I'll be more than happy to take you over my knee right now. We could play that game if you want." My thoughts trailed off as I became mesmerized by her slightly parted lips. "God, I want to fuck your mouth right now."

She seemed to squirm in her seat. "Do you now?"

"Yes. And go down on you. We can liken it to stress eating."

She burst into laughter.

"Glad you think it's funny because I am ten seconds from burying my face underneath that dress."

"We can't. We're going to be at the funeral parlor any minute."

My voice sounded thick and needy as I slid my hand underneath her dress, caressing her thigh. "Not if we agree to be late."

"You're serious?"

Instead of answering her, I picked up the phone to call my driver. "Louis, we're not quite ready to head to the funeral home. We'd like you to just drive around for a while. Circle back here in about thirty minutes."

"No problem, Mr. Morgan."

She bit her lip and shook her head in disbelief at me, and that made my dick swell even harder. I couldn't go to a wake with a hard on. So, this was an urgent matter anyway.

Soraya's back was against the leather seat. Sliding the material of her dress up her thighs, I knelt beneath her and spread her knees apart. Slowly removing her lace thong with my teeth, I could feel the wetness on the material against my tongue.

Fuck me. She was drenched.

Her ass writhed under me as I wasted no time moving my tongue in a slow up and down motion over her pussy. I wasn't just using the tip, but rather the entire length of my tongue to devour her, stopping only long enough to suck on her clit. She'd never been this wet for me. *Ever.*

Soraya ran her long fingernails through my hair and pulled. My mouth was covered in her arousal as I kept at it before deciding that I couldn't take it anymore. Sticking my fingers inside of her, I moved them in and out as I looked up into her glazed-over eyes. "I really need to fuck you."

"Yes. Please..." she muttered.

Oh, I could definitely get used to Soraya Venedetta begging.

Unzipping my trousers, I let them fall halfway down my legs before repositioning her so that she was on top. The leather was cold beneath me. Within seconds, she bore down on my cock, causing my eyes to roll back.

Her dress was riding up her waist, her bare ass exposed as she rode me while I looked up into her eyes. The feel of sinking into her had been just as incredible as I imagined it would be. I couldn't help pulling out the pins in her hair, undoing her updo, watching the tresses fall as she fucked me. Just like the night of the gala, she didn't protest; I knew she didn't want it up anyway.

The other times we'd had sex seemed gentle in comparison to this town car experience. This was rougher, carnal...pure, unadulterated fucking at its best.

When she let out a stifled moan, I came harder than I could ever remember coming. It felt so good to let out the tension that had been building all day. Nothing—not even my strenuous workout—had been able to soothe me like being inside of her had. Not only that, but Liam's death was a harsh and painful reminder of my own mortality and a reminder of what was important. Life was simply too short not to fuck like this all of the damn time.

"We're both a mess now," she said as she got off of me.

"I swear to God. You've never looked more beautiful to me, Soraya." It was the truth. Her face was flushed, her hair a mess. Pure joy in the face of death. I was so grateful not to have to face this night alone. So grateful to be alive.

She took out her compact and looked in the mirror. "I went from looking like Princess Grace to Roseanne Rosannadanna."

That made me chuckle. "And I fucking love it."

I had Louis stop at Macy's so that Soraya could use the bathroom to fix her hair and buy some new panties. We were officially late to the wake.

When we pulled up to the funeral home, my anxiety level

was sky-high again. Soraya now had her hair tied back into a low ponytail. She rubbed my back and said, "It'll be okay."

Thank God she was here with me.

Not only was it going to be difficult to see Liam's dead body, but it was the first time I'd have to come face to face with Genevieve in a very long time. But perhaps the most painful part was the fact that all of this reminded me of the last time I'd set foot in a funeral home: when my mother died.

The line was out the door, a sea of black, stuffy polyester. Old rich members of Manhattan's upper crust were discussing their stock portfolios when they should have just been shutting the fuck up. I couldn't see past the people in front of me. Not that I wanted to see anything in there. I wanted to go home, to my safe place inside Soraya.

Having to take a leak like no one's business, I whispered in Soraya's ear, "Keep our place in line. I'm gonna find a bathroom."

"Okay," she said, looking a bit wary of my leaving her alone.

I left the line and followed the path of Persian rugs to the restroom. After I'd pissed like a race horse, I was on my way back to Soraya when I spotted Liam's mother, Phyllis, comforting a little girl in the hallway. The child was crying, and it broke my heart.

While the girl's back was turned to me, she seemed to be about four years old. She had to be Liam and Genevieve's daughter. I'd never seen her before. I'd only known that Liam knocked Genevieve up pretty soon after I found out about their affair. At the time, that news had only made things worse. But at this moment, I felt nothing but sympathy for a child who'd lost her parent. I knew that kind of pain all too well.

Phyllis looked startled to see me, but I couldn't walk past her without paying my condolences.

I felt nauseous as I said, "Hello, Phyllis. I'm so sorry about Liam."

Looking distraught, she simply nodded and held the little girl tighter before walking away. I trailed behind them when I noticed a black pom pom had fallen out of the girl's hair onto the rug.

Clearing my throat, I walked a bit faster to catch up with them. "Excuse me. She dropped something."

When the girl turned around, it was the first time I'd gotten a look at her. Kneeling down and holding the pom pom out, I'd forgotten what I was supposed to say next. The wind had been completely knocked out of me. There were no words...just a complete state of disbelief and confusion. Because if I didn't know better, I would have thought I was looking into the face of my mother.

CHAPTER 15

Soraya

WHAT THE HELL WAS TAKING HIM SO LONG?

The line was moving faster than anticipated, and Graham had yet to return from the bathroom.

It was now possible to see the open casket. How upsetting it was to witness such a young, handsome guy lying there dead. I knew he had wronged Graham, but Liam didn't deserve this. I could see that he had blond hair and a handsome face. He looked so peaceful. I truly hoped he was in a better place.

Loads of white floral bouquets surrounded his casket with banners that read, *Son, Friend, Husband.* There were long, cream-colored candles lit. It was a beautiful setup. The best that money could buy.

I looked behind me. Still no sign of Graham.

My eyes then landed on her.

Looking stoic, she was sitting in the seat closest to the casket.

Genevieve.

My body went rigid, an unexpected surge of possessiveness running through me. Like Liam, Genevieve also had blonde hair. My boyfriend had been fucked over by Barbie and Ken. And I was more like the *Bratz* doll rebound.

My boyfriend. I guess he was, wasn't he?

Anyway, Genevieve was physically the opposite of me, petite with almost a ballerina's body. She was beautiful. While I hadn't expected anything less, I had hoped that maybe, by some chance, she would just be average-looking. Not the case.

But it wasn't just her looks that gave me an upset stomach. It was more so coming face to face with someone whom Graham had given his heart to. He'd loved her. I wasn't sure that he'd ever feel the same about me. Perhaps I never realized how much I wanted or needed that until this moment.

As she spoke to the people giving their condolences, I looked at her eyes. Those were the eyes that used to gaze into Graham's. I looked at her mouth. That was the mouth that kissed his lips, sucked his cock. I then looked down at her modest breasts hidden beneath a black sheath dress. My boobs were way bigger. That made me feel good for about a millisecond until my eyes traveled down to her thin legs. Those had been wrapped around his back.

Jesus, Soraya. Stop torturing yourself. So THIS was what full-blown jealousy felt like.

When I looked behind me again, the woman in back of me smiled. "How did you know Liam?"

"Um...I didn't. I'm actually with Graham Morgan."

"Genevieve's former fiancé?"

I swallowed the lump in my throat. "Fiancé?

"If it's Graham Morgan of Morgan Financial Holdings, yes. They were engaged to be married before Genevieve and Liam got together."

My stomach sank. *He'd asked her to marry him?*

"Right. Of course. Yes. I'm with that Graham Morgan. And you are?"

"Helen Frost. I'm a neighbor of Genevieve and Liam's. I sometimes babysit Chloe."

"That's their daughter?"

"Yes. She's four. Beautiful, dark hair, unlike her parents."

"Well, that happens sometimes." I shrugged.

Before our conversation could continue, my attention shifted toward the sight of Graham wading through the crowd toward me. He was staring blankly ahead, looking completely dazed. This whole experience was apparently even tougher on him than I thought.

"Are you okay?"

He nodded silently, but my gut told me that something was terribly wrong.

It was finally our turn to kneel at Liam's casket and offer a prayer. Clasping my hands together, I closed my eyes and said one Our Father and one Hail Mary. My heart dropped when I heard the words that came out of Graham's mouth.

"You bastard," he whispered under his breath. His eyes were watery, but he didn't full-on cry. His lower lip trembled. I just continued to look at him, confused at his sudden anger. We both stood up in unison, slowly heading toward the not-so-grieving widow. Genevieve looked strangely okay for someone who'd just lost her husband.

Her eyes seemed to brighten when she saw Graham. His body was stiff as she wrapped her arms around his neck and pulled him close.

You bitch.

"Thank you so much for coming, Graham."

Graham just stood there, staring at her.

Had he gone mute from shock?

She went on, "I appreciate it more than you know. I'll see you Friday for our meeting."

Meeting?

She was going to see him?

We were holding up the line, and he hadn't even introduced me. She finally peeled her eyes away from him long enough to notice me standing to his right.

She flashed a fake smile. "Who are you?"

"I'm Soraya...Graham's..." I hesitated.

He finally spoke. "Girlfriend," he said firmly as he placed his arm around my waist.

"Girlfriend..." she repeated.

Graham tightened his hold on me. "Yes."

"Avery told me you were seeing someone new, but I didn't realize it was serious."

"It is. *Very* serious."

Well, okay then. Good to know.

"Well, it's very nice to meet you, Soraya."

"Likewise. I'm so sorry for your loss."

And by that I mean...Graham.

Graham was giving her what looked like a death stare.

What the hell was going on? Why was he so angry all of a sudden?

He abruptly moved along to the next family member in line. We mechanically shook hands with every person in the lineup before reaching the end.

Letting out a sigh of relief, I said, "Well, that was painful. What do we do now?"

He looked like he wanted to say something but couldn't find the words. "Soraya..."

"What? Graham, what's going on? Talk to me."

"I can't right now. I'll lose it on someone. And it's not the right time nor place."

It wasn't long before I got the answer to my question when all eyes in the room turned to a beautiful, dark-haired little girl appearing at Liam's coffin. *Chloe.* She'd been MIA all night. I'd assumed Liam and Genevieve's daughter was kept away intentionally. I didn't think she was here at all.

The crowd seemed to still upon the heartbreaking sight of the girl weeping over her father's body. It made me feel guilty because my father was still alive, and I chose to have nothing to do with him. Hers was dead, and she would never have the option to see him again.

"That's so sad," I whispered to Graham.

He took a deep breath in and slowly let it out.

Almost at the same moment, Chloe turned around, allowing me the first look at her face. I literally gasped. Out loud. The wheels in my head started turning. When I looked over at him, he was staring at her with a look of disbelief.

"Had you never seen her before, Graham?"

His eyes were still planted on her when he shook his head and simply said, "No."

Suddenly, Graham's strange behavior made total sense. Because this little girl looked just like her father.

Her father, Graham.

There was no doubt in my mind. Graham was Chloe's biological father. My mind was racing. How could this have happened? How could they have not told him? Was it even possible that this could have been a coincidence? That she looked just like Graham, even though she was Liam's? In my heart, I knew the answer. Suddenly, I didn't know if I wanted to cry or punch someone out.

He tugged at my arm. "We need to leave before I do something here I'm going to regret."

I looked over toward Genevieve, who was oblivious to Graham's impending nervous breakdown as she chatted and flashed her perfect white teeth at the people in line.

"Okay. Okay, let's go," I said.

Back in the town car, Graham stared blankly out the window for the first ten minutes of the ride. Presumably still in shock, he didn't seem ready to talk about what we'd just witnessed, and I didn't want to push it.

He finally turned to me. "Tell me that was just my imagination."

"No. It wasn't. That little girl looked just like you."

He blinked repeatedly, still trying to process. "If she's my daughter, how could Genevieve have known all this time and not told me?"

"I wish I had an answer, but I don't. I guess you're gonna have to ask her."

Rubbing his temples, he said, "I have to think this through."

"I understand if you want to be alone tonight."

"No!" he said emphatically. "I need you with me."

"Okay."

That evening, there was no sex. Instead, Graham just held me, the enormous weight of his worry evident with each and every breath he took as he stayed awake, unable to sleep most of the night.

It seemed like the fun, carefree days of our relationship had come to an abrupt end tonight. Things were going to change in a very drastic way. As much as I wanted to be there for him, I couldn't help the fact that part of me was secretly putting on an imaginary suit of armor to protect myself.

GRAHAM HAD DECIDED THAT HE WOULDN'T confront Genevieve until their meeting on Friday. He figured he'd give her time to properly bury Liam before going on the attack about Chloe. I think he also needed the time to prepare for the inevitable truth as well as determine what his legal rights were. He was also bogged down with work, still trying to strategize on the takeover of Liam's company.

I'd decided that a couple of nights off from each other would be a good idea under the circumstances. Much to his dismay, I intentionally made plans with Tig and Delia two nights in a row and told him I'd be sleeping at my own apartment.

Truthfully, there were no plans other than just hanging out at the tattoo parlor. I really needed my friends' opinion on this situation.

They couldn't believe the story.

Delia was organizing her disposable piercing needles as she spoke. "This sounds like something out of *General Hospital*."

I had to bite my tongue. They had no clue of the irony in that statement. I had never mentioned that Graham watched it.

Tig had his feet up as he put out his cigarette and cracked, "More like *All My Children* if you get what I mean."

"Thanks a lot." I rolled my eyes.

He continued, "What I don't get is how this guy never considered the possibility that that kid was his."

"He'd never seen her."

"But he'd heard about the pregnancy, right? Couldn't he have done the math? It didn't dawn on him that it was, at least, possible?"

Feeling the need to defend Graham, I said, "They had stopped speaking. He didn't know the exact timing. He just assumed it was Liam's."

Tig lit another cigarette. "That's some crazy shit. You wake up one day and boom...instant family."

His words made me shudder. Tig had just articulated my absolute worst fear.

Delia knew I was upset when she turned to her husband. "Don't say that. He's not with that chick. They're not his family."

"Believe me, it's not like I haven't thought that very same thing," I said. "Not only was he once in love with her, but there's no other man in the picture anymore, and she's likely the mother of his child. Where exactly do I fit into this?"

Delia tried her best to talk me off the ledge. "You're jumping way ahead of things. He's not gonna want to be with her, especially after knowing she lied to him for years."

I sighed. "This woman is beautiful and cunning. I bet she's already trying to figure out how to make this situation work to her benefit. She'd scheduled a meeting with him to talk business even before he found out about Chloe at the funeral. She wants to merge Liam's company with Graham's."

"I bet she wants to merge a lot more than that," Tig cracked.

Delia walked over to Tig and shook him playfully. "Will you stop?" She looked at me. "Graham seems to really care about you. I have a hard time believing he's gonna fall for her crap."

Tig interjected, "I have a hard time picturing Soraya acting all Mary Poppins and shit with this kid. You have to look at the big picture here. Even if Mr. Big Prick doesn't end up with the girl's mother, Soraya still has to deal with raising someone else's kid if she stays with this guy. That alone is something to consider."

He was right. There were so many different layers to this problem.

"Soraya would be a good stepmother. We could dye the little girl's tips and pierce her ears." Delia smiled.

Tig blew out a huge waft of smoke. "You know what I think? I think you should bid Daddy Warbucks and Little Orphan Annie adieu. That's just my opinion."

That night, I'd finally changed the color of my tips again. They'd been green since the night of the gala. There was only one color that seemed to fit the current situation.

Code red.

CHAPTER 16

graham

IT FELT LIKE SORAYA WAS SLIPPING away from me. The excuse she gave me about hanging out with her friends was a load of bullshit. The worst part was that I couldn't even say I blamed her. Imagine if the situation were reversed. How would I have handled it, knowing that she'd given birth to another man's baby? That thought made me sick to my stomach. I felt so possessive over her; I just couldn't imagine it.

This week had been like a nightmare I couldn't wake up from. All I wanted was to go back to the way things were before the wake. Everything was so simple then.

I had so much work to get done but couldn't stop thinking about the two females infiltrating my mind: Soraya and Chloe.

If she really was my daughter, then I owed her so much. None of this was her fault.

Don't get ahead of yourself.

I needed that paternity test. There was still a part of me that wouldn't believe it until I had proof. I couldn't allow myself to get emotionally invested until there was no doubt that she was mine.

My secretary's voice interrupted my thoughts. "Ms. Moreau is here to see you."

Clicking my watch, I took a deep breath and said, "Send her in."

The door opened, and Genevieve strutted into my office like she owned the place. There was a time when she practically did. She, Liam, and I would spend hours strategizing in this very office until the wee hours of the morning. She'd given me endless blow jobs under the very desk she now sat in front of with her legs crossed. It seemed just like yesterday, except for the fact that my previous love for her had turned into what felt like hate.

"She placed a white box on my desk. I brought you your favorite cupcake from Magnolia. Peanut Butter. I remember how much you—"

"Fuck! Shut up about the cupcake," I spewed. "Is she mine?"

So much for a gradual lead in to the discussion.

Her eyes widened. "What?"

"You heard me. Chloe. Is she my daughter?"

She looked absolutely shocked as her cheeks turned red. How could she not have seen this confrontation coming?

When she didn't speak, I continued, "Why do you look so surprised, Genevieve? Did you really think I was going to see her at the wake and not ask you that very question?"

"I don't know, Graham."

"What you do mean you don't know?"

"I've been dreading this moment for five years. I don't

know how to possibly explain my thinking to you in a way that you'll understand."

"Well...I have all damn day. Figure it out." When she continued to be silent, I said, "Alright, I'll start then. You were fucking Liam and me at the same time, correct?"

"Yes."

"How long after we were last together did you find out you were pregnant?"

"A month."

"How far along were you?"

"Two months."

I threw a pen across the room in anger. "How the fuck could you do this?" Spit had flown out of my mouth as I said it.

Tears started to form in her eyes. "Can you try to let me explain?"

"I'm looking forward to watching you try to explain your way out of this, in fact."

She closed her eyes for a moment then said, "I was in love with both of you, Graham. I *truly* was. It was selfish of me to feel entitled to that, but I did. I wanted it to go on forever. Being with both of you was the best of both worlds. I knew that once you found out, that would be it. I'd told Liam that you and I had stopped sleeping together. He didn't know that I'd been with both of you at the same time. Apparently, you never told him otherwise."

"I barely spoke to either one of you after I caught you."

"I know. I'm quite aware. It still breaks my heart to this day." She gazed out the window for what seemed like minutes to gather her thoughts. Then, she finally spoke again. "When Chloe was born, her complexion was lighter than it is now. She didn't have much hair. It wasn't immediately evident that she didn't look like either Liam or me. As she became a toddler, I knew he was noticing how much she looked like you. He chose to ignore it. We both chose to ignore it. Things were so bad between the three of us at that time. And Liam loved Chloe more than life. He couldn't have faced the possibility that she wasn't really his."

"What about me? Did you think I would *never* find out?"

"Deep down, I always felt she was yours. And, to be honest, that made me happy. Things between Liam and me went sour pretty fast after we were married. I realized that I'd made a huge mistake. I still loved you so much and will always deeply regret hurting you."

"Again, I still don't understand how you could've kept this from me."

"I don't have an excuse, except to say that I didn't want to disrupt Chloe's life. And a part of me felt like I couldn't do that to Liam. Staying with him was the lesser of two evils because I knew you wouldn't ever take me back. So, I let things be the way they were. I was just trying to keep the peace." More tears fell from her eyes.

I refused to soften. "I want a paternity test immediately."

"I'm not going to fight you on that, Graham. I'll give you whatever you want. Time with her. The test. All that I ask is that if it turns out you're the father, please wait to tell her until she's a little older and can understand better. She just lost the only father she's ever known. And she's devastated."

"I would never do anything to harm her. I'm fine with not telling her for a while if that's in her best interest."

"I really do care about you. I never meant to hurt you. Please believe that."

"I want that test within a week, Genevieve. I'll make the arrangements so that I can be sure the results are accurate."

A look of panic suddenly washed over her face. "You're not going to try to take her away from me, are you?"

"I would never take a child away from its mother."

Genevieve sniffled. "Thank you."

"If it turns out she's mine, I want you to gather every single picture you have ever taken of her since the day she was born. Do you understand me?"

She didn't hesitate. "Of course."

THAT NIGHT, ALL I WANTED was to see Soraya. Smell Soraya. Sleep next to Soraya. My body felt like it was withdrawing from the strongest kind of drug. It had only been a few days without her, but it felt like a lifetime. It wasn't just the physical need. I missed her humor, her sarcasm, her laugh.

It was late. I had just left the hospital from visiting Meme, and I wasn't sure if Soraya would even still be up. My driver, Louis, had the rest of the night off. Without thinking, I grabbed my jacket and headed down to the garage.

I hadn't texted or called her first. So, driving to her place was a risk. But I couldn't chance her telling me not to come.

There was no parking near her apartment, so I had to walk two blocks in the pouring rain. When I finally got to her door, I pressed the buzzer to her apartment.

She sounded groggy. "Hello?"

I closed my eyes because I'd missed her voice. "Baby, it's me."

"Graham...it's late."

I leaned my forehead against the wall. "I know."

Without saying anything further, she buzzed me in.

Relief washed over me as I walked swiftly up the stairs two at a time.

My hair and jacket were soaked. I must have looked like a drowned rat. When she opened the door, she didn't immediately let me in. I didn't know whether she was going to kick me out or tell me to come inside. It was her call to make. I had no right to push after the mess I'd just brought her into. I took her in for a moment. She was completely unmade up in a thin, white night shirt. Her nipples were saluting me. At least *they* were happy to see me. She looked so gorgeous, even with her hair a matted mess.

The tips were red.

I was losing her.

"Oh, God. Come in. You're soaked."

Thank fuck for the rain. I wasn't above taking sympathy at this point.

She closed the door and disappeared for a moment, then came back with a towel. "Here. Give me that wet jacket."

I peeled off the top layer. My dress shirt underneath it was still dry. I should have stood outside for a while longer.

"What's going on? Is everything okay?"

"No. Everything isn't okay."

"I take it your meeting with Genevieve didn't go well today?"

"She admitted she wasn't sure that Liam was Chloe's father. She was fucking both of us at the same time and realized after we broke up that she was pregnant. She agreed to get Chloe DNA tested within the next week."

"I don't know what to say."

I looked into her eyes. "Say you won't leave me."

She looked away. "Graham...everything is so uncertain right now. I'm so confused."

"I feel the same way. My mind is spinning out of control, and there is only one thing I'm sure of right now. Do you know what that is, Soraya?"

She was staring at the ground, but lifted her eyes, looking up at me through her dark eyelashes. "What?"

"I want you. I want to be with you. I'm head over fucking ass about you, and I need to know you aren't going to leave me."

She cracked a small smile. "I think the saying is head over heels about you."

"Whatever." I wrapped my hands around her waist and locked them behind her back. "Tell me you aren't going to leave me over this."

"We don't know what's going to happen."

"I know what I want."

"Graham...things can change."

"I need you, Soraya. I've never said that to another woman in my life." I leaned my forehead against her and whispered, "I *need* you."

She nodded. "Okay."

Taking her face in my hands, I lifted it, so our eyes met. "No more bullshit avoiding me."

"I had plans with Tig and Delia."

I flashed her a look that called bullshit.

"Fine." She rolled her eyes. "I was avoiding you."

I leaned in and kissed her on the lips. For the first time since the funeral, the world seemed to stop spinning for a moment.

"Do you want to stay tonight?"

"Try to get me to leave."

That night, with my body wrapped around Soraya, I finally got some much-needed sleep. I'd even slept in late the next morning until the sound of my phone ringing woke me up.

CHAPTER 17

Soraya

I KNEW WHO IT WAS from the tone in his voice. Luckily, I was facing away from him, so I could listen to the whole conversation without having to pretend it didn't cut deep into me. It was bad enough another woman was calling his cell at seven in the morning while he was lying in my bed, but *the mother of his child* was another thing altogether.

Is this how it would be? Graham was not the type of man who would ever ignore a phone call if the woman who had custody of his child was calling. This bitch who had screwed him out of years of watching his daughter grow up could now interrupt his life at any given time of day. I had no doubt that she would use it to her fullest advantage, too.

"I'll make arrangements for a private lab to come to your home Monday at ten."

He was quiet as he listened. I heard the sound of her voice but couldn't make out the words. There were a few more curt exchanges, and then right before he hung up, his voice softened. "How is she doing?"

My heart ached for him.

After, I kept quiet for a few minutes, giving him some time. When I finally spoke, my back was still to him. "You okay?"

Graham hugged me from behind and kissed my shoulder. "I'm good. Sorry about that. She was calling to make arrangements for the DNA test."

I turned over and faced him. "She's still in love with you."

He looked down. "I'm not sure Genevieve is capable of love."

"She's beautiful."

"She doesn't hold a candle to you."

"She's smart."

"I'm more of a *smart ass* kind of guy."

That made me smile. Until I thought of other things that Genevieve beat me in. "She was your fiancé."

"Without commitment, it's merely a piece of jewelry."

I have no idea where it came from, my dark masochist side, I suppose. "Did you get down on one knee and propose?"

"Soraya..."

"I need to know."

"Why?"

"I have no idea. I just do."

"I didn't actually. It was more of a business deal than anything romantic. I took her to Tiffany's, and she picked out her own ring."

"Oh."

"When we split up, Meme didn't seem too surprised. One day over lunch, she asked me why I hadn't given Genevieve her engagement ring. The thought had never even occurred to me, to be honest. Meme had given me her ring when I turned twenty-one and told me that it belonged to whomever I eventually gave my heart to. My grandmother's ring was small and simple. It wasn't until the relationship had ended and Meme had pointed out the obvious to me that I understood the significance. There was never a question in my mind, given the choice between a small ring that meant a lot to me and a flashy rock, Genevieve would rather have had that rock. And I knew that enough to not give her my grandmother's ring. But I didn't stop to think about what that said about who she was."

"Wow. She sounds like a real fucking bitch."

Graham laughed. It was good to hear it. "That's what I love about you, Soraya. You call it like you see it. The first time you did it to me, I was pissed, but also hard as a rock."

I wrapped my hands around his neck and gave him a dirty grin. "You're a stuck-up suit who can't even remember his secretary's name."

Graham squinted and then quickly caught on. His lips went to my neck. "Go on."

"Most of the time, you don't even notice the people around you."

"Is that so?" His voice was gravelly, and his mouth nibbled its way up to my ear.

"You think women should just spread their legs for you because of what you look like."

His hand caressed its way down my body, landing on my bare thigh. He spoke directly into my ear as he nudged my legs open. "Spread your legs for me, Soraya."

I tried not to. I really did. But that voice...

"Spread for me, Soraya. I need to hear you moan my name."

"You're so confident you can..." He lowered his body down the bed, settling his shoulders between my legs. I was already wet, and his warm breath *right there* shot fire through my body. I quickly spread my legs.

By afternoon, all the confidence in our relationship that this morning had instilled was already starting to dissipate. Ida had me running errands for her since lunch time. In line at the bank, the man in front of me was with his daughter. She was probably around the same age as Chloe. Sitting on the seven train on my way to the printer, a couple was seated across from me. Their daughter was holding on to the pole, spinning around and around. It probably wasn't a profound moment for them, but for me, I saw a happy *family*. Reminders were everywhere I looked.

After my last errand for the day, I was standing on the platform waiting for my southbound train to arrive. Across the track, the northbound seven arrived. The word next to the circled seven caught my attention. *Queens.* Without thinking, I hoped on, just as the doors slid closed.

What the hell was I doing? I hadn't seen him in eight years. For all I knew, he might not even live in Queens anymore. When I exited at the Sixty-First Street Station, a northbound train was pulling up. Looking across, I considered going back where I'd just came from. I thought about it for so long, that eventually people had to walk around me while I stood frozen in place watching the train pull away.

His house was only about eight blocks from the station. Around the third block, my phone buzzed, and Graham's name flashed on the screen. My finger lingered over the

DECLINE button, but then I remembered what I told him last night. *I would be there for him.* I wouldn't avoid him anymore.

"Hey."

"Hey, gorgeous. How was your day?"

I was standing at the crosswalk waiting for a light to turn green. "Busy. Ida had me running all around the city doing errands." Just then, the light turned, and I stepped off of the curb. Out of nowhere, a cab pulled up in front of me, less than an inch from my toes. I banged on the trunk of the yellow car. "Hey, asshole. Watch where you're going!"

"Soraya?"

"Yeah. Sorry. A cabbie almost just ran over my foot."

"You're still in Manhattan?"

"Actually, no."

"Oh. Good. I just finished a meeting in Brooklyn. Where are you? I'll pick you up, and we can grab some dinner?"

I was quiet for a minute. "I'm not in Brooklyn."

"Where are you?"

"Queens."

"Oh. I didn't realize you were still doing errands."

"I'm not, actually." I swallowed. "I'm going to see my father."

Graham didn't ask me why I was going; the reason was pretty obvious. We talked for the rest of the walk, and I told him I'd text him when I was done so that we could have dinner. When I hung up, I stopped in my tracks, realizing my father's house was only two doors down. *What was I coming to say?*

I had no sense of time as I stood there, but it must have been at least a half- hour that I stared at his home. My emotions were completely out of control, and I seriously had no idea what the hell I was going to say, yet I was sure I needed to do this. *Fuck it.* I walked to his doorstep, took a deep breath, and knocked. My heart was racing as I waited. When no one came to the door, at first a sense of relief came over me. I was just about to turn and leave when the door opened.

"Can I help you?" Theresa squinted, and then her eyes grew wide. "Oh, my. Soraya. I'm sorry I didn't recognize you."

I forced a smile. "Is my dad here?" I was suddenly panicked and wanted nothing more than to leave. *Please say no. Please say no.*

"Yes. He's upstairs fighting with the closet door that came off the hinge. I think he's losing." She smiled warmly and stepped aside. "Come in. I'll go up and get him. He's going to be so excited you're here."

I stayed just inside the doorway, no different than how I would have felt entering a stranger's house for the first time. It's what he essentially was. A stranger. The walls were lined with family photos. My father's *new* family. They were smiling and laughing in every framed shot. Not a single picture of my sister or me. *I shouldn't have come.* A voice I hadn't heard in years interrupted my internal debate to flee.

"Soraya." My father was halfway down the stairs as he spoke. "Is everything okay?"

I nodded.

"Is your mother okay?"

That pissed me off. "She's fine."

Frank Venedetta strode to me, rattling my already shaky confidence. For a second, I thought he was going to hug me. But when I folded my arms across my chest, he seemed to take the hint. "This is a pleasant surprise. It's been too long. Look at you, you're all grown up. You look like your Aunt Annette. You're beautiful."

"I look like my mother." His side of the gene pool wasn't getting credit for anything good.

He nodded. "Yes, you're right, you do."

The eight years that passed had been kind to my father. He was over fifty now. A few silver flecks dotted his thick mane of black hair, but his olive skin hadn't aged much. He was a fit man; running had been his escape when we were kids, and it looked like he had kept up with it.

"Come in. Let's sit." Hesitantly, I followed him into the kitchen. "Coffee?"

"Sure." He poured us both steaming mugs and gave me a biscotti. My mother never let us have coffee when we were little. But the Venedetta side of the family was off the boat from Sicily; they thought if you were old enough to hold the mug, it should be filled with coffee. The same went for a wine glass. My best memories of my father were our mornings together in the kitchen after Mom left for work. Dad and I would sit at the table talking while we drank coffee and ate biscotti before I left for school. I even got up early in the summer to sit there with him. After he had moved out, I avoided the kitchen table in the mornings because it made me wonder if he was sharing coffee with Brianna—his new daughter.

"So. How are you?"

"Fine."

He nodded. I'd shown up on his doorstep, yet I was shutting down any conversation he started.

A few minutes later, he tried again. "Are you still living in Brooklyn?"

"Yes."

More nodding. Then a few minutes later. "What do you do for a living?"

"I work for an advice columnist."

"That sounds interesting."

"It's not."

A few more minutes passed. "Are you seeing anyone?"

Graham had called me his girlfriend the other night, yet I had never said it out loud. "I have a boyfriend."

"Are things serious?"

I thought about it for a minute. They were serious. We may have only known each other for a month, but it was the most serious relationship I had ever been in. "They are."

My father smiled.

"He just found out he has a daughter he knew nothing about with his ex-fiancé."

My father's smile wilted. He closed his eyes briefly, then opened them nodding as if it all made sense finally.

He took a deep breath and let out a loud whoosh of air. "I made a lot of mistakes in my life, Soraya. Did things I'm not proud of."

"Like cheating on my mother."

He nodded. "Yes. Like cheating on your mother."

"You left us. How do you leave your children?"

"I told you. I did things I'm not proud of."

"Do you regret it?"

"I regret hurting you, yes."

"That's not what I asked. Do you regret the choice you made? Choosing a woman over your daughters? Taking a different family as your own and never looking back?"

"That's not how it was, Soraya."

My voice got louder. "Answer the question. Do you look back and wish you made a different choice?"

He looked down ashamed but answered honestly. "No."

It felt like someone had sucker punched me in the stomach. "Did you ever love my mother?"

"I did. I loved her very much."

"What if Theresa didn't love you back?"

"What are you asking me?"

"Would you have stayed with my mother if Theresa didn't love you back?"

"I can't answer that, Soraya. That's not how it was."

"Were you and my mother happy?"

"Yes. We were at one time."

"Until Theresa."

"That's not fair. It's more complicated than that."

I stood up. "I shouldn't have come. This was a mistake."

My father stood. "The mistakes were all mine, Soraya." He looked me straight in the eyes as he spoke his next words. "I love you."

Everything from the last few days was bubbling to the surface. It felt like there was a tsunami coming, and I was about to get sucked under if I didn't run for it. So I did. I took off like a bat out of hell running out of his house. It wasn't the most mature moment of my life, but there was no way I was letting that man see me cry. I flew past the framed family portraits, flung open the front door and bolted down the six-step stoop two at a time. My eyes were burning, throat felt like it was closing, and my chest constricted. I was so intent on getting away as fast as I could, that I wasn't even paying attention to where I was going. Which is why I didn't see the man who was standing at the curb until I was wrapped in his arms.

CHAPTER 18

graham

I BARKED AT MY DRIVER to head to Queens before I even knew her father's address. Luckily, there was only one Venedetta in the borough, or I would have been knocking on doors. My gut told me her visit was not going to go well. Arriving on Catalpa Avenue, I had no idea if she was inside or not, so I settled in the back of my town car and waited. It wasn't long before the front door flew open, and Soraya was barreling down the walkway toward the street. I barely made it out of the car in time to grab her; she clearly hadn't seen me. The haunted look on her face, I wasn't so sure she was able to see anything at all.

She struggled in my arms at first. "It's me, Soraya."

Her eyes seemed to come into focus. I watched as they filled with tears and then she melted into my arms. Her full weight leaned on me as I tightened my hold around her. "I have you, baby. I have you." She made a gut-wrenching noise and then her body began to shake, tears streaming down her beautiful face. It physically hurt my heart. Seeing her like that, hearing that sound of pain come from deep within, it felt like someone had cracked open my ribs and gripped my beating heart in their hands only to nearly squeeze the life out of it.

I held her as tight as I could for a few minutes while we stood in front of the house. When I lifted my eyes and saw a man standing in the doorway watching us, a man who from the looks of him was without a doubt Frank Venedetta, I decided it was time to go. "Come on, let's get in the car." Soraya never looked back as I helped her into the backseat. But I did. Her father simply nodded and watched us pull away.

The ride from Queens was quiet. When her crying finally subsided, she kept her head on my shoulder and her eyes closed. I hated that this was all my fault. I'd fucked things up between us royally. Not only had the situation with Genevieve thrown a wrench into our relationship, but it had brought Soraya's old demons back to the surface. Now she was relating who I was back to a man who had disappointed her for most of her life.

Stroking her hair, I finally broke our silence. "I'm sorry. This is all my fault."

"I don't know why I went to see him. What was I expecting him to say?"

"It's only natural. You're trying to make sense of his choices because of everything going on."

"I guess..."

"I know you left upset, but did he tell you anything that helped?"

"No. He said he couldn't tell me if he would have stayed with my mother if he hadn't met Theresa."

Fuck. I shifted in my seat so we were facing each other. "Whether I have a daughter or not, even if I had not met you, there is no way in hell I would be getting back together with Genevieve."

"But you loved her at one time."

She stared down at the floor. "Soraya, look at me." Her head lifted, and eyes returned to meet mine. "The woman cheated on me with my best friend and then didn't tell me that I could possibly have a child. *For four years.* Trust and loyalty are important to me. I wouldn't even hire someone to work in my business who I couldn't trust, no less build a life with. We *are not* getting back together, no matter what." My next words came out slow, each one given careful consideration, yet I was still cautious about saying them. "Your father could have been involved in your life while he was married to another woman. People do it all the time. He made his choices. And if you ask me, he made poor ones. I am not your father."

Just then, Louis, my driver, interrupted. "Mr. Morgan? Are we heading back into Manhattan or to Brooklyn? The exit for the Belt Parkway is coming up."

"My place or yours?" I looked to Soraya.

I was relieved to hear a flash of my girl come back. "You're assuming an awful lot with that question."

"I'm just being a gentleman. You've had a tough afternoon. I know the perfect remedy to make you feel better."

"Of course you do."

"It's my duty, and I take it very seriously."

"You know what would really make me feel better?"

"Name it."

"You, not being a gentleman."

The corners of my mouth twisted up while my cock

hardened at the thought. I didn't take my eyes from hers as I spoke. "To my place, Louis." Then I whispered in her ear. "And to think, I was going to fuck you full of nice. You never cease to amaze me, Soraya. It would be my pleasure to leave the gentleman at the door and fuck you four ways dirty."

THE NEXT FEW DAYS, THINGS RETURNED to normal between Soraya and me. Her anxiety over the prospect of my having a child seemed to diminish. During the day, I threw myself into my work, and at night, I worked just as hard at pleasing Soraya. If she was going to be weighing her options soon enough, I needed to make her decision to cut me loose as difficult as possible. Pleasing her sexually was my favorite part of that plan.

On Monday morning, the lab came to my office at seven to collect my DNA. They had an appointment with Genevieve to take a sample from Chloe a few hours later. I'd paid a fortune for fast results and by Wednesday, I'd be certain whether I was a father or not.

A father.

Having never really had one of my own, the thought in itself was a novelty to me. If it was confirmed she was mine, there was no doubt I wanted to be involved in her life. Although I had no fucking idea what that looked like. What did a grown man do with a little girl who became his child overnight?

Monday night I had to go out of town, up to Boston for a quick meeting early Tuesday morning. My flight was delayed, and I was sitting in the airport reading the paper. Before Soraya, I started with the business section first. These days,

I turned to *Ask Ida*, before catching up on the market watch. Between soap operas and now reading an advice column daily, I was fast becoming a pussy.

> **Dear Ida,**
> **My mother was recently remarried. Bill, my new stepfather, has a nineteen-year-old son, whom I had never met until three weeks ago. Alec was away at college and came home to live with us for the summer. The problem is, I'm extremely attracted to Alec. I'm pretty sure the attraction is mutual since the sexual tension is so thick, sometimes it's hard to breathe. Is it wrong to be with my stepbrother?**
> **-Gretchen, Manhattan**

> **Dear Gretchen,**
> **While technically you are not blood-related, there is still a familial connection and many people will frown upon a relationship between the two of you. By your writing the letter, I suspect you think it's not right to be with Alec, and you're looking for someone to give you permission to go against your own beliefs. My advice to you is to be true to yourself, and the rest will fall into place.**

I texted Soraya.

Graham: I'd fuck you even if you were my stepsister.

Soraya: LOL. You read the column?

Graham: I do. I like to figure out which ones you have a part in responding to.

Soraya: How can you tell which ones I responded to?

Graham: I just can.

Soraya: Did I write today's response?

Graham: Do I get a prize if I answer correctly?

Soraya: I thought I gave you your prize last night.

Damn. That she did. For a few minutes, while she was sucking my cock, I thought about getting my own tongue pierced just so she could feel that cold metal ball on her clit. My staff would surely think I'd lost my mind entirely if I walked into a Monday morning staff meeting tripping over my words with a swollen, bedazzled tongue. It was bad enough this morning I was smiling in the middle of the meeting when my mind wandered.

When I didn't respond right away, Soraya knew what I was doing.

Soraya: You're thinking about last night, aren't you?

Graham: I am. And it makes me want to leave the airport and blow off my morning meeting. Blow off for a blow job?

Soraya: Perv. So...did I write any part of the response to poor Gretchen today?

Graham: Not one damn word.

Soraya: Very good. What about yesterday? The

woman who was stealing from her elderly uncle's change jars?

Graham: Prisons are filled with people who started with petty theft.

Soraya: OMG! How did you know? That was literally the only sentence she kept from my response.

Graham: I know you.

Soraya: That's a little bit scary!

Tell me about it. I'm scared fucking shitless these days.

My flight had just begun boarding when my phone buzzed in my hand. At first, I thought it was another text from Soraya. My smile dropped seeing Genevieve's name flash on the screen. I considered not answering it, but then I realized it could be about Chloe.

"Genevieve."

"Graham. How are you?"

"Busy. Is everything okay with Chloe?"

"She's fine."

"What do you want then?"

She sighed loudly into the phone. "You're going to have to learn to speak civilly to me. I don't want our daughter exposed to the way you bark at me."

"Our daughter? You're getting a little ahead of yourself, aren't you? The test doesn't come back until Wednesday morning."

"It's just a formality for me. I know in my heart she's yours."

"How fucking nice for you. Perhaps you could have shared that little bit of information a little earlier. I don't know...say...*four years ago*?"

"Stop yelling at me."

"Stop calling me."

Another sigh of frustration. If I didn't know better, I'd swear this woman had balls. Giant ones, bigger than her head.

"Listen. I'm boarding a plane. I need to hang up."

"Where are you going?"

"That's none of your damn business. I'm hanging up, Genevieve."

"Wait. I called for a reason. I want to be there when you get the results on Wednesday morning."

"No."

"What do you mean, no?"

"It's the opposite of yes. Perhaps you should have tried saying it four years ago when my best friend told you to spread your legs."

"Graham..."

"No. We're not a happy family waiting on the stick to show a plus sign. I'm waiting to find out if you've robbed me of four years of my daughter's life. Either way, it won't be a Hallmark moment, and you won't be sharing it with me."

"I'm coming to your office on Wednesday."

"I'm warning you not to."

There had been muffled sounds of traffic in the background, and they suddenly quieted. "Genevieve?"

The bitch had hung up on me.

CHAPTER 19

soraya

GRAHAM WAS SUPPOSED TO BE GETTING the results of the DNA test today. Even though he hadn't specifically asked me to be there, I wanted to surprise him. He said the results were due in sometime before noon, so I took the entire morning off from work.

In another show of solidarity, it was time get rid of the red. I'd dyed the ends of my hair blue which Graham knew was a sign that things were going well in my life. Whether I truly believed that or not, I knew that gesture would put him at ease about us.

Stopping at Anil's, I picked up two buttered bagels and two juices on my way to Morgan Financial Holdings.

Making my way through the glass doors, I no longer even bothered to check in with the receptionist. Instead, I just zipped past her and sashayed my way down to my boyfriend's office like I owned the place.

I could hear her scurrying behind me. "Ms. Venedetta?"

I flipped around. "It's fine. I thought Graham and I explained that we're involved. You don't need to announce me anymore."

"That's not why I stopped you," the receptionist said.

"Okay. What is it then?"

"Well...we...some of the employees here just wanted to thank you."

"Thank me?" I scrunched my forehead. "Why?"

"Ever since he started seeing you, he's been different. Nicer. Easier to deal with. I don't know if you have a magical vagina or what...but whatever it is you do, keep on doing it. You've made all of our lives a whole lot easier."

Some of the people sitting in nearby cubicles overheard her. One started clapping, and a few others followed. Standing there with my greasy paper bag, I was being applauded by these people.

Was I supposed to bow?

Graham must have overheard the commotion because his office door opened.

"What the hell is—" The frown on his face softened when he saw me. "Soraya." He smiled. "Did I miss something here? Why are they clapping?"

I looked back at the employees and winked. "I was just telling them a joke."

"I see. Well, why don't you move your one-woman show into my office then?"

The door shut behind us, and Graham backed me up against it, planting a firm kiss on my lips then said, "Everyone's crazy about you...just like me. This was a damn nice surprise."

"I didn't want you to go through this alone."

He placed his forehead on mine. "You know...I really

wanted you here. But at the same time, I wasn't sure if it would make you uncomfortable. I didn't want to pressure you, but I'm so glad you came."

"Well, I have a feeling I'm going to need to practice dealing with discomfort."

He cupped my cheeks. "Let's just take one day at a time. Can you do that for me?"

Nodding against his hands, I said, "I'll try."

We sat together eating our bagels for the next half-hour. Graham had his feet up on his desk and looked more relaxed than I anticipated. Through his office windows, the sun was shining, reflecting into his eyes that were glowing as he watched me eat. He seemed to be doing very well considering.

"You seem okay. You're not scared to get the call?"

"You know what? I was honestly feeling sick to my stomach until you got here. Knowing that you're here for me no matter what truly makes all the difference."

"I'm glad I could make it better."

"You make everything in my life better, baby. Everything."

He reached across the desk and grabbed my hand, gently placing a kiss on my knuckles. The sound of his intercom interrupted our moment.

"Mr. Morgan? Ms. Moreau is here. She didn't have an appointment but is insisting that I let you know she's here anyway. She says you'll know what it's in regards to."

My stomach felt unsettled as I withdrew my hand from his. "Genevieve is here?"

He closed his eyes and rubbed his temples in frustration. "Fuck. I told her I didn't want her to come for the results. I should've known that she wouldn't listen."

"Well, you can't exactly kick her out."

"Sure, I can."

198

"Believe me, I would love it if you kicked her to the curb right now, but how is that going to make things any easier if you find out Chloe is yours? You're going to have to deal with her whether you like it or not. The sooner you learn how, the better."

Deep in thought, he nodded to himself for a while. "You're right." Pressing the button, he said, "Send her in."

Our relaxing breakfast was officially over.

I threw away our food wrappers to distract myself from the jitters creeping in.

The door opened, and Genevieve entered the office, quietly closing the door behind her. She was dressed conservatively, wearing a gray pencil skirt and a cream-colored, sleeveless blouse that showed off her toned arms. Her scent was familiar—Chanel No. 5. It dawned on me that she was built a lot like the television host, Kelly Ripa—petite and svelte. She actually resembled her a bit.

Graham didn't even look over at her. He stayed silent, fidgeting with his watch, a nervous habit that until now, I almost thought he'd completely done away with.

Genevieve made eye contact with me first. "Soreena, I didn't realize you would be here."

"It's Soraya. And, yes, I'm here to support Graham when the results come in."

She took a seat. "So...you know everything."

"Yes. He and I don't keep anything from each other."

"Well, that's nice of you to be here for him."

Graham finally spoke to her. "I thought we discussed the fact that I preferred *you* not come here today."

"I need to be here, Graham. I'm sure you've given Syreeta an earful about what a bad person I am, but I'm here today to support you, too."

Graham's tone was stern. "It's Soraya. Not Soreena. Not Syreeta. So-RAH-ya. What is so hard about that?"

"Soraya....Soraya...sorry...I'm a bit nervous myself, okay? I didn't come here to make trouble. I'm just trying to be supportive as well. I realize that this whole situation is all my fault. I'm not denying that, but I can't change the past. I'm just trying to make things right moving forward. If I have to spend the rest of my life making up for it, I will." She looked like she was about to cry. Either she was truly upset, or she deserved an Academy Award. Graham remained unaffected by her mini breakdown.

Several minutes of awkward silence ensued as Graham went from fiddling with his watch to twirling the ends of a pen between his two index fingers.

He tossed it across the room and grumbled, "What the hell is taking them so long?"

Genevieve was trying her best to lighten the mood and looked down at my feet. "I like your shoes. What brand are they?"

"Michael Kors. They're not Louboutins or anything, but I like them. They're comfortable for wedges."

She smiled. "I like them, too."

Graham rolled his chair back and got up. He started to pace and seemed to be losing his cool, so I attempted to calm him down. "They said before noon, right? Well, there's still a little time."

He took out his phone. "I'm calling the lab." He put it on speaker.

A woman answered, "Culver Laboratories?"

"Yes. This is Graham Morgan. I was supposed to be getting a call before noon today with the results of a paternity test your lab conducted for me this week. We're three minutes away from the deadline. I'd like my results now, please. Arnold Schwartz indicated that he would oversee everything personally to ensure those results would be in by this morning. I have a special reference number he gave me if you need it."

"Yes, sir. That would be helpful."

As Graham gave her the information, I said a silent prayer that by some miracle, it turned out he wasn't the father. I wasn't sure if that made me a bad person or what. Until those results came in, there was still hope as far as I was concerned. What if there was a third man we didn't know about...one who was darker like Graham, maybe resembled him? Anything was possible, right?

The clicking of a keyboard could be heard in the background as the woman retrieved the information. "I'm going to put you on hold, Mr. Morgan. It seems that the results are in, but when they indicated that someone would call you to read them, they were apparently basing it on Pacific Time. But I do show here in the system that the test has been completed. I just need to see if we have authorized personnel available to give you those results."

He whispered under his breath, "Jesus Christ."

These people on the West Coast had no idea how much was riding on this. If they did, they'd surely hurry the hell up.

Genevieve exhaled and looked over at me. "This is very nerve-wracking."

I didn't know why she was making an attempt to talk to me. In any case, I was too worked up to respond. I turned my attention toward Graham. The relaxed demeanor from earlier was like a distant memory. He looked so worried. I think a part of him wanted Chloe to be his while another part was terrified for the opposite scenario, one where a little girl he had imagined as his own was left fatherless.

My insides felt like they were twisting, and I wondered if this was what happened when you truly loved someone, that you could physically feel that person's fear. His fear was mine. His pain was mine. His life had now merged with my own. I hadn't told him I loved him, but as I sat there feeling like my entire future depended on the next few minutes, I came to the conclusion that this had to be the real thing.

I loved Graham J. Morgan. Mr. Big Prick. Stuck-up Suit. Celibate in Manhattan. Fifty Shades of Morgan. I loved them all. I loved that he appreciated all of my idiosyncrasies. I loved that he protected me. I loved that he made me feel for the first time in my life like I was the most important person to someone—to him. The thing was, depending on these results, I would no longer be the most important thing. His daughter would and *should* always come first. That was the way it was supposed to be. That was what Frank Venedetta never understood.

A man's voice came on the speaker. "Mr. Morgan? Thank you for holding, This is Brad. I'm one of the lab managers. I apologize for the delay. I have your results."

Graham swallowed hard. "Alright…"

"There is, at least, a 99.9 percent probability that you are a match. These results are conclusive to prove paternity."

He took his palm to his mouth and let out a long, slow breath into his hand.

The man continued, "We'll be FedExing your hard copy lab results today. You should receive them tomorrow. Again, I apologize for the delay."

Genevieve covered her face and started to cry.

"Thank you," Graham simply said. He hung up the phone and looked straight into my eyes.

Trying to stay composed, I just kept nodding my head over and over in an attempt to convince him and myself that things were going to be alright.

"It's okay," I silently mouthed.

Deep down, I was far from sure of that. I knew I loved him. That was all I knew anymore. I just hoped that would be enough.

CHAPTER 20

graham

GENEVIEVE'S THREE-STORY BROWNSTONE was only about a mile from my condo on the Upper West Side.

I stood in front of the brick structure and lingered for a bit before entering. Once I officially met Chloe, there would be no going back.

I was a father now. It still felt like a foreign concept.

Genevieve and I had agreed that this first meeting would be a casual dinner. She would introduce me as a family friend. We would play it by ear, and when the time was right, it would be explained to Chloe that she actually has two fathers, one in heaven and one on Earth. Over time, when Chloe was comfortable with the idea, we would develop a fair custody arrangement. Genevieve was lucky that she'd decided to make this easy for me. Otherwise she would have had one hell of a fight on her hands.

I had badly wanted Soraya here with me tonight, but it made more sense for me to get to know my daughter one on one first before introducing any more new people into her life. Chloe had just lost the only father she'd ever known. She was still extremely fragile.

A wreath made up of branches and berries hung on the red door. Ringing the bell, I took a deep breath in before the door opened.

Genevieve smiled and nudged her head. "Come in, Graham."

Everything inside was either stark white, silver or gray. The décor was a lot like my own place, sleek and modern. It reminded me of just how much my taste had changed. I was much more into things of the colorful variety lately. Bright, bold colors.

The scent of aromatic spices filled the air, prompting me to ask, "What is that I smell?"

"Remember that homemade pad thai I used to make you? It was always your favorite. That's what you smell. I made it for dinner tonight."

I had to bite my tongue to keep myself from reminding her that I didn't remember much that happened before catching her blowing Liam. This was not the night for my typical jabs, though.

"Thank you. That was thoughtful."

"I just want you to feel comfortable here."

The only thing making me uncomfortable was Genevieve trying to play happy homemaker.

"Where is she?"

"Chloe is playing in her room. I figured it would be better to just let her come out and find you here naturally, rather than introduce you right off the bat. I don't want her to be suspicious."

Suspicious that her mother is a lying cheat who's

withheld her actual father from her since the day she was born?

"Whatever you think is best. You know her better than I do. That's not by my choice, of course."

"I know." Genevieve cleared her throat and walked toward the kitchen. "Make yourself comfortable. Can I get you something to drink?"

"Water will be fine with dinner, nothing for now." I took a seat in the living room, which was adjacent to the kitchen.

"Are you sure? I have cognac...merlot..."

Holding out my palm, I said, "I'm not going to be drinking tonight."

"Okay...just let me know if you change your mind."

"I know you," a sweet little voice said.

I turned around to find Chloe standing there. Her thick mane of long, brown hair covered half of her face. She was wearing adorable pink-footed pajamas and holding a teddy bear.

My mouth curved into a smile as I got up from my seat. "You know me?"

"You found my barrette...at Daddy's party."

That's right. I'd picked up the pom pom thing that fell out of her hair at Liam's wake.

I knelt down in front of her. "You're a smart cookie."

"What's your name?"

"Graham."

"Like Graham Cracker?"

"Yes. I suppose."

"You're a smart cracker!"

I chuckled. "You're very funny, Chloe."

Genevieve interjected, "Chloe...Graham is a friend of Daddy and Mommy's. He's joining us for dinner tonight."

"Did you know my Daddy died?"

"Yes. I'm very sorry for you. I know he loved you very much."

She walked over to the end table and picked up a framed picture, bringing it over to me. In the snapshot, Liam was looking lovingly over at her as autumn leaves fell around them. There was no doubt that he adored her. I wanted to feel bitter, but seeing the smile on her face in the photo made that impossible.

"That's a really great photo of the two of you."

"Thanks."

Struggling with what to say to her next, I asked, "Do you always wear pajamas this early?"

"Sometimes."

"They look very comfy. I wish they made those in my size."

She scrunched her little nose. "That would be silly."

"Yes. I suppose it would be."

She handed me her teddy bear and said, "Look! Teddy Grahams...like the little cookies." Then she started to belly laugh.

I laughed because *she* was laughing. "Clever."

"Dinner is ready!" Genevieve called out from the kitchen. She'd set up the dining room table. A large, white, rectangular platter was filled with the rice noodles and veggies she'd made. A plate of chicken nuggets and mixed vegetables was placed in front of what I assumed was Chloe's seat. The *Dora the Explorer* placemat was a dead giveaway.

"Graham, you said you just want water?" Genevieve asked.

"That's right."

"Chloe, you want your usual strawberry milk?"

Strawberry milk?

No way.

I turned to Chloe. "Strawberry milk? I love strawberry milk."

"That's my favorite."

"What kind?"

"Quik," she said.

I'd never had Nesquik milk in front of Genevieve. So, she had no idea what a crazy coincidence this was.

"That's wild. That's my favorite drink in the whole wide world, too." I turned to Genevieve. "Can I change my request to strawberry milk, as well?"

"Of course." Genevieve seemed amused.

In my daughter's presence, I would for the first time in my adult life drink Nesquik milk openly and shamelessly. I'd come out of the strawberry milk closet.

Chloe turned to her mother. "You have to give him a crazy straw."

"Oh, I don't think he wants one."

For Chloe's benefit, I looked at Genevieve like she was crazy for thinking I wouldn't. "Of course I do!"

Genevieve shook her head then placed a long, pink swirly straw in front of me. Chloe got a real kick out of watching me drink from it.

"You know, Chloe, I never realized how much better this milk tastes when you drink it from a crazy straw."

"I know!" she squealed.

The joy in her eyes was palpable. I could get used to this. It made me feel so good that the mere sight of a big lug like me doing childish things could put a much-needed smile on her face. This little girl had just been through a traumatic loss, but she was well-adjusted and loved by her mother. I had to, at least, give Genevieve that. She seemed to be a very good mother.

Throughout dinner, Chloe enjoyed watching me slurp my noodles. I would do it cross-eyed just to make her laugh again and again. Genevieve stayed quiet but observant, often resting her chin in her hand as she watched us. She was taking a step back, allowing Chloe and I to bond.

After dinner, Genevieve made Chloe wash her hands and brush her teeth. I wasn't sure what the rest of the evening held until Chloe came up behind me again and asked, "Are you sleeping over?"

"No. No, I'm not. But I'll stay a while. What's next on the agenda?"

"The what?"

I had to learn to make my language more kid-friendly.

"What do you like to play after dinner?"

"Dress up."

"Dress up?"

"Yes."

"What does that entail?"

"No tails. Dresses."

I chuckled. "Dresses?"

"Yes." Then she ran away, presumably to go fetch something.

I looked over at Genevieve as if she needed to translate all of this for me. "Dresses?"

"Chloe has a chest full of princess dresses and other costumes in her room. She likes to put them on over her pajamas and spin around in them until she tires. It's sort of a bedtime ritual."

Chloe came running back toward me. She was now dressed in a pink fluffy gown and was wearing a plastic crown. Before I could practically blink, a white, feather boa was placed around my neck.

"Chloe, Graham may not want to dress up like a lady."

"It's fine. I've been meaning to get in touch with my feminine side. It's been on my to-do list."

Chloe grabbed my phone and handed it to me. "Take a picture of us!"

I snapped a selfie of Chloe and me and instinctively forwarded it to Soraya. Not knowing her mood tonight, I second-guessed my decision to send it, but it was too late.

"I'll be back," Chloe said as she snatched the boa from around me. She took off back to her room, leaving Genevieve and me alone in the living room. A few stray feathers had fallen in her wake, landing on the rug.

"You're really great with her, Graham."

"This feels more...natural...than I expected."

"Of course it does. Because she's yours."

Before we could continue the conversation, Chloe came flying toward me again. This time, she was dressed in a red Christmassy looking gown with white, fur trim. She was holding a black top hat.

"Are you a snow princess?"

"I'm a Christmas princess." She placed the top hat on my head. "And you're Scrooge."

"I think there are a lot of people who would probably say you just typecast me, Chloe."

"What?"

"Nothing." I smiled. I had to keep reminding myself I was talking to a four-and-a-half-year-old.

The dress-up game went on for about an hour before Genevieve told Chloe that she had to go to bed.

"It's already a half-hour past your bedtime. Say goodnight

to Graham."

My daughter walked toward me. *My daughter.* I still had to get used to it. She stopped in front of my face. God, she looked so much like my mother. Mom would have loved her so much. That reminded me that I needed to set time aside to break this news to Meme.

I couldn't help taking my hands and cupping Chloe's cheeks. I didn't want to scare her, but I'd been wanting to do it all night, and this was my last opportunity.

"Goodnight, sweetheart."

"Will you come back?"

"You can count on that, Chloe." No truer words had ever come out of my mouth. She was going to have a hell of a time ever trying to get rid of me.

TONIGHT HAD DEFINITELY GONE BETTER than I could have ever anticipated.

Back in the town car, the warm feeling inside of me was quickly replaced with worry when I checked my phone and realized that Soraya never responded to the picture I'd sent her. A sinking feeling came over me. It wasn't like her not to respond to one of my texts.

I was an idiot.

A total fucking dumbass.

I should have never sent that picture.

My heart started to pound. Should I leave her alone tonight or head to Brooklyn?

"Just park in front of the condo, Louis. I'm not sure yet where I'm headed."

Just as the car came to a stop at my building, my phone buzzed with a text notification.

Sorry. I didn't get this until now. My phone was charging in the other room. You look adorable in a boa. Glad things went well. I think I'm turning in early tonight. I feel a little under the weather. Talk tomorrow. xo

Letting out a massive sigh of relief that she responded, I leaned my head back in the seat before rereading the message over again. I wasn't sure whether to head to Brooklyn or not. She said she wasn't feeling well. I picked up the phone and dialed her, but it went to voicemail. Was she ignoring my call or had she already gone to bed? Maybe she shut her ringer off. When the phone beeped to leave a message, I just started rambling.

"Hi, gorgeous. I'm sorry you're not feeling well. I just wanted to hear your voice before I turned in for the night. You're probably already in bed. Tonight went well. I want you to meet her when you're ready. But, Soraya, you need to know something. I don't think I would have been ready for this if it weren't for you. The man I was a few years ago is not the man I am now. I was a miserable person. Liam was the better father for her then. I'm convinced. But because of you, I'll be the kind of father she deserves now. Because you've taught me so much about what's important in life."

I paused.

Fuck.

Tell her you love her. Just tell her.

"Soraya, I—"

BEEP.

The damn thing cut me off.

CHAPTER 21

soraya

I HADN'T NOTICED THE TOWN CAR parked at the curb outside of my building until the window rolled down, and his sexy voice caught my attention. "Wanna ride, beautiful?"

I sashayed to the dark car. "That depends. What kind of a ride are you offering, Mr. Big Prick?"

Catching me by surprise, Graham opened the door, tugged my arm and pulled me inside and across his lap in one swift movement. The playfulness of his action had me smiling, even though it was morning and I hadn't had my second cup of coffee. *That was a rarity.*

I giggled, probably sounding like a schoolgirl, but couldn't help myself. "What are you doing here?"

"I came to give my woman a lift to work."

"Your woman? You sound like a caveman." *Which I secretly loved.*

He buried his face in my neck and breathed in deep. When his breath whooshed out, I felt tension leave his body.

"I missed you last night. You weren't feeling well. Are you better today?"

"I am, actually. I thought I was starting to come down with something. But a good night's sleep made me feel a lot better."

"You know what else can make you feel better?" His right arm was across my lap keeping me pinned in place while his other hand started to sneak up my thigh. I was wearing a skirt allowing him easy access.

"Let me guess, your penis? Your penis can make me feel better?"

"Now that you mention it, I'm sure it would. But that's not what I had in mind, actually."

"It's not?"

He shook his head slowly. "Actually, I've been fantasizing about how damn sexy you look when you come and I wanted to have the opportunity to watch you closely. I was thinking I'd like to finger fuck you on the way to work today. When I'm inside of you, I'm too distracted to really study your face."

"You want to study my face..." I twirled my finger around pointing in the general vicinity of my lap. "while you..."

"Finger fuck you. Yes."

I looked into Graham's eyes. He was dead serious. Without unlocking our gaze, I spoke to his driver, "71st and York, please, Louis."

Graham's pupils dilated as he pushed the button for the privacy divider with a smile that was a delicious cross between wicked and delighted. He was dressed for work in his usual custom tailored suit, looking every inch the powerful businessman he was. Yet in that moment, the only business he was focused on was me. That look in itself aroused me. So when he kept me on his lap and spread my legs open, I was already wet for him. He didn't have to work hard to get what he came for. Remarkably, feeling his eyes fixated on me the whole time didn't make me self-conscious. Instead, it actually heightened what I was feeling by knowing he was getting off on watching me.

We weren't even to the Brooklyn Bridge before I was finished. Sated, I sighed contently, resting my head against his chest. "This is so much better than the train."

He chuckled. "I hope you're referring to my services and not the mode of transportation."

"Of course."

His arms were wrapped around me, and he squeezed me before kissing the top of my head. "These services are available to you twenty-four seven, Soraya. Just say the word."

Enjoying the post-release serenity and the feeling of being wrapped in Graham's arms, I was quiet for a while—we both were. After we had crossed into Manhattan, I knew we didn't have much time left before we arrived at my office, and I felt guilty for not asking about last night yet.

"I loved the picture of Chloe and you with your boa that you sent last night. It looked like you had a good first visit."

"She's extraordinary."

I pulled my head from his chest to watch him speak. His eyes lit up as he spoke about her. "She's smart and funny. And sarcastic. And beautiful." He stroked my cheek. "She's a lot like you, actually."

"Her mother is smart and beautiful."

"How fucked up would it be for me to say I went home last night thinking I wished she was ours?"

"Pretty fucked up." I paused. "But also honest and sweet."

"I can't wait for you to meet her."

That was terrifying to me. "I'm not sure I'm ready for that."

Graham nodded as if he understood, although I saw the hurt in his eyes.

"But I want to hear all about her from you. I just think we need to take this slow. I don't really know the first thing about children, and we're still figuring our own relationship out."

I felt his body stiffen. "I've already figured our relationship out."

"I didn't mean..."

"It's fine. I understand, Soraya."

Dear Ida,

My boyfriend and I have been together for a little over four months. I love him, and he has told me he loves me, too. My concern is he doesn't make me feel special, wanted, or desired. He's never anxious to see me, and I often need to initiate sexual activity. I've attempted to speak to him about this, but it hasn't changed things. Am I being foolish for needing to feel wanted?

-Krista, Jersey City

I kept sorting through the daily mail, putting aside the ones that I thought had potential.

Dear Ida,
My boyfriend, Brad, and I moved in together six months ago. One week after we signed the lease, he lost his job....

Dear Ida,
My husband seems to have lost his sexual desire...

Dear Ida,
I'm dating a man who is thoughtful and caring. The problem is he's a slob and...

Dear Ida,
I fear I let the love of my life slip through my fingers a few years back. Everyone that I meet pales...

By the time I was done, I wanted to bang my head on the desk. I'd already felt like shit about the way Graham and I left off this morning. Reading about all these relationship problems made me realize how unappreciative I truly was. Here Graham was coming all the way out to Brooklyn to pick me up, putting everything out there by telling me how much he missed me (not to mention delivering a pretty damn spectacular early morning orgasm while taking no physical pleasure for himself), and what did I do? Make him feel like shit. *Nice job, Soraya.*

The thing was, I wanted him more than I even knew it was possible to want another human being. And that thought scared the living hell out of me. Even more so now that there was a child involved. I sat back in my seat and tried to imagine my life without Graham. It didn't take long to realize I was screwed. Because I no longer could. It also made me realize I was being one hell of a shitty girlfriend.

Taking a deep breath, I reached for my phone.

Soraya: I'm sorry about this morning. I do want to meet Chloe.

The little dots began jumping immediately. I wondered if he was having trouble concentrating because of the way we left things, too.

Graham: Are you sure?

Soraya: She's an extension of you, and I want to know all of you.

My phone sat quiet for a few minutes, and I waited impatiently for a response.

Graham: Thank you, Soraya.

Soraya: No. Thank you.

Graham: For this morning?

Soraya: For being the man you are.

I was relatively calm again after that. At least for two more days. Until Saturday when we were on our way to lunch to meet Genevieve and Chloe.

"YOU TOLD GENEVIEVE I was coming, right?"

"Yes."

"And she didn't object."

Graham's jaw flexed, and he didn't say anything. Then again, he didn't need to.

"She doesn't want me here," I sighed.

"It doesn't matter what she wants."

"Of course it does. She's Chloe's mother."

We were riding in the back of Graham's car, traffic was very light, and we were more than a half hour early for lunch. My nerves were already on edge and this new little piece of information—knowing Genevieve had voiced she didn't want me there—made my head pound.

"If she had a legitimate concern for the welfare of Chloe, I would have agreed to put off introducing you. But she didn't, and it's important to me." He reached for my hand and squeezed.

"What was her concern then?"

Again, that telling muscle in his jaw flexed. "It's not important."

Even though I wanted to know, I left it be. Mostly because we pulled up on 3rd Avenue and Louis interrupted. "60th is closed. Got some kind of a crane in the street, so they have the entire thing blocked off."

"That's fine. We'll get out here," Graham responded.

After exiting the car, he checked his watch before extending his hand to help me out of the back and didn't let go after shutting the door behind me. "Do you want to go to the restaurant early?"

"It's nice out. Why don't we take a walk around the block?" I figured sitting and waiting would be way more stressful than taking a walk on a beautiful day.

Midway through our stroll, we passed a dance studio, *West Side Steps*. "Is this where Chloe is?" Genevieve had told Graham that Chloe had just started a new session of dance classes not too far from *Serendipity 3*.

"I don't know." We slowed, but the large glass front

window was mirrored so no one could see in. After we passed, a woman's voice called after us.

"Graham." Turning back, we found Genevieve holding open the door to the dance studio.

"Genevieve." Graham nodded. "You remember, Soraya."

She flashed a practiced megawatt smile. "I do. How nice to see you."

Sure, it is.

"Class doesn't end for another twenty minutes. But you can watch through the viewing room. It's one-way glass so she won't see you watching her practice." Graham looked to me, and I nodded.

Inside, the viewing room was filled with parents. Most sitting around and chatting, not even looking through the glass at the class on the other side. Graham hesitantly walked to the window. The room was filled with four- and five-year-old girls wearing ballet tutus. I searched for Chloe amongst the sea of pink. She would have stood out even if she weren't the most adorable little girl in the room. Her outfit was neon green, where the other girls all wore pastels.

"She refuses to conform and wear what the other girls wear to class. I'm hoping she'll grow out of it."

Graham just kept watching the little girl in fascination. "I'm hoping she doesn't."

Genevieve's eyes narrowed on me. She was wearing a cream pants suit with a navy, silk camisole that was feminine, expensive and stylish, but certainly nothing you wouldn't find on a dozen women in the Upper West Side at any time.

"This is a new class for her. She used to come on Tuesday nights while her father..." She realized what she had said and corrected herself. "While Liam went to the gym across the street. The last session ended a few weeks ago, and I thought it was best to switch to the weekend so she wouldn't have to be reminded of the old routine."

Graham nodded.

A pregnant woman came by. "You're Chloe's mom, right?"

"Yes."

The woman's hands had been folded on top of her enormous belly before she extended one to Genevieve. "I'm Anna's mom, Catherine. Anna wouldn't stop talking about Chloe last week after class. I thought maybe we could get the girls together sometime."

"Sure. I'm certain Chloe would love that."

Graham had been riveted to the glass, his eyes following Chloe's every move, but he turned around to face Catherine."

The woman smiled. "You must be Chloe's dad. She's the spitting image of you, isn't she?"

Graham froze, staring at Genevieve.

Noncommittal, she introduced him. "Catherine, this is Graham Morgan."

The woman extended her hand and looked to me since I was now facing her, too. "Are you the nanny?"

That snapped Graham out of it. He wrapped his hand around my waist possessively. "This is Soraya. My girlfriend."

Graham didn't notice, but Genevieve caught my eye, and hers sparkled with amusement. *Bitch.*

We slipped out before the class ended, not wanting Chloe to find us there, and told Genevieve we'd meet her at the restaurant.

Out on the street, the fresh air felt good. I could finally breathe better. "That woman does not like me."

"She's jealous of you. She's always been insecure of her looks."

"Her? She's gorgeous."

Graham stopped on the street. "She's attractive, of course. But she's ordinary. Unlike you." He reached out and held my face with both hands. "You're extraordinary."

He was completely serious and the way he looked at me, the doubts that had again risen up inside of me were put to rest.

Chloe literally skipped into *Serendipity 3* fifteen minutes later. She hadn't changed out of her dance outfit, and it was impossible not to smile watching her. After a brief pause where Genevieve pointed to our table, she skipped the rest of the way to where we were seated. Graham stood.

"Chloe," he nodded and smiled.

"Cracker." She put all her weight behind her, reached back and slapped her hand into the air for Graham to high five. He was caught off guard, almost missing the hand connection. The exchange was comical. High-fiving was so... *not Grahamly*.

When he sat back down, I leaned in. "Cracker?"

He whispered back. "As in Graham. Apparently, I have a nickname."

"What's your name?" Chloe climbed up on her chair and kneeled. She was sitting directly across from me.

"My name is Soraya. It's nice to meet you, Chloe."

"Soraya?"

"That's right." *First try*.

"I love your hair. Mom, I want to do that to my hair."

Genevieve picked up the menu. "I don't think so."

"Are you Graham's wife?"

"No."

"Are you his..."

Genevieve again interrupted her curious daughter.

"Soraya is Graham's friend, sweetheart. Now, why don't you sit down on the chair properly?"

She shrugged. "But I like sitting on my knees. I can reach things better."

"Sit. If you need something, and you can't reach it, I'll get it for you."

Chloe pouted but planted her butt in the seat properly.

"Do you remember the time we came here after we landed the Donovan account?" Genevieve asked Graham.

"No." His response was quick. It was clear he remembered but was trying to move her from the subject.

Lowering her eyes to the menu, Genevieve smiled broadly. "That's too bad. But I'm sure you remember later that evening."

"Cracker, what are you going to get?"

"I don't know yet, Chloe. What are you going to get?"

She scrunched up her entire face and held her pointer finger to her nose in deep thought. "The iced hot chocolate."

"I take it you've been here before?"

"I used to come every week after dance with my dad." Chloe's face faltered. She directed her next question to me. "Did you know my dad, too, Soraya?"

"Ummm..."

Graham rested his hand on my knee under the table and responded for me. "She didn't get to meet your dad, Chloe."

"You know what my dad would get every week?"

"What's that?"

She wrinkled up her nose like something smelled. "Coffee."

Graham set down his menu. He hadn't even taken a look at it. "I'll have what you're having, Chloe."

She smiled so big, I could almost count all her little white teeth. When the waiter came to take our order, I ordered a frozen hot chocolate, too. Genevieve ordered just coffee. He left Chloe a tin can filled with crayons and a paper kids menu for coloring. She immediately set to work.

"What's your favorite color, Cracker?"

"Blue." Graham's eyes narrowed to the tips of my hair. "Yours?"

"Green. I wanted to paint my room green, but mommy said it wasn't beckoning of a little girl's room."

Genevieve chimed in. "Becoming. I said it wasn't becoming of a little girl's room."

Chloe shrugged and went back to coloring.

"So, Soraya. What do you do?" Genevieve asked.

"I work for a columnist. *Ask Ida*."

"The relationship column?"

"That's the one."

She fake smiled. "I'll have to remember that, the next time I'm looking for advice."

I nodded.

"How did you two meet?"

"Graham wrote into the column for relationship advice a few years back."

"He did?" Genevieve's eyes went wide.

Although I thoroughly enjoyed her reaction, I figured it was best not to screw with her too much. "I'm just messing with you. We met on the train. Well...sort of. Graham left his phone behind, and I found it."

"*Graham* was taking the train?"

"He did that day."

Graham squeezed my knee.

"Mommy doesn't take the train. Daddy and I used to take it together!" Chloe announced factually. Speaking of Liam didn't seem to upset her as I thought it would. She continued coloring and then her pointer finger returned to her nose. It was clear that it was her thinking position, and it was freaking adorable. "Will you come to my birthday party?"

I caught Graham's face wilt. *He hadn't known when his daughter's birthday was.* There was so much he needed to catch up on.

I responded. "When is your birthday?"

"May 29th."

"What kind of a party are you having?"

"A princess party. Will you come?"

My eyes flashed to Genevieve for assistance. "Her party is at our summer home in the Hamptons."

Chloe interjected, "It's big. You can stay with us."

"I was actually going to ask *Graham* if he wanted to join us, Chloe."

She made it clear the invitation was not a plus one.

Graham didn't seem to give a shit. "*Soraya* and I would very much like to attend your birthday party, Chloe. We'll see if we can make that happen. Thank you for the invitation."

When it was time to go, I saw in Graham's eyes he wasn't ready to leave his daughter yet. *His daughter.* It still didn't seem real. Out in front of the restaurant, Chloe gave me a quick squeeze goodbye and then turned to Graham. He crouched down at eye level on the street and spoke to her.

"Is there something special you want for your birthday, sweetheart?"

Her finger went to the tip of her nose while she looked up to the sky. When she looked Graham square in the eyes and delivered her answer, she couldn't have known the irony of fate. "I want my dad back."

CHAPTER 22

graham

IN A MATTER OF WEEKS, I went from Genevieve being a distant memory to her calling on a regular basis and showing up at my office unannounced.

I took off my glasses and scrubbed my hands over my face before pushing the intercom button. "Send her in."

Genevieve strutted into my office and planted herself on the other side of my desk in a guest chair.

"We need to talk."

"Is Chloe alright?"

"She's fine."

"Then what are you doing here, Genevieve?"

"I just said we need to talk."

I slipped my glasses back on my face and dug back into the pile of papers on my desk, not looking up when I spoke. "I'm busy. Make an appointment on your way out."

She sighed loudly but didn't budge. "Chloe's birthday party is a *family* event."

"And…"

"You should be there."

"I told you the other night when we spoke that we would attend."

"She's not family."

"Not yet, no."

Genevieve looked startled. "You can't be serious? Saying something like that? How long have you known each other? You have a daughter to consider now. As a father figure, you shouldn't be introducing our daughter to someone who you barely even know. Chloe could get attached."

"I'm well aware of that."

"You barely even know each other. What's it been? A month? Two months?"

"I know her better than I ever knew you."

"We spent nearly three years together."

"And yet I never knew the woman you were. The things you were capable of."

"That's not fair."

"On the contrary. I think I've been exceedingly fair with you. More so than you even deserve. You slept with my best friend, deprived me of my daughter for more than four years, and now you show up at my office unannounced to insult someone who I care deeply about."

"She's not right for you."

"Let me guess. You are?"

"Well…yes. We're on the same level, Graham."

"I don't think so. I would never have fucked Avery."

She flinched, but recovered quickly, straightening her back as she spoke. "She has a tongue ring. I saw it the other day."

"Yes. And it feels incredible on my cock."

Her eyes narrowed. "It won't last."

"Get out, Genevieve. I have work to do."

"I'm just trying to protect my daughter."

"*Our* daughter."

"That's what I said."

"Out." I pointed to the door.

"Fine." She stood. "But don't say I didn't warn you." She huffed off.

That night, I took Soraya out to dinner. Now that I'd squared away with Genevieve that Soraya would be with me for Chloe's party this weekend, the only thing left was convincing Soraya to go with me. She'd already voiced doubts about going. I didn't broach the subject during our meal, thinking it was better to ply her with good food and wine and make my move later in the evening.

The last hour I'd spent bringing her to orgasm first with my mouth, and then a second time as we made love, me spooning her from behind. When she let out a relaxed and comforted sigh, I decided it was time. Still behind her, I kissed a bare shoulder and molded my body around hers. "It would mean a lot to me if you came with me this weekend."

"I don't know, Graham."

I nuzzled closer. "I need you there with me."

"You need time with your daughter. And we both know Genevieve doesn't like me."

"It's important to me. I know you have your doubts. I want you to see that *we* can still work even though things have changed."

"Graham..."

"Please?" I asked softly.

"Fine." She sounded defeated, but I didn't care. I was selfish enough to take it any way I could get it.

"Thank you. I'll make it worth your while the following weekend. I promise."

IT WAS SOMETHING I'D BEEN THINKING about doing for a while anyway. With all of the changes happening lately, there was no better time than the present to bite the bullet.

When Louis dropped me off at Tig's tattoo parlor on Eighth Avenue, I was feeling pumped.

Bells chimed when I opened the door. As usual, it smelled like cinnamon incense and tobacco. Bob Marley was playing. Being here somehow oddly reminded me of my college days.

Tig put out his cigarette and greeted me. "Mr. Big Prick! When I saw your name on the appointment list, I nearly shit a brick. What the fuck? Has she finally driven you to lose your mind?"

"You didn't tell Soraya I was coming, did you?"

"No," Delia said. "When you called to make the appointment, you made it clear you wanted it to be a surprise, so we won't ruin it. Right, Tig?"

Tig led me over to the corner seat. "You have an idea what you're getting?"

"Yes. I know exactly what I want. I actually attempted to sketch it for you." Taking a piece of paper out of my pocket, I said, "My drawing skills aren't as good as yours, but it gives you an idea of what I have in mind."

Tig lit a cigarette and squinted to examine my attempt at tattoo design. "I recognize this." He chuckled. "Alright. I think we can do even better. Why don't you lie down."

I looked up at him as he prepped the needle. "Has she said anything to you about what's going on with us?"

He blew smoke. "You mean about your baby mama drama?"

"Okay. You obviously know I recently found out I have a daughter."

"If she did talk to me about it, I wouldn't fucking tell you anything, dude."

"Fair enough."

Damn. I wasn't going to get jack shit out of him.

The sting of the needle burned into my chest as he started the design. A few years ago, I would have never imagined getting a second tattoo in my lifetime. But somehow it felt natural to be doing this. It seemed like more than just marking my body. It was art, which in turn was an expression of love. Soraya had a way of getting me to see a lot of things differently now.

After several minutes of watching him work in silence, I blurted out, "I love her, Tig."

He stopped the needle and held out his hands. "Whoa... whoa. Why are you telling me this?"

"Because you're her friend. She doesn't have many close ones."

"Have you even said those three words to *her*?"

"No. I haven't had the right opportunity, but I will. I also get the impression that you still don't trust me, and I think it's important that you understand that despite recent developments, I'm in this for the long haul."

"Look, I'm not gonna bullshit you. I *don't* personally trust you. But Soraya seems too deep into this for me not, at least, to take you seriously. If she cares about you, then I'm gonna have to accept it and trust her judgment."

"Okay...well, I appreciate your honesty."

"Just remember what I said. Don't break her heart, and I

won't have to break your pretty face."

I swallowed my anger for Soraya's sake. "I heard you loud and clear the first time you threatened my life, Tig." If this guy was anyone but Soraya's best friend, I wouldn't have taken his shit, but I didn't need him badmouthing me.

When Tig finished the tattoo, he applied clear tape over it. I couldn't wait to show Soraya.

Delia came around the corner. "Since you're getting adventurous, MBP, I'd be happy to pierce something for you while you're here."

"MBP?"

"Mr. Big Prick."

"Oh, of course." I rolled my eyes and threw a wad of cash that was triple the amount I owed on the counter.

She took the money and placed it in the register. "So... cock ring? Whattya say?"

A protective shiver ran down through my dick from shaft to tip. *Ouch.* "Baby steps, Delia."

"Alright." She shrugged her shoulders. "Can't say I didn't try."

THE NEXT NIGHT, I COULD BARELY CONTAIN my excitement as I headed to Soraya's for a surprise visit after work. The bandage would be coming off, and I could finally show her my tattoo.

With Chloe's birthday party this weekend, revealing it to her tonight would be good timing. It would remind her how important she was to me.

I had worked late and made the decision to drop by unannounced with some of her favorite Mexican takeout.

Soraya buzzed me in no problem, but when she opened the door, her mood seemed off.

"Graham....I wasn't expecting you. Come in."

Pulling her toward me, I slid my hand down her back and gripped her ass. "Are you not happy to see me?"

"No, it's not that."

I placed the paper bag of food on her kitchen table. "I have a surprise for you. I couldn't wait to come here tonight to show you."

"What is it?"

Taking off my jacket, I said, "Let's eat first. I brought your favorite enchiladas from No Way Jose's."

Soraya was quiet all throughout dinner. Something was definitely off. I wondered if she was just nervous about going to the Hamptons this weekend.

I took her plate. "Want to talk about what's bothering you?"

Dodging my question, she said, "Not really. Tell me what the surprise is first."

It felt odd presenting the tattoo to her when she was in such a morose mood. It wasn't exactly how I'd pictured this moment, but I wasn't going to be able to hide it much longer since I had every intention of fucking her out of that bad mood later. She was going to see my chest one way or the other.

"Okay...this is something I've wanted to do for a long time. I finally bit the bullet and had it done. I hope you like it."

Soraya bit her lip in anticipation as I slowly unbuttoned my shirt. My heart was pounding. What if she thought it was creepy? Shit. It was too fucking late. She watched as I tore the tape off.

"It's still a little red," I said, oddly nervous.

She covered her mouth. "Oh, my God. Graham...it's..."

"Do you like it?"

Her eyes glistened. "It's amazing." She looked down at her foot. "It's exactly the same as mine."

"Of course. Tig did it to match."

She traced the area around my tat as she examined the tattoo placed strategically over my heart. It was Soraya's name written out in script. Underneath the letters was a smaller version of the same feather design she had on her foot.

"I thought the feather was the perfect accent to your name. Our story might have been different if I hadn't been able to use it to identify you back when we first met. I'm very thankful for that feather." She was still silently looking at it in awe when I said, "You know, it's no coincidence that the other tattoo I had was nowhere near my heart. You're the only woman who's ever fully owned it."

Tell her you love her.

Why is it so damn hard to just let it out?

Because you're afraid she won't return it.

Her hand was still tracing the tat. I covered her fingers with mine to stop the motion and to get her attention. "Soraya...I lo—"

"Graham, I'm late."

Late?

"What?"

"I'm late."

"You're late? What do you mean? Late for what?"

"My period. I'm late. I'm scared."

I blinked several times. "You think you might be pregnant?"

"I'm on the pill. It's unlikely, but I'm never late. So, I'm worried. I just looked at the calendar and realized it today."

Well, now her bizarre mood made total sense.

"Could there be other reasons to explain it?"

"I read that stress can cause a delay sometimes. So, I'm hoping that's what it is. This is the last thing you need right now."

"You're worried about *me*?"

"Yes. Of course, I am! You're just coming to grips with having one child. This would be too much." She buried her face in her hands. "Too fucking much."

I moved her hands down from her face and pulled her into me. "Soraya, I agree the timing wouldn't be ideal, but make no mistake about it, the idea of you carrying my baby brings me nothing but happiness. I don't think you're ready... no...but if it happened, I would look at it as a blessing."

She looked up at me. "Really?"

"Yes...really." I cupped her cheeks, smiled and repeated, "Really."

"Thank you for saying that because I've been so scared to even mention it."

"Don't be scared. You never have to go through anything alone again."

I needed to know.

"Can we take a test?" I asked.

"I don't know if I'm ready. I don't want to take it too early anyway, might get a false result. I'll wait until after this weekend...once we have the party behind us. Then, we'll do it."

"Whatever you want."

I knew from the look on her face that she was praying she wasn't carrying my baby.

Was I crazy for wishing the opposite?

CHAPTER 23

soraya

THE TWO-HOUR DRIVE OUT to East Hampton on Saturday morning was surprisingly smooth with little to no traffic. Considering it was Memorial Day weekend, we'd been expecting worse. It was still early in the season with cooler weather, so maybe the majority of New Yorkers hadn't yet begun their weekend retreats out of the city.

Graham had given Louis the weekend off, preferring to drive his Beemer to the Hamptons. He had the windows down, so my hair was blowing around wildly in the wind. We were both donning sunglasses. Life was good. I had vowed not to let my late period or the impending encounter with Genevieve today ruin this weekend getaway.

Graham had booked us a room at a bed and breakfast for tonight close to Genevieve's property. We'd be heading straight to the party, though, since he didn't want to be late. The backseat was filled with gifts wrapped in pastel paper. Apparently, Graham felt he needed to make up for all of

Chloe's birthdays that he'd missed. He'd ordered his secretary to practically clean out the girls' section at Toys"R"Us.

During the ride, Graham was being particularly attentive to my needs, asking me if I was okay, if I needed water, if I was cold. I knew the slim possibility that I could be pregnant was constantly on his mind. It was constantly on mine, too.

It hadn't really surprised me that he took the news that my period was late so well. Graham would be a wonderful father; he was already proving that. He was in a place in his life where he was ready for it. I, on the other hand, still wasn't even sure I wanted kids, so the prospect of a pregnancy, especially given the current situation with Chloe, was terrifying. We were definitely on different pages as far as that was concerned.

At one point during the ride, Graham turned to me. "Have you ever been to the Hamptons?"

"Never. Rockaway and Coney Island have been it for me. I've always wanted to go out there, though, just never had the chance, nor the money to book a place."

"I think you'll love it. There are a lot of little galleries and shops. We'll have to do some exploring tomorrow."

"I'm just happy to be getting out of the city. It doesn't matter what we do."

"Well, I'd like to take you on a real vacation soon. Work should calm down in the next couple of months. Think about where you'd want to go...St. Barts, Hawaii, Europe. There are so many choices. I'll charter a jet."

"Okay, Mr. Fancy Pants. But you can choose, because I haven't been anywhere. It doesn't matter anyway; I just want to be with you."

He squeezed my hand. "You're the first person who's said those words that I actually believe."

It was easy to forget how wealthy Graham was sometimes because he'd become so relaxed around me. He insisted he preferred things like eating on the floor out of cartons over going to high-end restaurants most nights. I often wondered if that was truly his preference or if he was just doing it to appease me or to make himself appear more down to Earth than he really was. I truly didn't need a private jet or an expensive vacation. In fact, I preferred the simple things.

As we pulled off the highway, my stomach started to feel unsettled. Being in the car was a nice little oasis that would soon be rudely interrupted.

Twenty minutes after driving through windy side roads, we pulled up to Genevieve's waterfront Hamptons' estate. The sprawling, wood-shingled home was partially hidden by plush green hedges.

Beyond the black, wrought iron gates, I could see just how massive the house was with its white moldings, arched windows and farmer's porch that wrapped around it. If it could talk, it would have said, *"You're officially out of your league, Brooklyn bitch."*

Graham left the presents in the car, deciding to retrieve them later. A woman in a gray housekeeping dress greeted us in front with mimosas. I took one and immediately put it back, forgetting that there was a small chance I could be pregnant. Damn. I really needed alcohol today.

"Go straight through the house to the French doors leading to the yard," she said.

Sensing my nerves, Graham protectively placed his hand on my back as we walked inside together.

The foyer had practically vomited lavender hydrangeas. Genevieve was in the large, white kitchen arranging even more of them when we passed through.

"Graham, you made it!" She smiled.

Brushing off her hands, she walked around the granite island to greet us. She looked like she was about to hug him but stopped herself, probably sensing his apprehension. Not to mention his grip hadn't left my torso.

Her eyes stayed fixed on Graham. "Chloe is outside playing with some of her friends. The adults are scattered about as well. You remember Bret Allandale. He's here with his wife, Laura. So are Jim and Leslie Steinhouse."

Since she had chosen to ignore me, I cleared my throat and said, "You have a beautiful home."

"Thank you. Graham picked this property out, actually."

Confused, I looked to him for clarification, but he didn't offer it. Instead, he just tightened his grip on me.

She continued, "This was our summer place...before things changed."

Graham finally spoke. "The house was in both our names at one point...until I gladly sold my share to Liam." He looked toward the doors leading to the patio. "We should go find Chloe." Graham led me outside without making further conversation with Genevieve.

A closed in-ground pool sat in the middle of the large backyard. To the left was a bright green tennis court. To the right was a large grassy area where at least a dozen little girls in flowy dresses were running around. A large, inflatable bounce house in the shape of a princess castle was set up along with a pink cotton candy station. There was also a makeshift outdoor beauty salon where the girls could get their hair done up like princesses. Genevieve had definitely gone all out.

Graham was looking toward the kids, trying to spot Chloe.

"So...this was *your* house, Graham?"

"Yes...only for a short time. I put it in both our names after we'd gotten engaged. Then, when I found out about what was going on, I didn't want anything to do with it. Genevieve's imprint is all over everything. It was easier for me to just sell it to Liam and be done with it."

"But you picked this house. It must have been hard to give it up."

"Yes. I loved how close it is to the water. The architecture also has a lot of charm."

"It certainly does. You have good taste."

He leaned in and nuzzled my ear. "I would say so."

I had to admit, knowing that this had been his and Genevieve's love nest at one time made me even more uncomfortable about being here.

I looked around at how conservatively everyone was dressed. In his white fitted Polo shirt, Graham blended in just fine. As always, I stuck out with my strapless royal blue dress and matching blue hair tips. I'd been itching to change the color but vowed to keep it blue so that Graham didn't think I was going off the rails.

When Chloe spotted Graham, she made a beeline toward him. "Graham Cracker!"

He knelt down with his arms open as she ran toward him then pretended to fall back when she threw herself into his arms. "Happy birthday, sweetheart."

When she pulled away, she looked up at me. "Hi, Soraya."

"Hi, Chloe." I bent down. "Can I have a hug, too?" We embraced, and she kissed me lightly on the cheek. Her mouth was sticky from the cotton candy.

She wrapped her little arms around Graham's neck again. "Will you come chase us?"

"Of course. You're the birthday girl. Whatever you want. Why don't you go back to your friends for a minute? I'll be right over, alright?"

Chloe nodded enthusiastically and ran over to rejoin the other girls.

He stood up. "Are you okay if I leave you alone with the wolves for a bit?"

"Of course. We're here for Chloe. I can deal with the rest of 'em."

He whispered in my ear, causing a shiver to run down my neck. "I'll make it up to you later in a big way. I promise."

Graham ran over to Chloe, and I watched amused as he took direction from her. Completely at her disposal, he ran in circles chasing the girls around. He towered over them. He was playing the role of some kind of monster. I chuckled as he dropped to the ground and let them clobber him. It was like he'd been attacked by an explosion of pink chiffon.

I couldn't help thinking that maybe the possibility of being pregnant with this man's child wasn't the worst thing in the world. The more I watched him out there, the more I realized I wanted to share a life with him. But it would never be uncomplicated; Genevieve would always be a part of it.

A conversation happening diagonally behind me turned my attention away from Graham and the girls for a moment.

"That's Graham Morgan out there."

"Yes. You know the story, right? That Graham is really Chloe's biological father?"

"Worst kept secret in the world if you ask me."

"Apparently, everyone knew but him."

"Crazy."

"Imagine. One woman and two good-looking guys like that."

"Sounds like one of your books, Elise."

"I know, totally."

"I guess Morgan went off the deep end for a while after Genevieve left him for Liam. Cut ties with a lot of people. He was really in love with her. Apparently, after he found out about the affair, he was so heartbroken, he came down here and shattered half the windows in this house."

"Are you kidding?"

"No."

"Wow. I'd have an affair just to see Stanley get half that passionate about me."

"Gen's paid for her mistakes, poor thing. Widowed at such a young age. We all acted foolishly when we were young. She didn't deserve this predicament."

"Well, it's nice to see him here for the little girl."

"I wonder if they'll reunite for the sake of their daughter. They make beautiful children together."

"That would be a happy ending to a tragic story, wouldn't it?"

The only happy ending he'll be getting is from me, bitch.

A few minutes later, I'd been so preoccupied thinking about what those women were saying that I hadn't noticed Graham sneak up behind me to plant a kiss on my neck. The gossipers had taken notice, though. Their eyes were practically bugging out of their heads. Their little happily-ever-after fantasy was quickly challenged by Graham's public display of affection with someone they probably assumed was working the party.

I couldn't help myself when I turned to them and smiled. "Plot twist."

Graham looked confused but didn't question me about it. He examined my face. "How are you holding up?"

I put on my best happy smile. "Good."

"Chloe wants to open her presents, so I'm gonna head out to the car to get them."

"I'll help you."

Graham and I made three separate trips back and forth to retrieve all of the gifts. When we returned, Genevieve was placing a massive cake that was shaped like a ruffly dress down on the table. All of the little girls swarmed around it like flies.

Genevieve had hired a professional photographer. When it was time for Chloe to blow out her candles, she waved for Graham to come around and get in the picture.

The photographer had Genevieve and Graham pose for several pictures with Chloe. The sight made my stomach churn because my mind kept replaying what those women were saying. It wasn't that I didn't want Graham in the picture next to his daughter, but seeing him so close to Genevieve was unnerving. The photographer probably assumed they were married. Seeing the three of them together made me wonder what would be happening right now if I weren't in the picture. This scene was like a glimpse into the crystal ball of what could have been. Would Graham consider taking her back if it weren't for me? He'd told me he wouldn't, but it might be different if I didn't exist in his life. I could be the very thing that is keeping that little girl from having her parents together. My own childhood came to mind.

Was I Chloe's Theresa?

My thoughts turned to Graham, who was walking toward me with two ceramic plates of cake. Apparently, this children's party was too high-end for paper goods.

"It's chocolate." He winked. "Your favorite."

I didn't have the heart to tell him why I'd lost my appetite;

even chocolate wouldn't be able to heal the anxiety that came from the realization that I was a potential homewrecker. So, I forced the cake down as we stood together and watched as Chloe started opening her gifts.

One hour and piles upon piles of wrapping paper later, I really needed to use the bathroom. I'd been downing nothing but water and decaf coffee since alcohol was out of the question. Graham was assembling some of Chloe's toys and hadn't noticed me slip away.

The upstairs bathroom window afforded me the perfect view of where Graham was standing down below, showing Chloe how to ride a pogo stick. Feeling so conflicted, my heart clenched as I looked at Chloe's sweet face, which was essentially a reflection of Graham's face. Was I keeping this girl from the perfect fairytale of living under the same roof with both parents?

Then, I looked over at him. The man who I loved who probably wasn't even sure that I loved him. I wanted him for myself. And that made me feel guilty. I was pretty sure if I did want kids, he was the only man I wanted as the father.

I pried my eyes away from the window and sat down on the toilet. Looking down at my underwear, I spotted it immediately. Bright red. I'd gotten my period. My stomach sank.

I'd expected to feel relieved, but it was the opposite: utter disappointment. It revealed a truth that I wasn't even fully aware of until that moment: a part of me *had* wanted a baby with him even if I wasn't quite ready. Because I loved him. Instead of relief, the blood symbolized a loss of something I didn't even realize I wanted until now.

Thankfully, my dress was a dark color, and I'd thrown a pair of spare panties and a tampon in my purse just in case this very thing happened. I left the bathroom with a little less hope than I'd walked in with, knowing that I'd also have to break the news to Graham tonight.

As I walked down the hall, I stopped at Liam and Genevieve's wedding picture. I looked into Liam's eyes in the photo and whispered to him under my breath. *Boy, you sure left a mess behind. I hope you're in a better place.*

If I thought I was having a bad day before, it became abundantly clear that the worst was yet to come when I saw who was waiting for me at the bottom of the stairs.

"Genevieve."

"A word, please, will you, Soraya?" Without giving me a chance to respond, she motioned for me to follow her and began to walk toward a set of French doors.

Feeling emotional from what had just transpired up in the bathroom, she was the last person I wanted to speak to at the moment. Yet I followed along like a puppy. She closed the doors behind us.

"Have a seat." She gestured to a brown leather couch. Unlike the rest of the house that was bright and airy, this room was dark and masculine. Built-in bookcases lined the walls, and a massive cherrywood desk was positioned on one side of the room. Genevieve walked behind the desk and opened a cabinet. She pulled out an ornate crystal liquor bottle and two glasses, pouring amber liquid into both before offering one to me.

"No, thank you."

"Take it. You may need it." Her tight smile was laced with more spite than sweet.

Screw it. No reason to abstain anymore. I took the glass and sucked half of it back in one gulp. It burned a path from my throat to my stomach.

"I thought it was time the two of us had a little woman-to-woman talk."

"And since you've cornered me into a room, I assume whatever it is you want to talk about isn't something you want Graham to hear."

"That's right. Some things are just better off between women."

"Well, go ahead, Genevieve." I settled back into the couch. "Get whatever bitchy thing you want off of your chest so we can all move on."

"Alright. I won't beat around the bush then." She sipped her drink. "I want you to stop fucking my daughter's father."

"Excuse me."

"What part didn't you understand?"

"You have no right to tell me what to do."

"That's where you're wrong. Your actions have a direct impact on my daughter. She deserves a family."

"Graham's being involved with me has nothing to do with Chloe."

"Of course, it does. You're being selfish."

"*I'm* being selfish. You slept with Graham's best friend then didn't tell Graham he was Chloe's father for four years so your husband wouldn't leave you. And *I'm* the selfish one."

"We're not talking about me."

"Like hell, we're not. You only want Graham away from me so you can attempt to dig your claws back into him. This has nothing to do with the welfare of your daughter."

She let out an exaggerated sigh. "You wouldn't understand, Soraya. You aren't a mother."

I felt it in that moment. A gurgling of emotions beginning to bubble their way up from within. The bathroom and now her not too subtle reminder. "No. I'm not a mother."

"This is a chance for Chloe to have her family. Graham and I have a lot in common. We share a common business, travel in the same social circles and have a child together."

"He doesn't love you."

Genevieve laughed. "You can't really be that naïve, can you? Believing some ideologic notion that love will conquer all."

"No, but..."

"We're compatible, and I'm the mother of his child. If you were to disappear, after a few weeks, I'd be back sucking him off under his desk, and he would forget you even existed."

I flinched. Being in a highly emotional state, the visual of her under Graham's desk was as if I was struck with a physical blow. She smiled like a wolf that'd just found a lame sheep. Then went in for the kill. "We've fucked right there on that couch you're sitting on. This was, after all, his office. It's the only room I didn't redecorate after things ended. It reminded me of him." She shrugged and finished the remnants of her glass.

"If you think that Graham would come back to you, after what you did to him, you never really knew him very well."

"Tell me, Soraya. Who is the one woman in Graham's life he values more than anyone?"

"His grandmother."

"And he still mourns the loss of his mother after more than ten years. Can you honestly tell me that *family* doesn't mean everything to that man?" She stood. "He'll get over you. He won't get over not waking up in the same house as his daughter every day."

CHAPTER 24

graham

"ARE YOU FEELING OKAY?" I'd gotten stuck talking shop with Bret Allandale for three-quarters of an hour. Finding Soraya in the yard looking out at the sunset over the water, I wrapped my hands around her waist and stood behind her.

"I'm good."

Without thinking, my fingers stroked her flat stomach. There were people milling around the yard, so I lowered my voices. "The thought that my child could possibly be growing inside of you, inside this beautiful body, is absolutely incredible."

"Graham..."

"I know. You don't think you're ready. But I think you will be an amazing mother. How pissed would you be if I admitted a part of me *hopes* you are pregnant? That way you'll have no choice but to put up with me." I pulled her hair to the side and kissed her neck.

"Can I ask you something?"

"Anything."

"If I were pregnant, you'd want to raise the child together?"

"Of course, why would you even ask that?"

"I don't know. I'm just tired and emotional, I guess. It's been a long day."

"Well, then, let's get you out of here soon. You should probably be off of your feet anyway."

After the sun fully set, I decided it was time to make our exit. I'd caught Chloe yawning twice, and it didn't look like she was going to make it much longer either. She was sitting at a kiddie-sized table with another little girl molding something out of hot pink Play-Doh. I pulled a tiny chair out for Soraya with a wink, and we both sat.

"What are you building?"

"A snowman."

"A pink snowman?"

She stopped kneading the clay and looked at me like I had just said something ridiculous. "It's a girl snowman."

"Did you enjoy your party, Chloe?" Soraya asked.

"I did. But it's not over. My birthday lasts for the entire weekend."

Soraya chuckled. "It does, does it?"

Chloe nodded fast. "Tomorrow morning, when we wake up, we're going to have chocolate chip pancakes and strawberry milk."

"I'm sorry we're going to miss that. That sounds delicious," I said.

"Why would you miss it? Do you sleep late?"

"Actually, I don't. But we're not staying here tonight, sweetheart."

"You don't want to have breakfast with me?"

"Of course, I do."

"Who's going to put together the rest of my toys in the morning? Mommy said you would put together my car and my dream house."

"She did, did she?"

"Pleeeeeeease."

I looked at Soraya, unsure of how to say no to my daughter. I had limited encounters with children, and the thought of disappointing her when I'd only just met her was not something I was ready to do. Soraya covered my hand with hers and squeezed.

"How about this, Chloe? Graham and I can come back early tomorrow and have breakfast. Then he can put together your presents."

"Really?"

Soraya gave me a reassuring nod before I turned back to Chloe with a smile. "Really, sweetheart."

We did a quick round of goodbyes, and then Genevieve walked us to the door. "Chloe is very excited you're coming back in the morning. It's too bad you won't be staying overnight. There's plenty of room." She seemed to turn her attention to Soraya. "I know she would love waking up to having her father under the same roof, even though she might not know who you are to her yet."

"What time is breakfast?"

"Avery is driving out from the city in the morning to join us. She'll be here by nine. So why don't we say nine-thirty?"

"That's fine. We'll see you in the morning."

"I'm looking forward to it, Graham." Genevieve put her hand on my arm and lowered her voice. "Chloe is lucky to have you. I know I made some big mistakes, but I hope for her sake we can move past them. I'd really like for Chloe to know her father...have a real family."

SORAYA WAS UNUSUALLY QUIET during the short ride to Harbor House Bed and Breakfast even after checking in. Once we climbed into bed, I pulled her close and tried to coax her into talking about what was going on inside that beautiful head of hers. "Talk to me. You're not yourself tonight." Her head rested on my chest right over my heart, and I stroked her silky hair in the dark.

The list of shit that could be bothering her was endless these days. We were spending the weekend visiting a home that I used to own and a daughter who I just met...while my possibly pregnant girlfriend was slighted at every opportunity by my ex. Why was I even fucking asking what was wrong? It would be simpler to ask what was right. Although that answer was easy for me. *She* was right. Even with all the chaos swarming around, I didn't remember a time in my life when anything felt so right to me. *We* were right.

"I'm just tired."

"So it has nothing to do with spending time with my fucking bitch of an ex or having newly discovered I have a four-year-old daughter or the possibility you could be pregnant. Am I missing anything?"

She chuckled quietly and then sighed. "You're missing breakfast with Avery. That ought to be a blast."

"Ah. Yes. Nothing like a double bitch fest for breakfast."

Soraya went quiet again after that. I hated to go to sleep without the air clear, but it had been a long day, and she needed her rest. After about ten minutes, her breathing became slow and steady, and I knew she had fallen asleep. Staring into the dark while I held her tight in my arms, I realized we didn't really need to rehash the day. Sometimes the words that are left unspoken are the ones that most needed to be said.

"*I love you, Soraya,*" I whispered to my sleeping beauty. "*I fucking love you.*"

"WHAT TIME IS IT?" SHE STRETCHED her arms over her head, and the sheet that was covering her body slipped down revealing her nipples protruding through her white ribbed tank top. I had been quietly sitting at the desk on the other side of the room working since five but stalked to the bed unable to resist putting my lips on some of that exposed skin.

I lowered the sheet more and pushed up her tank top, dropping a line of kisses on her stomach. "It's almost eight-thirty. You were really out." Venturing higher, I licked the underswell of one of her breasts.

"Mmmm..." The sound she made shot straight to my dick. "What time is breakfast again?"

"I'm about to have my morning meal right now." Lifting her tank fully over her breasts, I sucked in a nipple. Hard. Her fingers threaded through my hair.

"Graham..."

"Hmmm..." I moved to the other nipple and swirled my tongue, looking up at her. "What can I do for you, gorgeous? Would you prefer I eat you, or we play hide and seek with my cock?"

Her eyes fluttered closed as I bit down on her nipple. When a throaty moan fell from her lips, I thought I might have a teenage boy moment. *Get ahold of yourself, Graham.*

Crawling further up her body, I spoke with my lips against her mouth. "What's it going to be? Part of me needs to be inside of you now, Soraya. Decide if it's my tongue or my dick." I kissed my way from her mouth to her ear and back again before concluding if she wasn't going to respond, I would just start below the waist and work my way up until I was done. Making my decision, I pulled my head back to tell her and what I found was a kick in the gut. Tears were rolling down her face.

"Soraya? What the..."

"I got my period."

"Oh, sweetheart..." Closing my eyes, I leaned my forehead against hers.

"It's okay. I...I...really didn't want to be pregnant anyway." She wiped her cheeks. "I just got caught up in the moment of it all. Seeing you with your daughter, realizing what a good father you are going to be, I guess I just wanted to be part of that."

"There's nothing I would like more. It may not be today or tomorrow. But we're going to have that someday."

"How can you be so sure?"

"When it comes to you, I have no doubts."

"God, Graham. Why does it hurt so much? I feel like I've lost something even though I never had it to lose." She cried for a long time while I held her. Once the floodgates opened, everything came pouring out. The ache in my chest seeing her distraught was almost more than I could bear. I had to choke back my own tears more than once. When she finally calmed, I wanted so much to tell her I loved her, but I was afraid she would think I only said it because she was upset.

"Why don't you stay here, and I'll swing by to have breakfast with Chloe and then come back. The last thing you need is Genevieve right now."

"But I want to say goodbye to Chloe."

"Well, then how about this? It's only a few miles to the house. I'll take a cab over this morning and have breakfast, so you can spend a few hours in bed. Then when you're feeling up to it, you can come by and get me, and say goodbye to Chloe."

She nodded. "I'd like that. I don't think I can handle Avery and Genevieve for too long."

"Then that's what we'll do." I tilted her chin to force her eyes back to mine. "We're going to get through all of this. I promise. Okay?"

I had no idea at the time, but some promises just couldn't be kept.

CHAPTER 25

soraya

THE HOTEL ROOM WAS TOO QUIET after Graham left. Alone with my thoughts, I picked up the phone and put it down, at least a dozen times. Who would I even call? There was no one I could really count on for an unbiased opinion. My situation was too close to home for my mom or my sister. There was always Delia. But she'd been with Tig since she was fourteen and truly believed in fairytale endings. Her reality didn't involve a small child, a cunning ex, or growing up with a father who forgot her and a mother who was too sad to leave the house for years.

Faced with slim pickens for genuine guidance on my situation, I did something I never thought I would do—I fired up my laptop.

> **Dear Ida,**
> **I've been dating a man for almost two months who I've fallen deeply in love**

with. A few weeks ago, he found out he
has a child with his ex-girlfriend. It's a
sordid tale, but essentially she cheated
on him, lied about who the father was,
and kept him from knowing his child
for years.

Or course, his ex is beautiful, smart,
and they share a passion for the
business they both work in. In most
areas, the two of them are way more
compatible than we are together. To
make matters worse, she's made it
clear to me that she wants him back.

The problem is, he really cares about
me, and I also don't want to hurt him.
I really need an unbiased opinion
here. Should I bow out gracefully
and let him have an opportunity to
rekindle his relationship with his ex,
so that they can be a real family? I love
him enough to make that sacrifice.

-Theresa, Brooklyn

Writing the letter had an unexpected cathartic effect on
me. I wasn't expecting Ida to give me any pearls of wisdom.
More often than not, her advice was utter crap. But the act
of writing the letter seemed to help me put all of my feelings
into perspective. It also helped me realize, until the day came
where I made a decision to actually bow out, Genevieve
wasn't going to screw with my head anymore.

The drive over to the bitch's compound, I blasted the
music and sang along at the top of my lungs. In the moment,

I completely understood why athletes always seemed to have headphones on before an event. They needed to be pumped up to avoid allowing their doubts and fears taking over.

Pulling into the long driveway, I parked and stared at the stately home. It was beautiful out in the Hamptons, but my ass definitely belonged in Brooklyn. Exiting Graham's car, the front door opened, and a woman walked out. She took one look at me, and an evil smile slowly spread across her flawless face.

"Samira. How lovely of you to come."

I plastered my best fake smile on to match hers. "Ainsley. So splendid to see you."

Avery looked amused. She lit a cigarette, which surprised the shit out of me. "What's it been seven, eight weeks? I'm shocked. Graham usually takes the trash out each Tuesday."

"You know what they say: one person's trash is another man's treasure."

She sucked a long puff of smoke into her lungs and then proceeded to blow out a half dozen perfect O smoke rings. I hadn't seen anyone do that since my Uncle Guido quit smoking his filterless Lucky Strikes back in the nineties.

"You know, smoking gives you cancer." I leaned in and whispered. "And wrinkles."

After two more puffs, she ditched the cigarette out in an oversized planter. "Eventually, he'll bore of you and come to his senses. A good blowjob, or whatever service you provide that is keeping him slumming these days, will eventually even get old."

"I'd ask your husband if that was true, but I'm guessing by the stick that's stuck so far up your ass, that the poor man hasn't had good head in a lot of years."

Inside, the house was quiet except for the clickity clack of Avery's heels. "Where is everyone?"

She poured herself a cup of coffee. Of course, she didn't offer one for the guest. Looking at me over her mug with a sly grin she said, "You mean the happy family?"

"I mean Graham and Chloe."

"Mom and Dad and their beautiful offspring are down at the beach, taking their daughter for the inaugural swim of the season."

"That's nice."

"When Graham and Genevieve bought this house, they used to fuck like rabbits in the ocean. Come to think of it, their daughter may have even been conceived there."

This bitch was truly a piece of work. I forced out yet another *that's nice* doing my best to pretend she wasn't getting to me. But the truth was, I couldn't help but get jealous at the thought of Graham and Genevieve. Obviously, they'd had a sexual relationship. I just didn't need to visualize what that looked like.

I walked to the wall of sliding glass doors that lead to the yard and further down, the beach below. A hundred yards off in the distance was Graham and Genevieve. They were both in the middle of undressing and Chloe was jumping up and down excitedly between them. It was excruciatingly painful to see the man who I was in love with frolicking on the beach with another woman.

When they were both stripped down to just suits and skin, I watched in what seemed like slow motion as Chloe took the hand of each of her parents and the three of them ran for the surf hand in hand. *A modern day Norman Rockwell featuring Barbie and Ken.* The visual made my chest have a crushing sensation.

Avery walked up close behind me, watching over my shoulder. "What a happy family they could be. Look at the smile on Graham's face."

Graham *was* smiling. He was laughing and splashing in the water with both Chloe and Genevieve. He truly looked content.

Avery sipped her coffee. "Homewrecker."

I slid the glass door open and stepped outside. When I turned around to slide the door closed, Avery was smiling victoriously. She didn't budge when I slammed it closed in front of her face.

ON THE RIDE HOME, Graham held my hand as he drove. "How are you feeling?"

"Better."

"Thank you for coming with me. I know it wasn't easy for you."

"I'm glad you got to spend time with your daughter. She's an amazing little girl."

Graham lit up. "She is, isn't she?"

"Have you and Genevieve spoken about your plans to tell her that you're her father?"

"Genevieve thinks it's best not to say anything quite so soon. She thinks we should continue to spend time together so that when we finally do tell her, she's already comfortable with me. She suggested I come for dinner again this week."

Of course she did. "That's probably a good idea."

Our conversation had never been so stilted. I was pretty sure we both felt it, yet neither one of us knew how to fix it. Although Graham kept trying. "So what did you think of the Hamptons?"

"You want me to be honest?"

"Of course."

"I think the landscape is beautiful. The ocean, the homes, all the boats down at the marina. But it's not someplace I could ever imagine myself wanting to spend my summers. The people just seem so...homogenous."

"That's a good way to put it. It's never been my favorite place either. Actually, it's very different in the off-season. I always preferred to come out in October or November. There's still a lot of farmers and fisherman who live out there. The town is very different when it's just locals."

"If it's not your favorite place, why would you buy that house?"

"Genevieve wanted it. And if we're being honest, at the time, the status symbol of having a home in the Hamptons seemed important."

"It doesn't anymore?"

Graham squeezed my hand. "My priorities have changed."

"If you were to buy a summer home now, where would it be?"

He responded immediately. "Brooklyn."

I chuckled. "You'd summer in Brooklyn?"

"I'd summer inside of you. It doesn't matter where I am anymore."

CHAPTER 26

soraya

WEDNESDAY NIGHT, GRAHAM HAD DINNER at Genevieve's with Chloe. I found it difficult to sit home and keep my mind off of picturing what the three of them looked like together at the dining room table sharing a meal. So rather than go straight home, I stopped by Tig and Delia's tattoo shop, and we pigged out on sushi and sake. By nine-thirty when it was time to close up, I was sufficiently full and buzzed enough that I was finally ready to go home.

Stripping out of my work clothes, I plugged in my phone and slipped into bed. Just as I closed my eyes, the bell sounded. Since he hadn't texted all evening, I had a feeling Graham might stop by. I went to the door and pressed the button to buzz him in, then slipped the latch from the top lock open and waited to hear footsteps at the door.

I opened it, smiling, just as his knuckles lightly rapped on the door.

Seeing the man on the other side made my smile immediately fall.

"Dad? What are you doing here?"

He took off his hat and crossed it over his chest. "Can I come in?"

"Sure."

This morning, I'd asked God for a sign as to how I should handle my relationship with Graham. It made me wonder if He sent Frank Venedetta as some sort of twisted messenger.

I walked over to the kitchen cabinet. "Can I get you something to drink?" On edge, I accidentally let the wooden door slam shut after I got myself a glass.

My father took a seat at the table. "Water will be fine."

The smell of Old Spice filling my kitchen brought me straight back to my childhood.

"I think I'm going to need something stronger," I said, opening a bottle of merlot.

"Okay, then, in that case, I'll have what you're having."

"Wine, it is." I poured two glasses and handed one to him.

He smiled. "This is nice. Never thought I'd be enjoying a glass of vino with my daughter tonight."

I cut to the chase. "What brings you here, Dad?"

He took a sip then let out a long, slow breath. His expression turned serious. "I've been thinking about coming to see you for a while but kept putting it off because I didn't want to upset you."

"So, why tonight?"

"It just felt like it was time."

"Say what you came to say."

"The day you visited me, you asked me a direct question that I didn't really know how to answer. You wanted to know whether I would have stayed with your mother had Theresa not loved me back or if perhaps I'd never met her. I wasn't prepared for that question at the time."

"You figured out the answer?"

"I've thought about it a lot these past several days. The bottom line is, if Theresa hadn't come along, I do believe there is a very good chance your mother and I would still be married today. It's hard for me to admit that because I don't want you to blame Theresa for my actions and personal choices."

"But you also told me that day that you don't regret the choices you've made, which means you don't regret hurting us. That's really hard to accept."

"No. That's not what I meant. I love you and do regret hurting you, but I don't regret falling in love with Theresa."

"How could you claim to have loved us when you left like you did?"

My father rested his head between his hands before saying, "It's not that simple. There are different kinds of love, Soraya."

"The love for your children should come first."

He closed his eyes as if my words stung then paused before speaking again. "Sometimes life throws you a curveball, something you never saw coming. We have to make decisions about whether we want to be true to ourselves or honorable to those we love. If I'd never met Theresa, I probably would have been perfectly happy with your mother because I wouldn't have known the difference. But because I did meet her and developed a strong connection to her, I knew what I'd be missing if I let that go. There was no going back."

"And what exactly did Theresa have that Ma didn't? Was it purely sexual?"

"Not at all. It's hard to explain. It's just a level of chemistry, Soraya, a kind of magnetic attraction between two people that I hadn't felt with your mother or with anyone before. I could have ignored it. I chose not to. It was selfish. I'm not denying that."

"But you don't regret it."

"There isn't a single yes or no answer to that question. I regret that you and your sister were hurt by my actions, but I don't regret following my heart. There would have been regret either way. I chose the selfish route, the one that hurt you the most, and for that, I'm sorry."

"I don't know that I could do the same thing if I were in your shoes."

"Then you're a better person than me, sweetheart."

"You just told me that you would still be with my mother today if you hadn't made a selfish choice. Your children would have avoided years of self-doubt. As an example, I wouldn't have the trust issues I have with men today. My mother wouldn't have been nearly hospitalized for depression. You might not have been the most satisfied if you'd stayed, but your family would have been better off." Tears were starting to saturate my eyes. "So, basically, we suffered the consequences of your actions."

"And for that, I'm truly sorry, Soraya. That's what I really came here to say more than anything."

I just kept nodding silently, trying to process it all. "I don't know that I'm ready to accept your apology, but I do appreciate it and am glad you came by. I've learned a lot from this conversation. I've needed guidance lately."

"Does this have to do with that wealthy man you're seeing? He gave me quite the dirty look the day he picked you up from my street. He must really care for you. We apparently have a lot in common. Because whether you know it or not, I do love you very much."

"You know what? You and Graham do have a lot in common, more than you probably realize." I sniffled.

He's you, and I'm Theresa now.

Chloe is who I once was.

Before leaving to head home, my father stayed for a second glass of wine. I also put out some that I'd picked up during a trip that Graham and I took to Little Italy.

Things were by no means fixed between Dad and me, but we agreed to keep in touch. At least one relationship with a man in my life was heading in the right direction. Unfortunately, Dad's visit only left me more tormented about Graham.

THE SIGNS WERE EVERYWHERE that night.

Graham had called me to say that Chloe had a high fever and bad ear infection. She apparently couldn't sleep and asked him to stay and read to her to take her mind off of it. I told him to take care of his little girl and that we would get together tomorrow.

In the meantime, I happened to go online and noticed that Ida had submitted her responses that were to be published in tomorrow's paper. One of them was the answer to my email. Before reading it, I took my wine glass out of the sink and poured the remainder of the bottle. I took a deep breath to prepare myself.

> **Dear Theresa,**
> **As much as you appear to be enamored with this man, I think you already know the right answer to your**

dilemma. All bets are off when there is a child involved.

While you indicate that his ex was the cause for the demise of their relationship, she has apparently come to the conclusion that she made a mistake, one that she wants to rectify for the sake of their child. The fact that the choice to end their relationship wasn't directly his (but only a result of her straying) leads me to believe that he could still harbor feelings for her. You indicated that they are quite compatible which is, even more, troubling. It sounds to me like this could turn into a messy situation for you as time passes.

You also mentioned that you don't want to hurt him. Perhaps, if he felt that you wronged him in some way, he would be more likely to get over you quickly. You could, for example, give him the impression that there is someone else in the picture.

Do the right thing and find a man without baggage. Give this one back to his family. When it comes to getting involved with men who have children, I have a motto: smart over heart.

My stomach was in knots. While Ida just helped solidify the conclusion I was starting to draw on my own, it was still hard to absorb the harshness of that reply. I knew that walking away was the right thing to do, but how do you walk away from the best thing that ever happened to you?

She had a point too: there was no way Graham would let me go easily unless he thought I'd betrayed him. Cheating was the one thing he would never tolerate. The thought of deceiving him like that was so painful that it made my skin crawl. I honestly couldn't see another solution, though. There was certainly no way I could look him in the eyes and tell him I didn't love him. I had to get him to break up with me out of anger, and there was only one way to do that.

Was I insane for considering pretending to cheat just so he'd leave me? Or was it an honorable and selfless move for the sake of a child's well-being? I almost couldn't believe what I was pondering.

After tossing and turning the entire night, I came to a decision and devised a reluctant game plan. Tomorrow, I would give myself one last night with him, enjoy him, let myself love him one last time. Then, I would begin the process of distancing myself until I could figure out how to make it appear that there was someone else. I reminded myself that while I couldn't go back and change my own childhood, I had the power to change Chloe's.

This was going to hurt like hell. I couldn't do it alone. There was only one person I knew who wouldn't try to talk me out of it.

I picked up my phone and sent a text to Tig.

I need your help.

CHAPTER 27

graham

THIS PARENTING THING wasn't for sissies.

Even though Chloe didn't know I was really her father, I treated her no differently than if she did. I made sure she got to see me almost every day and made her a top priority.

Last night was particularly rough because I'd never dealt with a sick child before. Genevieve thought it would be a good idea if I took the lead in caring for Chloe. If my daughter was going to be spending time at my place eventually, I needed to know how to take care of her in sickness and in health.

Chloe mainly just wanted me to hold her and read to her. The poor thing had pus coming out of her ears and was burning up. I felt helpless because there was nothing I could do to really make her feel better aside from just being there. She was growing more attached to me every day. It proved that despite the distance between us over the years, there was such a thing as an innate connection between a father and child.

Thank God Soraya was being so understanding about all of it. I missed her like crazy. I was starting to have serious withdrawals. As much as I loved spending time with my daughter, I needed to see my girlfriend tonight. I needed to feel her pussy wrapped around my cock. I needed to fist a handful of that sexy raven hair. I needed to hear that sound she made when she came with me inside of her. Shit...I needed to tell her once and for all how much I loved her.

Luck was on my side because Chloe was feeling a bit better. The antibiotics were starting to kick in. After having an early dinner with her, I headed straight to Soraya's. I was going to have the car pick her up and take her to my place, but she said she preferred I come to her. I'd joked that I'd be happy to come anywhere she wanted tonight.

When she opened the door, I immediately buried my face in her neck, breathing in her vanilla perfume. That smell practically got me high.

"Fuck. I've missed you," I said against her skin. "How did you get even more gorgeous?"

It was a relief to see that the tips of her hair were still blue. A tight, matching royal blue dress hugged her heaving chest. As much as I wanted to rip that dress down and suck on her nipples hard, I'd equally just really missed her smile, her laugh, her snarky attitude. Even though we hadn't been apart for very long, being immersed in fatherhood felt like I'd been a world away from the other important part of my life. I loved my daughter, but my home was with Soraya.

Lowering my hand down her back, I asked, "You hungry?"

"No. You mentioned you had dinner with Chloe, so I just grazed on stuff."

It seemed like something was bothering her. "Something on your mind?"

She hesitated. "No."

"What did you want to do tonight? We could go get a drink, see a movie, whatever you want."

"Can we just stay here?"

"You know I'll never complain about getting you all to myself."

"How's Chloe doing tonight?"

"She's much better. The doctor put her on penicillin, and the ear pain's gone down significantly."

"I'm so glad to hear that."

My eyes wandered over to the sink. I noticed that there were two dirty wine glasses. A rush of adrenaline hit me.

Two glasses? Who the fuck was here?

"Did you have company?"

Her face turned flush. "Um...actually, my father came by."

While relieved for the explanation, it bothered me that she hadn't told me. "Really..."

"Yeah. He showed up here unannounced last night."

My heart sank, because I knew under normal circumstances, she would have come to me about this. Seeing him couldn't have been easy for her. Even though I knew the answer, I asked her anyway. "Why didn't you say anything to me about this?"

"You were with Chloe. I didn't want to bother you. Anyway, it was fine. We just talked. It wasn't as bad as I imagined it might be to see him after the way I left his house that day."

"What did he say to you?"

"You know what? I don't want to waste this night rehashing all of that. My father and I...we're actually fine. It was an okay visit."

"You sure you don't want to talk about it?"

"I'm positive."

"Okay." I pulled her into me and planted my forehead on hers. "You know what I was thinking? Maybe we should go to Italy for our vacation. I want to kiss the ground of the land that brought me you. I've never been there. We could visit the Amalfi Coast. What do you think?"

"I'm sure Italy is beautiful."

"You didn't answer my question." I pulled back to examine her face. "You don't seem as excited as I thought you'd be. We don't have to go there. We can go somewhere else."

She placed both of her hands around my face and said, "You're amazing. I'd be lucky to go anywhere with you." Yet she wasn't smiling when she said it.

What the fuck?

"Are you alright? You seem down. Are you sure your father didn't upset you?"

"I'm okay."

"I don't believe you."

She stayed silent, and it was starting to seriously alarm me.

I brushed the back of my hand along her cheek. "You know you can tell me anything, right? I know that the stuff with Genevieve and Chloe hasn't been easy for you. I need you to talk to me when things are bothering you, not keep them inside. There's nothing we can't work through as long as you don't keep things from me."

"There's nothing to talk about. My mood is just off tonight. Can we just go lie down?"

I examined her face before responding, "Sure."

Despite her explanation, an ominous cloud seemed to

follow us as we headed into her bedroom. I whipped my tie off. As I unbuttoned my shirt, Soraya was just sitting on the bed, watching me. I loved the fact that she was so enthralled with my undressing, but to be honest, it was a little odd and uncharacteristic for her to just be staring at me like that. She was definitely not acting herself tonight.

Throwing my shirt on the chair, I said, "You don't want to talk, then I'm gonna have to find another way to make you feel better."

She stood up and walked over to me then slowly traced her index finger around the tattoo of her name over my heart. "The fact that you did this means so much to me. I don't think I ever really expressed that enough."

"*You* mean so much to me. You brought me back to life, Soraya. This was the least I could do to express how I feel. It represents how you're always with me, even when we can't physically be together because of work or Chloe. Ultimately, knowing you're there for me and that you have my back is what's getting me through."

She continued to stare at my ink when she asked, "Will you make love to me?"

"Was there ever a question about whether that would be happening right now?"

"No, but I want take it slow tonight. Savor it."

"I can do slow."

Sex couldn't solve everything, but I was sure as hell going to try to fuck her out of this funk she was in. I was going to show her with my body exactly how much I loved her, that there was nothing we couldn't get through as long as we stuck together both literally and figuratively.

She reached up and started to kiss me passionately in a way that almost felt desperate. As we collapsed onto the bed, her grip around my neck was tight as she pulled me to her, spreading her legs open wide.

"Please," she begged.

Seeing her bare and spread eagle like that, I immediately had to remind myself of her request to take it slow, because in that moment, I just wanted to ravage her pussy.

As I entered her, she let out the most beautiful gasp into my ear. Moving in and out with a slow and hard intensity, I realized that there was definitely a difference between pure, unbridled fucking and making mad, passionate love. You had to be truly in love with someone to achieve the latter. And I was definitely in love with Soraya in a way that I had never been with anyone before. It was time to let her know.

As I sunk into her, trying not to crush her with the weight of my eager body, I whispered into her ear, "I love you so much, Soraya." Withdrawing and thrusting all the way into her again, I repeated, "I love you."

She responded simply by grasping onto me tighter, bucking her hips and guiding my body. I wanted so badly for her to return those three words back to me. Instead, she remained silent until I felt wetness on my shoulders.

She was crying.

"Baby, what's wrong?"

My heart was beating faster. Had I been delusional in thinking that she was handling everything okay? Was it all unraveling?

When I slowed my movements, she muttered, "Don't stop, Graham. Please don't stop."

Frustrated, I picked up the pace, fucking her harder than I meant to. She screamed out in pleasure as her muscles pulsated around my cock. I came so hard, emptying inside of her.

Our chests rose and fell as we panted on top of one another.

She looked into my eyes for the longest time and seemed to be struggling with her words. What she finally said nearly undid me.

"Your name may not be tattooed over my heart, but it will always be etched into my soul. I've spent over two decades thinking I was incapable of being loved. Thank you for proving me wrong. You've changed my life."

Even though it didn't contain the three words I hoped to hear, in many ways, it meant even more.

We made love three more times that night, each time more intense than the last. While Soraya finally fell asleep in my arms, a foreboding feeling kept me awake.

OVER THE NEXT WEEK, it started to become clear that I'd had good reason to be worried. Soraya gave me a different story every night as to why she couldn't see me.

Her sister needed help moving.

Her mother wanted to go shopping.

She had plans with Tig and Delia.

Dread multiplied each day as I thought back to our last encounter, which while sensual and passionate had elements of bizarre behavior on Soraya's part.

As much as her words about my changing her life touched me, I couldn't help obsessing over the fact that not once had she used the word love. With each passing hour, that omission seemed to have growing significance.

Maybe she *didn't* love me.

Either way, something was wrong, and I needed to get to the bottom of it. I tried hard to give her the space she apparently wanted. I focused on Chloe to take my mind off of the fact that Soraya was distancing herself from me.

By week's end, though, she'd left me with no choice but to wait in front of her apartment until she showed up. Supposedly, she was with Tig and Delia again. But that sure as *fuck* was not who she came strolling down the street with hand in hand at nine o'clock at night.

CHAPTER 28

Soraya

IT ALL HAPPENED SO FAST.

Marco and I had just left Tig's shop. Since Graham and I hadn't seen each other in a few days, I had a suspicion that he might show up unannounced one night this week. I just had no idea which night it would be. Our plan for tonight was the same as last night. We'd sit around, watch movies, and wait to see if Graham surprised me with a visit. If he did, I would let Graham see Marco inside my apartment and tell him that I was sorry, I'd met someone, and that I didn't mean to hurt him.

It wouldn't be that hard to believe. Sitting next to Marco on the subway, even I had to admit that we looked more like a couple than Graham and I ever did. With his olive skin, spiked dark hair, Italian horn around his neck, and bulging biceps, he was more like Pauly D. from *Jersey Shore* than a man who commanded a boardroom. In all honesty, before

Graham, he *was* my type. Although not Marco, specifically. We'd known each other way too long for that.

Marco was Tig's cousin; we'd all been friends since we were kids. Even though I hadn't seen him in a few years, I knew he would do me the favor of pretending to be my boyfriend. When Tig called him down to the shop on Monday, he'd agreed to do it even before I'd explained the circumstances.

"You okay, dollface?" Marco squeezed my knee.

"Just nervous."

"You want to go over what you want me to say if he shows, again?"

"No." I forced a smile. "We have the plan down."

So I thought.

But what I didn't plan for was Graham standing outside of my building before I even got there. He was leaning against his car, looking down, texting on his phone. Luckily, I saw him before he saw me. Jumping into panic mode, knowing what was about to happen, I quickly grabbed Marco's hand. When Graham looked up and saw me, I actually watched the moment I broke his heart play out on his face. Even from halfway down the block, his eyes lit up for a split second when he caught sight of me. That light was quickly extinguished when he saw the tall, dark, tatted hipster I was holding hands with.

My heart was completely eviscerated seeing the hurt in his eyes. I'd practiced the things I would say to him over and over a thousand times, yet when he stormed to us on the street, I was unable to speak.

"Soraya? *What the fuck?*"

I stared down at the sidewalk, unable to look Graham in the eyes. Marco figured out what was going on and jumped in to ad lib.

"You must be Grant. Soraya told me there was a possibility you could show up before she had a chance to talk to you."

"Talk to me about what? Soraya? What the *fuck* is going on?" Graham was practically screaming at this point.

"Dude. Calm down. She was going to tell you. We just talked about it last night at dinner."

"At dinner? Last night? Soraya! Answer me. What the hell is going on?"

When I didn't respond and still didn't look at him, Graham reached for me. Playing the part of a protective boyfriend came naturally to Marco. He stepped partially in front of me and got in Graham's face.

"Dude. I'm only going to warn you once. Keep your hands to yourself, and don't touch my girl. I don't want to have to kick your pretty boy ass out here on the street."

"*Your girl?*"

Everything happened so quickly after that. Graham took a step back, then began to turn away, only to rear back and throw all of his weight behind a punch that slammed into Marco's jaw. A loud cracking sound made acid rise up my throat, and for a second, I thought I was going to vomit right there on the street. I wasn't immediately sure if the sound was Marco's jaw or Graham's hand breaking. My heartbeat was pulsing so loudly in my ears; for all I knew it could have been the sound of my own heart shattering.

Marco staggered back a few steps, his hand going to his jaw in an attempt to ease the pain. But I'd grown up watching Tig and Marco brawl, and I knew a little thing like a broken jaw was *not* going end this fight. Before I could get between them, Marco lunged at Graham. The two men collided, and Marco slammed Graham up against a parked car.

"Stop!" I'd finally managed to speak. "Please, stop! Marco, no!"

Graham somehow managed to toss Marco aside, and then he was standing in front of me, his chest heaving up and down, knuckles split and bleeding. Without thinking, I reached out for his injured hand. "Graham."

He pulled away from my touch as if it was fire. "Say it, Soraya."

I looked down.

"Say it! Tell me you're a fucking cheater and I'm a God damn idiot. Because even though I'm seeing it right in front of my eyes, I *still* don't want to believe it."

Tears rolled down my face. I couldn't look at him.

When he spoke again, his voice was low and pained. He sounded broken. "Look at me, Soraya. Look at me."

I finally mustered the courage to raise my head. Staring into his eyes, tears streaming down my face, I told him the absolute truth. "I'm so sorry, Graham."

His eyes closed for a moment before he turned, got into his car, and drove away without another word. I watched, sobbing, until I could no longer see a trace of his car.

What had I just done?

"DON'T BE SUCH A PUSSY." Tig's hands were cupping his cousin's face. He had showed up with Del fifteen minutes after Marco and I came inside my apartment. I hadn't even realized Marco had called them.

"I really think that should be done in the emergency room." It was the second time I'd voiced my opinion that Marco's obviously dislocated jaw should be reset in the hospital.

"It's fine. I've done it before. Three times when he was doing that stupid kickboxing shit." He handed Marco the bottle of Jack he had brought with him. "One more swig, make it a good one."

Poor Marco gulped from the bottle then stood in front of his cousin with his eyes closed. "Ready."

"On three. One..."

"Fuuuuuuccck!" Marco let out a bloodcurdling scream, and I ran to the bathroom. This time, I really did vomit.

When I came back, Tig chuckled. "I forgot what a girl you are."

"You said on three and did it on one. You didn't give me a chance to run out of the room."

"Of course I did it on one. Who the fuck actually does it on three when the person is tensed up and waiting for it?"

"How the hell would I know?"

"Get your loverboy a bag of peas, will you, babe?"

I dug into the freezer, searching for a bag of something frozen. But I didn't even have any vegetables. "I don't eat peas."

"What else you got?"

I pulled out a box of Choco Tacos—ice cream in the shape of a taco. Tig pulled one from the box and handed it to his cousin. "That's perfect. A taco for the pussy who gets his jaw dislocated by a suit."

Marco winced bringing the frozen ice cream to rest against his cheek. "Throws a good punch for a pretty boy."

"I take it that things didn't go exactly as planned?" Del had held me in her arms until I'd finally stopped sobbing. By then, Tig was playing doctor with his poor cousin.

"Not at all. We never even made it into my apartment. He saw us on the street, so I panicked and grabbed Marco's hand."

"That must have given him a good visual."

I blew out a deep breath. "It was awful. He was so hurt, Del."

"You knew he would be. You think he bought it?"

I nodded my head, silent tears again streaming down my face. "He did. Honestly, I don't think there was any other way to do it. Even seeing me holding another man's hand and hearing Marco call me his girl, he *still* wanted confirmation. He believed in us so much, he didn't even want to accept it when it was right before his eyes. He's been that way since the day I met him. I never knew a man could be so unwavering in his love and support. It was the most beautiful part about him."

When my shoulders began to shake again, Del wrapped me back in her arms. "He's going to give that to his little girl. You wanted to do this for her. That part of him won't change. It just won't be you he's devoted to anymore."

CHAPTER 29

graham

"REBECCA!"

Was it so hard to find competent people these days? I smacked the intercom button down again, yelling louder. *"Rebecca!"* There was no way she couldn't hear me the last ten minutes. The entire damn office had to have heard me, even though my office door was shut. With no response, I went in search of my secretary. Her desk was empty, and it looked like she wasn't in today, even though she was sitting there when I walked in only three hours ago. Grumbling to myself with a stack of papers, I headed to reception.

"Where is Rebecca?"

"Who?"

"My secretary. She's not at her desk again."

"Oh. You mean Eliza."

"Whatever. Where is she?"

"She quit this morning, Mr. Morgan."

"She what?"

"She quit."

"Jesus Christ. It's impossible to find dependable staff anymore." I tossed the stack of papers I was holding onto the reception desk. "I need five sets of these."

A little while later, there was a knock at my door. "*What?*"

The receptionist held the photocopies I'd asked for, along with a stack of newspapers. "Where would you like the copies?"

I pointed with my finger, without looking up from my work. "On the credenza."

"You haven't been taking your newspapers out of your mail slot this week, so I brought them to you."

"I don't want them."

A few minutes later, I still hadn't looked up, and I realized that the receptionist was still in my office. Sighing, I acknowledged her, not that I wanted to. But seeing as she was standing on the other side of my desk staring at me, she left me little choice. "What?"

"Ava. My name is Ava."

"I know that."

"May I say something, Mr. Morgan?"

I tossed my pen on my desk. "You've already interrupted me, so spit out whatever it is you'd like to say, and get it over with."

She nodded. "I've worked here for two years now."

Really? "And..."

"Do you know how many secretaries you've had in that time?"

"I have no idea. But since you're wasting my time, I'm going to assume you're about to enlighten me."

"Forty-two."

"In a city this size, it's pretty damn amazing how difficult it is to find good help."

"Do you know why they leave?"

"I'm not sure I care."

"They leave because you're normally a tyrant to work for."

My eyebrows jumped. "Is that so, Ava?"

"It is, Mr. Morgan."

"So why are you still here? You just said yourself that you've been here for two years."

She shrugged. "My dad used to be like you. Plus, we don't have that much interaction since I'm up at reception all day. Most days you whiz by me and don't even acknowledge my existence. Which is fine with me."

"And your point to all this is? Are you *trying* to end your two-year streak of putting up with me? Because in about ten seconds, I think you will have succeeded."

"No, sir. The point I wanted to make is that...well...a few months ago you started to change. Eliza, your secretary, was here for almost six weeks, and she actually seemed to like her job."

I stared at her, but said nothing, forcing her to continue.

"Until a few days ago. When Angry Mr. Morgan walked back in. I don't know what happened, but whatever it is, I'm sorry. And I hope we get Nice Mr. Morgan back again real soon."

Nice Mr. Morgan? He was the asshole who got stepped on. "Are you done yet, Ava?"

"I am. I'm sorry if I upset you. I just wanted to say you seemed happy. And now you're not."

I picked up my pen and proceeded to bury myself back in my work. Ava took the hint this time. Just as she was about to walk out, I asked, "What happened to your dad?"

"Pardon?"

"You *said* your dad used to be like me."

"Oh. He met my stepmother. Now he's different."

"Leave the newspapers on the credenza and don't let the door hit you on the ass on your way out."

I POURED MYSELF A DRINK and stared out my office window. It was dark already. For the last three days, I left the house before the sun rose and returned in the middle of the night. I was exhausted, and it had nothing to do with lack of sleep. The anger that I'd been carrying around was physically draining. Blood boiled in my veins. I was distraught, rejected, betrayed, filled with fury. Hurt squeezed the cold muscle that had replaced the warm heart inside my chest—a heart that had only just begun to thaw after meeting Soraya.

I'd been betrayed before. Fuck, Genevieve and Liam were my best friend and fiancé. When shit went down with them, I'd lost two people who had been the biggest part of my life for years. Yet that loss felt nothing like this. No, there was no comparison. This was utter devastation—the type of loss you feel when you lose someone to death. I still couldn't get over what Soraya had done to me...what she'd done to us. Never would I have thought she was capable of being unfaithful. The woman I fell in love with was open and honest. It made me question if I had ever really known her at all.

My phone vibrated in my pocket, and just as I did for the last three days, my hopes rose longing to see Soraya's name flash on the screen. But, of course, it wasn't; she was gone. I gulped back the contents of my glass and answered.

"Genevieve."

"Graham. What's going on? Where have you been?"

"I've been busy."

"Chloe is starting to ask questions. You've canceled on seeing her two nights in a row. She's very vulnerable right now after losing Liam and needs consistency. She needs *you*, Graham. Somehow, she's already grown attached."

I closed my eyes. The last thing I wanted to do was let Chloe down. I'd canceled because I didn't want her to see me this way—unhappy and angry. But I was a parent now. I needed to get my head out of my ass for the sake of my daughter. "I'm sorry. It won't happen again."

"What's going on with you?"

"Nothing that concerns you."

"Is something going on with that girlfriend of yours?"

I ignored her question. "How about if I come for breakfast in the morning and then take Chloe to school?"

"That would be good." The phone went quiet for a minute. "Chloe isn't the only one who misses you, Graham. I like having you around."

"I'll see you at seven tomorrow, Genevieve."

After I hung up, I set my empty glass on the credenza. The pile of newspapers that Ava had left were still there. *The City Post*, the paper that *Ask Ida* was printed in each day. I picked the top one up and stared at it. I'd intentionally avoided going anywhere near the paper, unable to trust myself not to scour the *Ask Ida* column for traces of Soraya's words. The last thing I needed was to read her giving advice to some poor schlep on the topic of love or cheating. *No fucking way.* I threw the paper back on the pile and decided to call it a day.

"MOMMY SAID YOU LIKED BANANAS in your pancakes." Chloe and I were sitting at the dining room table finishing our breakfast and strawberry milk. Genevieve had gone upstairs to get dressed for work.

"I do. And chocolate chips, too. My grandmother used to make banana chocolate chip pancakes for me all the time when I was your age." I leaned to my daughter and whispered, "You want to know a secret?"

She nodded her head fast.

"Sometimes she still makes them for me. And they're even better than your mom's."

Chloe belly laughed. The sound was the best medicine in the world for me; nothing could stop my face from smiling when I heard that. I'd kept away from my daughter to protect her from what I was feeling, worried my sour mood was contagious. Yet the reality was, it was the other way around—it was Chloe's naturally happy-go-lucky disposition that was contagious. This little precious girl had lost a man she loved as her father only months ago, and yet here she was smiling. If she could do it, I could, too. My daughter was inspiring.

I reached over and cupped her cheeks. "I've missed you, sweetheart."

"You didn't come see me for a few days."

"I know. I'm sorry. I was caught up in something. But that won't happen again."

"Can we go see your grandmother one day for breakfast?"

Not only was she inspiring, but she was also full of good ideas. "She'd love that. I've told her all about you, and she can't wait to meet you."

"Can Soraya come, too?"

My chest tightened at even the mention of her name. I could still actually visualize the four of us together. Myself and the three most important women in my life. My daughter, Meme, and the woman I loved. It was raw to speak of, but I wouldn't lie to my daughter. "I'm sorry, Chloe. She won't be able to come with us. But maybe you and I could go together this weekend?"

Genevieve picked that moment to walk back into the dining room.

"Are you mad at Soraya?" My eyes caught briefly with Genevieve before I answered my daughter.

"Sometimes things don't work out between adults and they stop seeing each other."

"Why didn't things work out with you and Soraya? I liked her."

I took a deep breath. "I liked her, too." Glancing at my watch, I changed the subject. "You're going to be late if we don't get you going. I thought I would drop you at school today, if that's alright with you?"

Chloe ran to get her things while Genevieve and I cleared the last of the dishes from the dining room table. "Will you join us for dinner, tonight? I'm making another one of your favorites, chicken parmigiana."

I had assumed Genevieve was going to attempt to discuss what she'd just overheard about me and Soraya. I was relieved when she seemed to move on. Maybe Genevieve and I could do this co-parenting thing better than I anticipated. "I'd like that. Thank you."

GENEVIEVE WAS ALL DRESSED UP when I arrived, wearing a very form fitting blue dress that showed off her figure. She was always a beautiful woman, but motherhood seemed to have added a little to her curves making her more voluptuous. I handed her a bottle of her favorite merlot I'd picked up on my way over. She'd been feeding me meals for the last few weeks; it was the least I could do not to show up empty-handed. "Are you going out tonight?"

"No. I wasn't planning on it. Why do you ask?"

"You look...nice."

She smiled. "Thank you."

"You're welcome."

"I need to stir the pasta. Why don't you come into the kitchen and open the wine for us?"

Genevieve pulled two crystal glasses from the cabinet, and I uncorked the bottle as she went to work at the stove.

"Is Chloe upstairs?"

"She's actually not home yet. Her best friend, Emily, invited her over for a play date. Emily's mom called a little while ago to ask if she could stay for dinner. I hope you don't mind. Lately, I've just had a difficult time saying no to anything she asks. After Liam moved out last year, she was really stuck to my side. Then, after he passed, she didn't want to play with any of her friends. I found it encouraging that she wanted to have dinner with Emily, so I told her she could stay. I'm sure she'll be back by the time we're done."

I hated the thought of Chloe not wanting to play with her friends. When my own mother was sick, I had gone through a similar withdrawal. Looking back, I realized I was afraid to leave her. If I went somewhere, something might change or happen. Genevieve made sound choices for Chloe. "You're good at being a mother."

She was surprised at my compliment. "Thank you, Graham. That means a lot to me coming from you."

Over dinner, we talked mostly about work. I'd forgotten how easy it was to speak to her. It had been years since we had any real conversation. After we finished our meal, I poured us both a second glass of wine.

"This is nice," Genevieve said.

I nodded.

"Can I ask you something personal?"

"Will it stop you if I say no?"

She smiled. "Probably not."

"What happened between you and Soraya?"

"I'd rather not talk about it."

"I understand."

There were so many unanswered questions in my head. Maybe it was finally time to get some answers. "Can I ask you a personal question?"

Her eyebrows jumped. "Anything."

"You sure about that?"

"Let me get us something stronger than wine first." I finished my second glass of wine while Genevieve disappeared to the kitchen. She came back with two glasses of cognac. "Why don't we go sit in the living room?"

Genevieve slipped off her high heels, then joined me on the couch. We were both quiet, sipping our drinks for a while. I stared at the floor when I finally spoke, "What made you turn to Liam?" It was a question I'd spent the better part of a year wondering about. The recent occurrences had obviously brought it to the forefront of my thoughts once again.

She blew out an audible breath. "I asked myself that same question a million times. The answer isn't so simple. I was selfish. I liked the attention that Liam gave me. You were so busy and wrapped up in growing your business that I think I felt a little neglected. That's not to say it's your fault. Because it's not. I just wanted to be the center of your world—the reason that you liked getting out of bed each morning. Don't get me wrong, we were compatible on so many levels. We had our work, and the sex was nothing short of spectacular ever. But I just never felt like I was the love of your life. Liam made me feel that way. The problem was, after we broke up and I was with Liam, I realized he wasn't the reason *I* got out of bed each morning. You were."

I glanced up at Genevieve for the first time. Four years ago I could never have understood what she was talking about. I had thought she was the love of my life. Until I met Soraya. I had to force myself to get out of bed these last few days since she wasn't in my life anymore.

I nodded. "Thank you for being honest with me."

"It's the least I could do."

I gulped back the remnants of my glass and stood. "I think I need another one. Would you like a refill?"

"No, thank you."

The next tall glass of alcohol left me feeling even more relaxed. Genevieve and I moved our conversation to lighter topics, and I settled into the couch comfortably waiting for my daughter.

"Graham?" Her tone had changed, and she hesitated until I was looking her in the eyes. "I'm sorry. I know I've said it before, but I want you to know that I mean it from the bottom of my heart. I hate that I hurt you, and I wish I could do it all over again and take back all of my selfish decisions."

"Thank you."

"I've matured since then. Having a child taught me a lot about myself. I don't need to be the center of anyone's universe anymore, because she's mine."

"I can see that."

It wasn't until I stood to go to the bathroom an hour later that all of the alcohol really hit me. I'd had a drink in my office before I left, two glasses of wine over dinner, and it had to be four cognacs. Drunk was never a sensation I enjoyed. The feeling of not being in a clear state of mind was normally something that I despised. But tonight, it felt good. My shoulders were relaxed, and the anger that I'd been carrying around seemed to have lightened a bit as well.

After I relieved myself, I went in search of another refill for my perpetually empty glass and then stumbled my way back to the living room. Genevieve wasn't there, and it was quiet. I sucked down half my glass and shut my eyes, leaning my head back against the couch. I must have fallen asleep for a few minutes before Genevieve's voice woke me up.

"Chloe just called while I was upstairs getting changed and asked if she could sleep at Emily's. She was so excited. I just couldn't say no. I'm sorry. I hope you're not upset with me for not asking you first."

"As long as she's happy, I'm happy. It's late. I should get going anyway." I stood from the couch and wobbled a bit.

"Why don't I make you some coffee first. Then you can call your driver or a cab, rather than take the train."

"That's probably a good idea." The couch was so comfy, I plopped myself right back down on it and closed my eyes. That was the last thing I remembered doing until Genevieve's voice woke me hours later in the middle of the night.

"Graham?"

"Hmm..."

"You fell asleep."

"Shit." I scrubbed my hands over my face. "Sorry. I'll get going."

I was covered with a blanket, and the room was dark, but the hall light illuminated the room enough to see Genevieve in front of me. She was wearing a long silk robe that was tied at the waist.

"I'd much rather you stay. But..." She untied her robe and let it fall open. Hesitantly, her hands reached up, and she slipped the silky material from her shoulders. The robe puddled at her feet as she stood before me, *fully naked*. "I woke you hoping you'd come upstairs to bed instead of staying on the couch."

CHAPTER 30

Soraya

A BAD DREAM HAD CAUSED me to wake up in a sweat. While I couldn't remember it clearly, it involved Graham and Genevieve naked. It was so upsetting that I couldn't fall back asleep.

The occasional car passing by provided small glimpses of light as I sat in my dark bedroom with that same dreadful feeling of doubt that had kept me up almost every night since the fiasco with Graham and Marco.

Did I do the right thing?

What if he didn't end up with Genevieve?

What if it was all for nothing?

Those kinds of thoughts would race through my mind. I also constantly wondered where he was and what he was doing, namely if he was doing *her*. He'd walked away from me so hurt; it wouldn't have surprised me one bit if Genevieve took full advantage of the situation the second she found out.

His lasts words continued to haunt me.

"Look at me."

My chest felt constricted. I was either the most selfless woman on Earth or the stupidest. Regardless, the pain of losing Graham was simply not subsiding. I doubted that I would ever stop longing for him, but would it get even a little easier? So far, the passage of time hadn't helped.

Whether he was drowning his sorrows in someone else or not, I knew that Graham was out there somewhere devastated. He'd really loved me. Somehow, I was sure he *still* did, even if he was disappointed in me. Love built to last simply doesn't unravel that fast. I truly felt that ours would have stood the test of time had I not ended things.

When the first glimmer of sunlight appeared through my window, I picked up my phone. Delia was always up at the ass crack of dawn. Constantly needing reassurance that I'd made the right decision, I called her the first opportunity I could.

She picked up. "Again you didn't sleep?"

"I know. Something has to give. I'm a mess. I haven't even had the energy to dye my tips red."

"Now, that's how I *know* you're in trouble."

"Seriously, right? I'm still wearing the blue as if my entire world hadn't turned upside down!"

"Listen, Rainbow Brite, I was talking to Tig last night, and he agrees that the two of us need to get away."

"You and Tig?" I panicked. "You can't leave me alone now!"

"No...you and me! Like a girls' trip. You need to get out of the city. Everything here is a reminder of Graham."

"Where exactly would we go?"

"Well, seeing as though you don't have a millionaire boyfriend anymore, we obviously have to think about cost, but anyway, I think I have the perfect solution for that."

"Okay…"

"I told you my brother Abe works in Japanimation? He's over in Japan now, actually."

Groggily making my way to the kitchen to start some coffee, I yawned. "You want to go to Japan?"

"No! Abe owns a condo right near the ocean in California. Hermosa Beach. It's currently empty. We could stay there for free. I looked at tickets last night, and they're reasonable, in the three-hundred dollar range. What do you say?"

Anything would be better than staying here in this funk. I couldn't remember the last time I took any kind of a vacation.

The decision was an easy one. "You know what? Yes. Let's do it. Let's go to California."

GROWING UP IN BROOKLYN, I'd always dreamt of seeing California, a setting glorified in many of the television shows I'd grown up watching. Even though I was probably the opposite of a stereotypical California girl, I'd itched to see the Pacific Ocean and experience the carefree living I'd always associated with the Left Coast. It always seemed like the polar opposite of Brooklyn.

Delia's brother Abe's place was right on the water. As I sat on the sand, listening to the crashing of the waves, thoughts of Graham were never far behind. Delia was back at the condo sleeping in, and I was taking advantage of the alone time to enjoy the quiet beach before it became crowded.

My attention drifted diagonally across the sand to the only other people on the beach. A woman and a little girl were sitting next to each other with their legs crossed in child's pose, a position I recognized from the one yoga class I ever took.

Their eyes were closed as they breathed in and out, taking in the sounds of the ocean. Desperate to calm my mind, I did something I normally never would. Approaching them, I asked, "Do you mind if I join you?"

"Not at all," the woman said. "We're almost done with our warm-up meditation, though. Take a seat on the sand and do what we're doing."

Closing my eyes, I willed the anxious thoughts of Graham and Genevieve away and tried to focus simply on my breathing and the sounds around me. Over the next half-hour, I followed along as this mother and daughter moved together with synchronized precision, teaching me various positions such as downward dog. I tried not to think about the fact that they reminded me a bit of Genevieve and Chloe. This girl was only a little older than Graham's daughter.

I definitely felt calmer by the time we were finished.

The woman handed me a water from her bag. "Are you from around here?"

"No, actually. I'm here for the week, visiting from New York."

"I've always wanted to go to New York!" the little girl said, turning to her mother.

"Maybe your father and I can take you next year."

Excitement filled the girl's eyes. "Really?"

"Do you take a lot of family trips?" I asked them.

"Mostly short weekend ones, yes. My husband and I share custody of Chloe with her mother."

I nearly choked on my water. "Did you say Chloe?" I turned to the girl. "Your name is Chloe?"

"Uh huh." She smiled.

"That's a beautiful name."

"Thank you."

Turning to the woman, I asked, "So...you're her stepmom?"

"Yes."

"Wow. I just assumed..."

"That she's my daughter? Because we're close?"

"Yes."

"Well, you'd be right. She *is* my daughter. I don't consider her any less of a real child because she's not blood-related to me."

"I'm lucky to have two moms," Chloe said.

I nodded in silence. "Yes, you are."

"Well, we have to run. Chloe has ballet practice." She held out her hand. "I'm Natasha, by the way."

I took it. "Soraya."

"It was wonderful to meet you, Soraya. Hope you enjoy your stay in Hermosa Beach."

"Maybe we'll see you in New York next year!" Chloe said, jumping up and down.

I smiled. "Maybe. Thanks again for the yoga class."

Left alone again on the sand, I contemplated what that encounter meant. In the days leading up to my ending things with Graham, I'd been looking for signs to justify that my leaving him was the right thing. I wasn't looking for any signs at all today, yet that one hit me in the face like a ton of bricks.

Chloe.

That was no coincidence.

I'd never once considered that a child might view having a stepmother as gaining a parent rather than losing one to another person. My own personal experiences had been guiding my decisions. Theresa never even tried to get to know me, let alone acted like a second mother. She never made an effort to include me in anything that my father and her daughters did together. It wouldn't have been like that with Chloe and me. Why had I never thought of it this way? Fear, stress, and guilt had blinded me, and now I was seeing things for the first time from an entirely different perspective—now that it was too late.

LATER THAT AFTERNOON, Delia and I were relaxing in the air-conditioned living room after an afternoon at the beach.

I'd impulsively picked up my phone and opened up the text message chain between Graham and me, looking through all of the old texts from the beginning of our time together. The very last one from him was sent the morning before he caught me with Marco. It simply said, *I love you.*

Delia didn't know what I'd been doing for the past several minutes. She probably thought I was just surfing the Internet. When she noticed the tears start to fall from my eyes, she came around and suddenly snatched the phone from my hands.

"Looking at old texts from Graham? That's it! I'm taking this and shutting it off. I didn't take you all the way to California for this shit."

"You can't just take my phone!"

"Watch me," she said, holding down the power button. "You'll get it back in New York."

CHAPTER 31

graham

MY PHONE VIBRATED just as I was leaving the office.

"Hello, Genevieve."

"Why haven't you answered my texts?"

"Busy day."

"I was hoping you could come by after work. We need to talk about what happened between us."

"I'm already on my way there to see Chloe."

"Alright. We'll see you when you get here."

The last thing I was in the mood for was to rehash the other night with Genevieve. Up to my ears in work from having been preoccupied over the past few weeks, the last two nights I'd skipped going to see my daughter again because it was way past her bedtime by the time I left work. That couldn't happen again. I planned to have dinner with Chloe before heading back to the office after hours.

Rain drops were pelting the windows of the town car. Almost every night on the way home, I'd instinctually go to text Soraya, forgetting for a split second that we were done. Then that awful acidic feeling of reality souring in the pit of my stomach would linger. It angered me that I'd trusted her so fully. After what happened with Genevieve and Liam, I was probably the least trusting person around. But I would have trusted Soraya with my life. How could I have not seen a change of heart coming? The whole thing just didn't make any fucking sense.

"Not sure how long I'll be here, Louis. I'll text you when I'm ready to head back to the office," I said as we pulled up to Genevieve's brownstone.

Genevieve greeted me, taking my wet jacket and hanging it up.

She stood there awkwardly, playing with her pearls. "About the other night...I—"

"Can we please not discuss this until I've seen my daughter?"

"Okay." She looked down at the floor. "She's in her room."

Chloe was playing with her dollhouse. "Graham Cracker! I missed you."

Bending down and pulling her into a hug, I said, "I missed you, too, smart cookie."

"Are you still sad?"

"What do you mean?"

"About Soraya?"

"Why do you ask?"

"Your smile isn't as big as it usually is."

She was so perceptive. Apparently, she didn't take after her clueless father. The last thing I wanted was for my daughter to think that something was seriously wrong with me or that it might have been her fault. Trying to wrack my brain for a way to explain, I ultimately decided that it was better to just be honest.

"I am a little sad, Chloe, yes...about Soraya. But that's not why I wasn't here over the past two days. I got out of work very late, but I won't let another two days go by without coming to see you again, okay?"

"My daddy used to work late a lot."

I wondered how much of that was actually work or Liam just fucking around on Genevieve.

"He did, did he?"

"So, when will you stop being sad?"

"Not sure, but you know what? I already feel better just being with you."

"That was how I felt when I met you. After my daddy died, you made me feel better even though I was still sad."

I AM your Daddy.

And I love you so much.

Pulling her into me, I kissed her forehead. "I'm glad I could do that for you."

Chloe and I played with her dollhouse for a bit until Genevieve entered and knelt down to join us. I could feel her staring at me, knowing she was eager to discuss things. After the other night, I was apprehensive about being alone with her again. Although with Chloe home, not much was going to be able to go down.

"Dinner will be ready in five," Genevieve said before exiting the room.

Genevieve had baked a homemade prosciutto and fig flatbread pizza for us and a plain cheese one for Chloe. She kept filling my wine glass with Cabernet, and I let her, knowing it would help take the edge off of whatever discussion we were going to have later.

After I tucked Chloe in and read her a bedtime story, Genevieve was waiting for me in the kitchen, polishing off the last of the wine.

Before she could open her mouth, I said, "There's really no need to get into it."

"I need to apologize again. I came on too strongly. I don't know what came over me. Seeing you lying there so comfortably in my house, it just took me back. That, coupled with the fact that we'd had too much to drink—"

"It wasn't the alcohol, and you know it. You've made your intentions very clear for some time."

"You're right. Inebriated or not, I want you back, Graham. I'll do whatever it takes to have the opportunity to make you happy again."

"You thought that showing me your pussy was going to make me forget everything—what you did?"

When Genevieve disrobed in front of me that night, I'd jumped up off the couch and demanded that she put her clothes back on. She'd actually seemed shocked at my rejection.

"Did you assume that because of my breakup with Soraya, that I was going to give in? What happened with Soraya won't change the fact that I simply can't ever trust you again, Gen. And while I think you'd be great for a quick revenge fuck, I'm sure as hell not going to screw my child's mother if I have no intention of ever being with her."

"You're not thinking straight, Graham. We have a small window of opportunity now to change our daughter's life. I'm not going to be able to wait around for you forever."

"Let me save you some time." I leaned in. "Stop waiting."

"You don't know what you're saying. How can you just close the door on that possibility so easily?"

"You closed the door, Genevieve. You closed it and threw away the key."

"I made a mistake!"

"Shh. You'll wake her," I said. Closing my eyes for composure, I took a deep breath and said, "Chloe will always have my love. You, as her mother, will always have my respect. But you lost your chance at a future with me the day you decided to betray my trust. I want my daughter to have self-respect. I need to set a good example by holding onto my own." Unable to tolerate any more of this conversation, I walked over to where my jacket was hanging and put it on. " My driver is outside. I need to get back to the office. Thank you for dinner. I'll be back tomorrow night."

MY OFFICE WAS COMPLETELY DARK except for a small amount of light coming from the green banker's lamp on my desk. Fidgeting with my watch, all I could think about was that fucking pile of newspapers taunting me from the across the room.

Over the past week, I'd repeatedly nixed the idea of going through all of the *Ask Ida* responses for any potential clues into Soraya's mindset. Between admitting my sadness to Chloe and the argument with Genevieve tonight, I was feeling weaker.

Bringing the stack over to my desk, I sifted through each edition's *Ask Ida* column like a lunatic. After thoroughly dissecting over a dozen responses, nothing stood out as unusual. That is, until I got to response number twenty.

A woman had written in with a dilemma about whether or not she should break up with her boyfriend whom she was deeply in love with—all so he could get back with the mother of his child. *For the sake of the child.* I looked at the date, which was shortly before we broke up. The other details outlined exactly what happened with Genevieve and me.

My heart started to hammer against my chest.

The name: *Theresa, Brooklyn.*

Theresa was her stepmother's name.

If there was any doubt that Soraya had written in the question, the response only confirmed it. Ida's advice was to break up with the boyfriend and suggested that "Theresa" make it appear as though she were cheating on him so that the poor fool would cut her off more easily.

"Smart over heart," Ida had advised.

I threw the newspaper across the room. Everything was starting to make sense.

Soraya lied.

She wasn't really dating that guido. She was pretending to. Anger over Ida's response transformed into elation. I'd never been happier to learn that someone had lied to me in my entire life.

I read the beginning of the question again. ***"I've been dating a man for almost two months who I've fallen deeply in love with."***

She'd fallen in love with me.

Deeply.

I froze, paralyzed first by shock, then intense relief, then an overwhelming urge to just get to her.

I fell deeply too, baby. So fucking deep.

I immediately picked up my phone and dialed her number.

It kept ringing and went to voicemail.

I dialed it again.

Same thing.

I wrote out a text.

Where are you?

There was no answer for five minutes. I texted again.

I need to see you. Are you home?

Unable to wait any longer, I grabbed my coat and called for Louis to pick me up.

When we arrived to Soraya's apartment in Brooklyn, there was no answer. Looking up at the window, I could see that the lights were off.

Where the fuck was she?

"Where to next, sir?" Louis asked as I returned to the car.

"Eighth Avenue. Tig's Tattoo Shop."

When we arrived, I told Louis to wait outside; I was going to need that car ready to book it once I got Tig to tell me where she was.

Tig blew out the last of his cigarette. "Suit! What the hell are you doing here? It's late. We're about to close."

"Where is she?"

"She's not here."

"Where is she?" I repeated louder.

"She's in California with Del."

"California?"

"Yeah. They went on a girls' trip. Just the two of them."

"Where are they staying?"

"I'm not telling you where they're fucking staying. You're her fucking crazy ex!"

"I need to call the hotel. She's not answering her phone. Actually, call Delia. Tell her I need to speak to Soraya."

"No."

I approached him, getting uncomfortably close to his face. "Give me the info, Tig. You have no idea what I'm capable of in this state of mind."

"Oh, I know what you're capable of, pretty boy. You wrecked my cousin Marco's jaw."

Tig seemed to realize that he'd slipped up. *His cousin.* He was in on the act.

"He's not her boyfriend at all, is he?"

"I didn't say that."

"I read the fucking Ida column, Tig. I know she made the whole thing up. Whether you admit to it or not, I know the truth. You need to tell me where she is."

"What are you gonna charter your fancy jet to California? With your money, I'll let you hire a private investigator. You're not getting her whereabouts from me."

A light bulb went off in my brain as I walked over to a small box hidden in the corner of the shop. "What's this over here? Your stash of weed? I bet the cops would love to know about this."

"You wouldn't do that..."

"I will do *anything* to get to Soraya right now. Do I look like I'm kidding?"

"Jesus, your fucking eyes are demonic."

"Tell me where she is, Tig."

He angrily scrolled his phone then wrote an address down on a scrap of paper before throwing it at me. "Here. It's Del's brother's condo in Hermosa Beach."

I patted the paper to my chest and walked backward toward the door. "Thank you. No hard feelings. I wouldn't have snitched on you. Soraya would never speak to me again. And I couldn't risk that because I really fucking love that woman."

"Whatever, MBP." For the first time, though, Tig looked like he actually believed me. He shook his head, his mouth curving into a slight smile. "You'd better not hurt her, Suit."

I'D HOPPED THE NEXT commercial flight to LAX.

When I arrived at the condo, no one was there. Soraya's phone continued to go to voicemail as did Delia's. At least, I knew she'd be coming back here. According to Tig, they were scheduled to be here another few days.

Taking a walk down to the beach, I decided I needed to let her know I was here. I started shooting off a series of texts to her, pouring out my heart, even though she hadn't been responding to any of my messages.

I hadn't been paying attention and somehow knocked into a muscular man walking a little spotted goat.

What the fuck?

"Watch where you're goin', Mate," he said with an Australian accent.

"Sorry, man. My head is not together today."

"You alright?"

"I'm looking for someone."

He nodded his head knowingly. "A woman."

"What gave it away?"

"You remind me of myself a few years back, roaming this beach, lovesick over my Aubrey—oblivious to everyone around me. It all works out if it's meant to be, you know."

"Why are you...walking a goat?"

"It's a long story. If you want to take a walk with us, I'll give you the deets, get your mind off the woman for a bit...till you find her."

His name was Chance Bateman. He was a former Australian soccer star, now living in Hermosa Beach. He told me the story of how he'd met his wife, Aubrey, at a rest stop in Nebraska. They went on an adventurous road trip together but ended up getting separated for some time after. But things worked out in the end.

I proceeded to share my own story with him. The one

big similarity was that we'd each met our women in the unlikeliest of places.

"Think about it, Mate. These are not coincidences. An Australian and an uptight princess from Chicago happen to connect in the middle of bumfuck Nebraska. Yet, she was my soulmate. And you...you said you didn't normally take the train. For some reason, that morning you did. You have to trust in fate. It's all written. Doesn't matter if it's today or in two years, if it's meant to be, it will happen one way or the other."

Chance looked down at his phone. "Gotta run. You're a good chap. If it all works out with your lady, you should bring her by our house for some brekky before you leave town."

This guy was probably one of the most charismatic people I'd ever met.

I smiled for the first time in what felt like forever. "I just might take you up on that."

He patted me once on the shoulder. "Good luck, Mate."

As if to say goodbye, the goat let out a long, "Baa."

Watching him walk away with the animal, I shook my head in amazement. I shot out one additional text to Soraya, still unsure if she'd received any of my other texts from earlier.

I just ran into a man walking a fucking goat.

CHAPTER 32

soraya

DELIA WAS IN THE SHOWER. It was my one opportunity to see if I could locate my phone. She'd agreed to shut off hers, too. We'd been living without our phones for over twenty-four hours, and I was seriously getting the shakes.

Ransacking her purse, I couldn't believe it was that easy. She'd simply put it in the most obvious place. She must have trusted me when she obviously shouldn't have.

The apple appeared on the screen as the phone powered on.

My heart sank.

Several missed messages and texts.

They were all from Graham.

Did something happen?

Scrolling up to the top of the text chain, I swallowed nervously as I read from the beginning.

Where are you?

I need to see you. Are you home?

You lied. I figured it all out.

You forgot one very important thing when you did what you thought was right. You can't make me stop loving you.

If I'm not happy, my daughter can sense it. She already has. I know you think your life would have been better if your parents were together, but did you ever consider that maybe it would have been worse? If your father were physically present but depressed and withdrawn as he longed for another woman?

My daughter will understand that my love for you doesn't have anything to do with my love for her. Your father sucked at communicating that. I will learn from his mistakes. You will help me. We will do it together.

My heart started beating out of control when I read the next message.

I just landed in Hermosa Beach. I'm coming to you.

Fuck. You're not home. Tell me where to find you.

I'll come back.

I'm at the beach. All I can think about is holding you again, kissing you and smacking that ass so hard for ever believing that I could be better off without you.

The last text made no sense but caused me to chuckle.

I just ran into a man walking a fucking goat.

POOR DELIA, HER HEAD WAS FULL of shampoo when I burst into the bathroom rambling on about Graham's texts. I'd expected her to be angry that I had broken our pact to forego cell phones, but she wasn't. After she rinsed off, she hopped out of the shower and found me rummaging through my suitcase for something other than the grungy, haven't-been-washed-in-three-days, sweatpants I was wearing.

"Are you okay?"

"I was wrong. I shouldn't have made the decision for us. I love him, Del. Graham's right. I wouldn't be taking him away from his daughter. I'd be giving her another person in her life who loves her. I'm not Theresa. I want to be involved in Chloe's life. I realized last night that I wasn't just mourning the loss of Graham. I'd also lost a little girl I loved."

"What are you going to do?"

"Drop down on my knees and beg for forgiveness."

Del snort-laughed. "He's a man. If you drop to your knees, you won't be able to beg for anything. Your mouth will be too full."

She had a point. Stripping out of my clothes, I ran back into the bathroom in a bra and panties to wash up. As I used the facecloth to wash my face, under my arms, and all of the important parts, I spoke to Del. "I owe him such a big apology. I hope I haven't ruined things for us. He seems to understand why I did it already. I just hope I can make things right again."

Del leaned against the bathroom door as I brushed my teeth. She was holding some of my clothes and held them out to me when I finished. "Here. Wear this. Your tits bulge out of the top of that shirt. That'll go a long way toward making it right again."

I smiled as I slipped on my pants. "These tits are how it all started, ya know."

"And that feather on your foot. I get credit for some of this, too, since it was my husband who inked you with the identifying mark that helped Mr. Big Prick solve the Soraya puzzle."

The mention of the tattoo on my foot made me look down. My feet were bare, and I stared at the feather. Graham had gotten the same one inked over his heart. How could I have thought that being without him was good for either of us? We'd been together a little over a month when he'd made my name permanent on his body. He was the most romantic, arrogant, stuck-up suit I'd ever come across in my life. And he was perfect for me.

Washed and dressed, I flitted back into the bedroom in search of some perfume. Del continued to follow me around. "Are you going to text him, or just wait for him to show up here again?"

"I don't know. What do you think I should do?" My heart was racing with anticipation. If I had to wait much longer to get to him, it might explode.

Del was quiet as I brushed out my hair and slipped on my flip flops. Then she picked up the phone and called Tig. I half listened as she spoke. When she hung up, she grinned at me. "I have a plan for you to reunite with MBP."

"A plan?"

"Do you trust me?"

"Of course I do."

"Then take off your shirt again."

CHAPTER 33

graham

A FEW BLOCKS FROM WHERE Soraya was staying, I stumbled upon an old red caboose that was turned into a diner. Smiling, I decided to go in and grab a cup of coffee. I'd traveled all morning and then walked the beach for hours waiting to hear back from Soraya. Some caffeine was definitely in order if I was going to have the stamina to go at it as hard as I planned to when I finally got my woman back in my arms.

"I'll have a large, black coffee," I said to the waitress as I slid into the booth. The entire inside of the restaurant was retrofitted to function as a diner, yet much of the original interior of the railroad car was intact. I was sitting in an actual train seat when my phone buzzed in my pocket. Seeing Soraya's name on my screen made my entire body instantly jumpstart back to life. I swiped to open and was surprised to find it wasn't a text at all. It was a picture. Or *pictures*, actually. Very unexpected ones. *A picture of her gorgeous tits, a picture of her sexy legs, and a picture of her very fuckable ass.* The three shots were similar to our first text exchange, the photos she had left behind on my phone when she stormed out of my office. Only I could see these photos were taken recently from the tan lines that now marked her skin. Her middle finger that was flipping me off between her cleavage that first time, was noticeably absent from the new photos. I saved the pictures to my iPhone and texted back immediately.

Graham: Where are you? Those are my tits, legs, and ass. I'm coming to get them.

As I sat inside the diner waiting for her response, I got a sense of déjà vu. That guy walking a goat today was absolutely right. Here I was, sitting in a train car, looking at pictures of the tits, legs, and ass of a woman who drove me nuts. *Again.* There were no coincidences in life. This journey we took, however fucked up of a turn it made, was meant to happen for us.

Soraya: I'm out with Delia. I won't be back for a few hours.

I raked my fingers through my hair in frustration. I needed to see her now. If that wasn't physically possible, I at least needed to know for sure that we were on the same page.

Graham: Tell me I'm right. I can't wait any longer. You didn't cheat, and you did this for me and Chloe?

The wait as she texted back was agonizing.

Soraya: I asked Marco to pretend to be with me. He's Tig's cousin. I would never have really cheated on you.

Graham: You should have talked to me.

Soraya: I know that now. It was stupid.

Graham: It was, and I'm going to put you over my lap and spank your ass as punishment later.

Soraya: Promise?

Graham: I want to promise you lots of things, sweetheart. But I'd prefer to do that in person. What time will you be back?

Soraya: I'm not sure. I'll text you when I get back to the condo. Where are you?

Graham: A few blocks away, sitting on a train.

Soraya: A train?

Graham: Don't worry. It's immobile. I'm not going anywhere without you.

Soraya: Promise?

Graham: Nothing will keep me from you, Soraya.

I sat in that train for more than two hours waiting. Soraya had said she would text me when she arrived back at the condo, and my patience was dwindling. Unable to sit still any longer, I walked the boardwalk until my phone finally buzzed.

Soraya: I'm back.

Graham: On my way.

Delia's brother's condo was on the sixth floor, unit 6G. I pushed the button for the elevator and waited impatiently. The light above the doors slowly illuminated each number as it climbed the floors. The damn thing was crawling and still needed to make its way back down. I couldn't wait that long. Finding the door to the stairs, I started up the first of six flights. By the third set, I should have been starting to slow down, but instead, I began to take them two at a time. My heart was beating out of my chest, yet I wasn't even slightly winded. I *needed* to get to her. At the start of the sixth flight,

I full-on ran the rest of the way up. When I reached her floor, I flung open the hall door and continued to sprint down the hall. Adrenaline was pumping through my veins when I arrived in front of unit 6G.

I tried to take a deep, calming breath, but it was impossible to relax. My chest heaved up and down. *I need to see her so badly.*

I knocked and waited.

When it finally opened, I froze for a moment.

Soraya.

God, she was fucking incredible.

She was standing at the door wearing only a hot pink bra and panties, and her tips were dyed hot pink to match. Never in my life had I seen such beauty. I stood there for a full minute, just taking her in. Then, I finally spoke. "What does hot pink mean?"

She looked me in the eyes. "Love. It means I'm in love."

My eyes closed. For a second, I thought I might pussy out right there at the threshold and cry. I was so fucking happy, my emotions needed an outlet.

"I'm afraid to come in."

"Why?" Her face momentarily dropped.

"Because there's so much I want to do to you, so much I feel right now, I'm afraid I won't be gentle."

Her cheeks flushed a bit. "I don't want you to be gentle. I want you to be you. A bossy, stuck-up ass with an unexpectedly sweet side. A dad that is going to love his daughter unconditionally no matter what, and never leave her behind. And a dominant partner in bed who sometimes needs it a little rough. I want all of you, Graham."

I stepped inside and shut the door behind me. "Oh, you're going to get it all, alright. My mouth, my hand, my fingers, my body, my *cock*." Taking her into my arms, I kissed her with everything I had.

Between kisses, she apologized over and over again. "I'm sorry for what I did. I thought I was doing the right thing."

"I know you did. Just promise me you'll never push me away again, baby."

"I promise."

I surprised her by lifting her off her feet and cradling her in my arms. "Since you answered the door in that outfit, I'm guessing Delia isn't here."

"She has family in Hermosa Beach. She's staying at a cousin's for the night."

"Remind me to send her a thank you gift. Perhaps a car."

I began walking down a hallway looking for a bedroom. When I set her down on the edge of the mattress, I realized that her foot was bandaged. "What happened here?"

"I fixed my tattoo."

"The feather one?" *She changed the one I had replicated on my chest?*

"Yes." She leaned down to the dressing and slowly peeled part of it back. I held my breath until I realized she hadn't changed the tattoo, she had added to it. Just as I had done, there was a name scripted above the feather. *Graham.*

Having no words, I leaned in and kissed her. When we came up for air, she pointed her eyes back down at her foot for me to follow. "Don't you want to see the rest of the changes I made?"

I squinted my eyes. "More ink?"

"Go ahead, take it off." She bit her bottom lip and lifted her shapely leg up.

If there was any doubt in my mind that she was the perfect woman for me, seeing what she had done would have erased every last shred of it. I stared down, emotions choking me up. "I don't know what to say. It's beautiful." Written in the same script as my name above the feather was *Chloe*, beneath it.

"I love you, Graham. And your daughter, too. I know it's early, and we need to go slow, but I want to be part of her life. I want to be involved. You were right. Just because of how things worked out with my own father, doesn't mean it can't work. I want to pick her up from dance classes and burn cookies with her on weekends. I want to watch her grow up and learn from her incredible father. I don't just love you, Graham…" I caught a tear as it fell down her check. "I love Chloe, too."

Hearing those words, it felt like a huge weight was lifted off my shoulders. *She loves me and my daughter*. It was the first time since I was a child that I felt like I had a real family again.

"I came in here with so much pent up emotions that I was nervous I wouldn't be gentle with you. But somehow, you softened me. I love you, too, gorgeous…more than anything. I'm in better control now, although I still need to be inside of you. Tell me…" I began to strip out of my clothes. "Do you want me to make love to you now and fuck you hard later. Or fuck you hard now and save sweet for seconds?"

She didn't answer right away. I made quick work shedding my clothes, and as I hooked my fingers into my boxers, I stopped and looked to her for an answer. "What's it going to be, Soraya?" I pulled down my boxer briefs, revealing I was fully ready for her, either choice she gave.

She licked her lips. "Fuck first. Sweet second."

"Good choice." She was sitting on the edge of the bed. I removed her panties and felt the wetness already between her legs before I lifted her. "Wrap your legs around my waist."

I moved us to the wall, pinned her back against it, and wasted no time lifting her onto my cock. "Fuuuck." I let out a groan as I pulled her down onto me. It was amazing that it had only been less than two weeks since the last time I was inside of her. The way that I longed for this, made it feel like an eternity that we were apart. I tried to go slow at first, making sure her body was ready for me. But when she moaned and told me she loved me and loved *my cock* inside of her, all bets were off.

I pounded into her hard and fast. At one point, I worried that I was hurting her because of the sound of her body slamming repeatedly against the wall. But when I tried to go easier, she begged for me to go even harder. There was nothing better than hearing the woman you loved telling you that she loved your cock and wanted it harder. We both came long and hard, yelling out as we released together at the same time. I was sure the neighbors had to have heard. Hell, I *wanted* them to hear. I wanted the whole fucking world to know what this woman did to me.

I mumbled against her lips, "I fucking love you, Soraya Venedetta."

"I love you, too, Suit. I think I fell in love with you before I even met you."

I smirked. "It must have been my incredible charm over text."

"Actually, you were pretty much an asshole. It was the pictures you kept on your phone that made me realize that there was a beautiful man underneath that heart of steel."

"I like the pictures that I received this morning much better than the ones that were there before we met. Perhaps I should make daily snapshots like that part of the restitution you owe me for the grief you've put me through."

"I can do that. You're easy."

"I didn't say that was *all* your restitution."

"Let me guess, you'll take additional payment in the form of blowjobs?"

"That sounds like a start."

Her eyebrows jumped. "A start? How long will I be indebted to you to make amends exactly?"

I cupped her cheeks. "I'd say sixty should do it."

"Sixty days? I think I can handle that."

"*Years,* Soraya. I expect sexy snapshots and blowjobs for the next sixty years."

Her face turned serious. "There's nothing I would actually like more."

"Good. Because you really didn't have a choice in the matter. This was the first and last time you'll leave me."

EPILOGUE

soraya

CHLOE SLURPED HER FROZEN HOT CHOCOLATE as we sat together at *Serendipity 3*. Graham kept texting me. He was freaking out because he was stuck in traffic after taking Meme to her first day back at Jazzercise class this morning. I knew he wanted tonight to go perfectly, but I reassured him that Chloe was content and that there was no reason for him to rush.

Of course, I understood why he was nervous. To Chloe, though, it was just like any other night having dinner out with us.

"Can I have a sip?" I asked.

She nodded and repositioned the straw to face in my direction.

"Mmm. That's so good. No wonder why you like it."

Chloe rested her chin in her palms and confessed, "My mom got mad at me this morning."

"Why?" I asked with my mouth full of the beverage.

"I wanted pink hair like you."

Genevieve must love me.

"Uh oh. What did you do?"

"I was painting my hair with my watercolors."

Trying not to let her see me laugh, I smiled inwardly. It touched me that she wanted to be like me.

"Chloe, don't try to color it again. It doesn't work anyway as you probably discovered, right? Someday, I'll do it for you the right way if you still want pink hair by then."

She was beaming. "You will?" I loved when I could see Graham's expressions in her face.

"Yeah. But not anytime soon."

I made a mental note to look for some hot pink clip-in extensions for the next time we'd play dress up. Chloe and I had a ton of fun on weekends when she stayed with Graham and me. She loved to put on my dresses and attempt to walk in my heels. I was sure Genevieve would have flipped if she knew half the things we did. To Chloe, I was more like a fun big sister than a disciplinarian.

A few months after reuniting with Graham in Hermosa Beach, I moved out of my Brooklyn apartment and into his condo. While I liked having my own space, it didn't make sense to keep the apartment when my insatiable man insisted I spend every night in his bed. So, I gave in, and honestly, it made life easier since now he only had to go back and forth between two places—Chloe's house and ours.

When Graham walked into the restaurant, he was weaving around tables, looking flustered.

"You made it!" I smiled.

"Damn traffic."

"Damn is a swear, Graham Cracker," Chloe chided.

"Give me some sugar, Sugar Cookie," he said to Chloe as he leaned his cheek in for a smooch.

Graham gave me a chaste kiss on the lips then sat down. He was sweating and took a napkin to his entire face. He looked at me, and I placed my palm on his knee.

"I love you," I mouthed.

Fresh beads of sweat formed on his forehead. After the waitress brought him a water and a menu, he began nervously ripping apart a different napkin. When he started to click his watch back and forth, I knew he was about to do it. Then, he began to speak.

"So, Chloe, there's something I need to talk to you about tonight," he said.

Chloe just continued to sip her drink while she looked at him innocently with her big doe eyes.

He continued, "I've been keeping something from you."

"Did you take one of my toys home by mistake?"

He laughed nervously. "No. It's about your dad."

"What about Daddy?"

Graham inhaled slowly then exhaled. "Your father, Liam...he loved you very much. I know losing him was hard. He'll always be your dad. But there are different kinds of dads. Sometimes, children can have more than one. Like your friend, Molly, for example. She has no mother but two dads who are married. What I'm trying to say is...I'm actually one of your dads, too."

She was silent then said, "Were you married to my father who died? Mom told me having two dads is called being gay."

"No." Graham looked at me, and we both couldn't help but laugh a little. He continued, "I was with your mother before him. Genevieve and I made you together. I didn't know about it at the time, though. Then your mother and your father, Liam, got married. Liam fell in love with you and became your dad. He believed he was your *only* dad. I only found out you existed after Liam passed away. When I saw your face, I knew you were mine. I know it's confusing, baby girl." He placed his hand on her chin. "See how much we look alike? That's because you're my daughter."

She reached her little hand over to his face and began to examine his features. It was adorable when she said, "I always thought I knew you from somewhere."

"Yeah. From the moment we met, right? That's because we're connected." Graham smiled.

"You're really my dad?"

"I am," he whispered, his voice shaky.

"Wow." Chloe stayed still for a moment as she processed everything. Then, without warning, she leapt into his arms. Graham closed his eyes, looking so happy and relieved.

I just sat back and enjoyed the sight of them hugging tightly. Chloe's reaction confirmed that we'd made the right decision to tell her tonight. Genevieve had originally given us trouble about it. She wanted to be here, but Graham promised to sit down with the two of them after he dropped Chloe back home later.

There was a reason for the timing of this conversation.

When Graham flashed me a questioning look over Chloe's shoulder, I nodded, giving him silent approval to give her the other piece of news.

"So, Soraya and I sort of have something else to tell you."

Her eyes widened with excitement. "You're taking me to Disney World?"

"No." He chuckled. "But we'll go there someday, alright?"

I chimed in, "You know how you always said you wished you had a brother or sister?"

"Yeah?"

Graham placed his arm around me. "Well...that's about

to happen. Soraya and I are having a baby. That means you're going to be a big sister."

At first, Chloe didn't say anything, but when she started to jump up and down for joy in her seat, Graham and I let out a collective sigh of relief. She got out of her seat and walked over to me. "Where is it?"

"It's in here." I pointed to my belly as she placed her hand on it."

"Is it going to come out with pink hair?"

I laughed. "No. But we'll find out who he or she looks like in six months."

She started to speak into my stomach. "Hey, in there! I'm your sister." Graham and I looked at each other and smiled. When Chloe looked up at me, I nearly lost it myself when she said, "Thank you."

"You're welcome. Thank you for being so sweet to me." The truth was, if Graham's daughter hadn't opened her heart to me, I didn't know that he and I could have lasted. Her innate goodness made that possible.

The waitress came by and asked, "Is everything okay over here?"

Chloe proudly exclaimed, "Yes. I'm gonna be a big sister, and I have two dads. I'm gay!"

She clearly misunderstood what Genevieve had explained about her classmate's parents, interpreting it to mean that any person with two dads is automatically gay. We'd have to explain it to her later.

The waitress thought it was adorable.

Graham interjected, "You know, the word gay means happy."

Chloe smiled with her head still on my belly. "Then, I'm very, very gay."

GRAHAM

SEVEN MONTHS LATER

Dear Ida,
It's been a while since I've written to you. You might remember me as Stuck-Up Suit, Celibate in Manhattan, Fucked in Manhattan and Fifty Shades of Morgan. Same guy. Well, tonight, I'm happy to say I've earned a new name: Poopface in Manhattan. That's right. I just looked at myself in the bathroom mirror and noticed that I literally have shit on my forehead. Don't ask me how it got there. You know what the funny thing is? I've never been happier in my life. That's right. This guy with shit on his face is deliriously happy! That realization prompted this message. You remember that smart-mouthed girl I met on the train—the one I used to write in about? Her name is Soraya. I knocked her up. Can you believe it? She gave birth to my son a month ago. I've trapped her forever, and now she's producing little dark-haired, Italian Morgans. I have a son, Ida. A son! Thus, the shit on my

forehead right now. Pretty sure it's from when I changed his diaper a little while ago. Yes, the poop is still there. I haven't wiped it off yet because...have I mentioned...I'm deliriously happy? I haven't gotten sleep in six days. SIX DAYS, Ida! I didn't even know humans could survive on no sleep, but apparently you can! I'm proof. You know why it's all good? Because I'm DELIRIOUSLY HAPPY. On no sleep. There's one thing, though, that my life is missing. See, Soraya won't let me make her an honest woman. She thinks she has to lose all this baby weight, fit into a fancy, white dress and walk down an aisle. Our date is set for six months from now, but I just can't wait another day. I want her to be my wife. I know we don't need a piece of paper to validate what we have, but I'm selfish. I want it all because I love her so much. So, my question to you is...what can I do to convince her to marry me tomorrow?

--Poopface in Manhattan

I pressed send, and Soraya's phone chimed. I watched as she read the message I'd just sent—not to Ida's email account—but directly to her.

She was sitting right next to me in bed with her big, beautiful tits hanging out as she fed our son, Lorenzo.

Lucky kid. He's doing what I'd like to be doing right now.

She laughed to herself then typed away on her phone for a while before hitting send.

My phone vibrated.

> **Dear Poopface,**
>
> **Perhaps a better name for you would be Sleepless in Manhattan because from the sound of your rambling message...you are wired. I think while you are "deliriously happy," your son keeping you awake is turning you into part zombie, part spaz. By the way, no one has ever looked sexier with shit on their face, but please wipe it off. That said, you are officially the best father in the world to our children, Chloe and Lorenzo. That poop on your forehead right now is just another example of that. I've never loved you more. I'm starting to realize that if making it legal means that much to you, then it's the least I could do to thank you. I say tomorrow we head down to city hall and make me a Morgan.**
>
> **Love always, Mrs. Morgan in Manhattan.**
>
> **P.S. We'll take the train.**

THE END

ACKNOWLEDGEMENTS

Thank you to all the amazing bloggers who have supported our collaborations. Without your posts, reviews, and deep love of books, our success would not have been possible. We are forever grateful for everything you do to bring new readers to us every day.

To Julie – The third musketeer. Thank you for your support and friendship.

To Elaine – Thank you for your attention to detail in making sure *Stuck-Up Suit* was nice and clean. Ida wouldn't have been happy with typos ☐

To Luna – We can't wait to see Graham and Soraya come alive through your imagination.

To Lisa – For organizing the release and all of your support.

To Letitia – For the beautiful cover that IS Graham J. Morgan.

To our agents, Kimberly Brower and Mark Gottlieb – For making sure people hear and see our stories in so many different places!

To our readers – Thank you for following along on our crazy ride. You never know when and where you'll meet your true love—a rest stop, a train ride...we can't wait to bring you more chance encounters. Thank you for your continued support and enthusiasm for our books! We would be nothing without you!

Much love Vi & Penelope

ACKNOWLEDGEMENTS

OTHER BOOKS BY VI KEELAND

Life on Stage series (2 standalone books)
Beat
Throb

MMA Fighter series (3 standalone books)
Worth the Fight
Worth the Chance
Worth Forgiving

The Cole Series (2 book serial)
Belong to You
Made for You

Standalone novels
The Baller
Cocky Bastard (Co-written with Penelope Ward)
Left Behind (A Young Adult Novel)
First Thing I See

OTHER BOOKS BY PENELOPE WARD

ROOMHATE

Sins of Sevin

Cocky Bastard

Stepbrother Dearest

Jake Undone (Jake #1)

My Skylar

Jake Understood (Jake #2)

Gemini